PRAISE FOR T

'I flew through the pages of this well-crafted historical thriller'

'I am hooked on historical fiction, especially women in World War II. This book includes all the intrigue of espionage, secrets, German paperwork – and of course, murder. It was just what I was looking for!'

'*The Silent Woman* will keep you turning pages long into the night, and eagerly awaiting the next installment of Catherine Carlisle's story'

'I highly recommend this book to both lovers of historical fiction and those that have an interest in pre-war Europe as a whole'

'This one is a page turner. Couldn't put it down! I highly recommend this book, and I can't wait until the next one'

'You are transported to another time and lifestyle in such a way you feel you have lived it'

'Will certainly read the next book with these characters'

'I thoroughly enjoyed this historical novel'

TERRY LYNN THOMAS grew up in the San Francisco Bay Area, which explains her love of foggy beaches and Gothic mysteries. When her husband promised to buy Terry a horse and the time to write if she moved to Mississippi with him, she jumped at the chance. Although she had written several novels and screenplays prior to 2006, after she relocated to the South she set out to write in earnest and has never looked back.

Terry Lynn writes the Sarah Bennett Mysteries, set on the California coast during the 1940s, which feature a misunderstood medium in love with a spy. *The Drowned Woman* is a recipient of the IndieBRAG Medallion. She also writes the Cat Carlisle Mysteries, set in Britain during World War II. The first book in this series, *The Silent Woman*, came out in April 2018 and has since become a *USA Today* bestseller. When she's not writing, you can find Terry Lynn riding her horse, walking in the woods with her dogs, or visiting old cemeteries in search of story ideas.

The Family Secret

TERRY LYNN THOMAS

ONE PLACE. MANY STORIES

HQ
An imprint of HarperCollins*Publishers* Ltd
1 London Bridge Street
London SE1 9GF

This paperback edition 2019

First published in Great Britain by
HQ, an imprint of HarperCollins*Publishers* Ltd 2019

ISBN: 9780008330835

MIX
Paper from
responsible sources
FSC
www.fsc.org
FSC® C007454

This book is produced from independently certified FSC™ paper
to ensure responsible forest management.

For more information visit: www.harpercollins.co.uk/green

Typeset by Palimpsest Book Production Ltd, Falkirk, Stirlingshire
Printed and bound in Great Britain by
CPI Group (UK) Ltd, Croydon CR0 4YY

In memory of my father, Walter Wayne Tombaugh.

CHAPTER 1

June, 1940

I should never have kissed her. Thomas Charles tried to push Cat Carlisle out of his mind, took a deep breath, and turned his attention to the city he had called home for years. He had only been away for two months, yet so much had changed. A tension hung in the air so heavy he could taste it, hot and thick on the back of his throat. His collar stuck to the back of his neck as sweat broke out between his shoulder blades. For the briefest moment, he thought about going back to his flat and crawling into bed. The sling that held his injured arm felt like a wool blanket. Exhausted and weak, he trudged towards Piccadilly Circus, his shoulder throbbing with every step. His thoughts – as they often did – returned to Cat and the unfinished business between them. His kiss. Her rejection. His sudden departure. It had taken Thomas Charles three years to fall in love with Cat Carlisle. *And I lost her with one kiss.*

Piccadilly didn't have its usual spark. He hadn't yet seen a double-decker bus. The statue of Eros had been taken away,

Thomas imagined for safe keeping, leaving a yawning chasm in the roundabout. He passed the fruiterer where the lady behind the counter kept the best apples for him. The men who used to stand outside smoking cigars and talking about the state of the world were gone now. The shop windows had been covered up with large pieces of plywood. Someone had haphazardly nailed a large poster to one of the boards depicting a young boy gazing at a British solider. The caption read, 'Leave Hitler to me, sonny. You ought to be out of London.'

Many women and children had evacuated to the country. The women who remained dressed in the smart style of office workers, independent women who spent their days toiling in offices and their nights frequenting night clubs and dancing to big band music. They walked along the street at a clipped pace with a sense of purpose. Many carried gas masks in a small box which hung from a leather strap. Thomas shook his head, remembering the brutal bombing of Guernica in April of 1937. This war would be different. Gas masks wouldn't be of much use. It would be incendiary and brutal. Invasion was imminent. Hitler was coming. After Churchill's rousing speech to the House of Commons, the people were ready.

Thomas caught a glimpse of a tired-looking man with gaunt cheeks and dark circles under his eyes in one of the few shop windows that hadn't been boarded up. He walked on. After a full minute, he realized the tired man was him. 'I look like hell.' He said the words out loud, not caring if anyone heard him talking to himself. He was out of breath and moving slowly. The time had come to reflect and evaluate, make changes in his life where necessary. The question was whether or not those changes would include Cat Carlisle.

The bookshop was just two blocks away. Thomas moved with his usual sense of awareness, deeply inculcated from his years spent doing dangerous things for a man he didn't really trust.

By the time he arrived at the back-alley antiquarian bookshop, he was ready to sit. The walking journey had weakened him. His shoulder throbbed and he longed to take off the sling which held his arm still and safe against his body. The alley was deserted, not surprising given the early hour. The tailor shop next door stood vacant, its doorway full of leaves and rubbish, its owner in all likelihood having fled to the countryside. Out of habit Thomas ducked into the alcove, ignoring the crunch of glass under his feet, counted to five, and surveyed his surroundings. Through the reflection in the glass across the street he had a good view of the surrounding footpath. Still empty. Certain he hadn't been followed, he stepped out of the safety of the tailor shop's doorway.

A bell above the door of the bookshop jangled as he let himself in. The old man who used to sit behind the counter had been replaced by a younger woman, probably in her early thirties. She had cropped raven black hair, fair skin, and thin lips doused in a layer of startlingly red lipstick. Thomas gave her a quizzical look as she looked up from the book she was reading.

'Where's…?' Thomas was embarrassed that he didn't even know the old gentleman's name.

'You mean my father, Frank? He took my children to Scotland.'

'And you decided to stay?'

The woman reached under the counter and set a small pistol with a mother of pearl inlaid grip on the counter. 'When the Germans come marching through the streets, I'll start shooting. Sir Reginald's in the back office. Turn the sign to closed and lock the door, would you?' She turned her focus back to her book. Thomas did as she asked and walked along the ancient wooden floor towards the tiny office in the back. Sir Reginald Wright sat on a rickety chair reading a tattered copy of *The Warwickshire Advertiser.*

Thomas and Sir Reginald had been having their clandestine trysts in this office for decades. The tiny room faced an alley,

3

with windows so grimy the room was cloaked in a patina of perpetual gloom. Disorganized files were stacked precariously in one corner. The desk held a brass banker's lamp in need of a polish, and – as usual – loose papers covered the surface. Sir Reginald had taken off his hat and set it on the corner of the desk. His cane – black with a silver lion's head – leaned against the wall. Thomas took in the pinstripe Savile Row suit, the impeccable tie, and felt the familiar irritation raise its ugly head. Sir Reginald didn't even raise his eyes as Thomas entered the room.

'That newspaper's rather out of date, wouldn't you say?' Thomas looked for another chair. When he didn't find one, he cleared a spot on the crowded desk and sat on it, not caring about the impropriety of his actions. For years Thomas had loyally served the Crown under a convoluted chain of command that led through Whitehall and straight to Downing Street. He had survived war, hand-to-hand combat, and a stint in a German prison camp. Sir Reginald had promised a long rest after his latest mission. It seemed as though his superior was going to renege on his promise.

Sir Reginald ignored Thomas as he shook the paper and carefully folded it before setting it on top of the stack next to his chair. Just being in Sir Reginald's presence set Thomas on edge.

'I'm here, Reginald. Why did you want to see me?'

'How's the shoulder? Infection cleared up?' Sir Reginald leaned back in his chair and crossed his legs. He surveyed Thomas with his rheumy eyes. Thomas wondered when the old man would finish with this business. God knew, he was ready to leave it all behind. He thought about moving to the country, spending his days doing research and writing in earnest, not just as a cover for his various missions. Of course, Cat would be with him. They would marry … He turned his focus to Reginald. 'Fine, thank you. My stay in the hospital proved beneficial.'

'Haakon commended you. I thought you'd want to know. He credited you for keeping your head in Nybergsund.'

'I wasn't the only one who kept a cool head,' Thomas said. 'It was a group effort, believe you me. I'm just grateful they came willingly. I wouldn't have relished forcing the King and the Crown Prince to come to England against their will.'

'Agreed. Now, onto more pressing matters—'

'No. I'm not interested in pressing matters. I'm finished. We had a deal. No more. I'm not fully recovered from the events in Norway. My shoulder isn't healed yet. I'm tired and physically weak. I was assured a long rest would be forthcoming, and I intend to take it.' He wondered what Reginald would do if he simply got up and walked away. Would the old man come after him? Send some henchmen to do his dirty work?

'You can't walk away from this, Thomas. You're too far in. Trust me when I tell you civilian life would not suit you. You're not fully recovered yet, so you don't appreciate how you enjoy the excitement. This type of work gets in your blood. You'd grow bored in months, maybe weeks. You and I both know you've grown accustomed to the money. Have you thought about finding a situation that pays you as well as I do? And, just in case you're not feeling appreciated, I need your delicate expertise.'

Liar. Thomas watched as Reginald fussed with his gold cufflinks. They had been doing this dance for years now. How many times had Thomas told Reginald he was finished with this business, only to have Reginald ignore his words and send him on another mission, often more harrowing than the last one?

'If I say no?'

'But you won't.' The old man stared at Thomas through heavy lidded eyes. He hurried on, not giving Thomas a chance to object. 'You're to go north, to a small village in Cumberland called Rivenby, under the guise of a rest cure. Take Cat Carlisle with you. I've arranged a house for her. When you approach her, tell her you've found her a house, you want her and the child safe when the bombs come. Scare her. Tell her they will come. She'll be of use to you. She grew up in Rivenby, lived there until her parents died and she moved to London with her aunt. She'll provide an in for you socially.' Reginald tossed a sealed envelope onto Thomas's lap. The envelope slipped to the floor. The old man watched as Thomas bent to pick it up, as if he knew Thomas's attitude would change now given Cat Carlisle's involvement.

Thomas let himself get carried away by his fantasy of a life with Cat in a quaint village. They'd have a garden, and a house filled with sunlight. *Oh, Cat. I hope I've not ruined it between us.* He shook his head, focused on the dingy room and the miserable man who sat before him. After thirty years, Thomas knew there was no such thing as an easy mission. Why did he think there would be one now? When he spoke, his voice was calm and steady. 'And the nature of the mission?'

Reginald rubbed a hand over his face. For a fleeting moment Thomas saw the exhaustion there.

'This is serious business, Thomas. One of ours has been murdered. She was a major player in the last war, a brilliant cryptographer. She worked in the field before we discovered she had talents in code breaking. She's made her fair share of enemies. Two weeks ago someone tampered with the brakes of her car. It crashed and she died. I'm afraid an enemy from long ago has tracked her down.

'She has a son, a Phillip Billings. His picture is in the packet, along with a scant dossier. Phillip's quite the Lothario. Actually lived in a house owned by his boss's wife, if you can believe that. She doted on him, bought him clothes, a car, the two were attached at the hip.'

'Her husband didn't mind?' Thomas asked.

'Apparently not. In any event, she caught him with another

6

woman and kicked him out of the house. Despite a wardrobe full of tailored suits, she wouldn't let him have anything but the clothes on his back. She was spiteful, tried to convince the police that he made off with a rare diamond necklace. Phillip came close to getting arrested, until the lady's maid – she was rather involved with Phillip too, if the gossip is accurate – found the necklace hidden in her mistress's desk. So Phillip returned to Rivenby penniless. He spends money like a lord and has accumulated a fair share of gambling debts.'

'Does his mother have anything in her possession the Germans could use now? Something they would buy? It just seems far-fetched they would come after her now. Codes and tactics have changed since 1919.'

Reginald shook his head. 'Not sure.'

'Local police?'

'Treating it as a homicide. Investigation ongoing. The woman's name is – was – Win Billings. She's got a niece she doted on, named Beth Hargreaves. Beth's husband died six years ago. They've got a daughter, Edythe, who is 18 years old. The two have been living with Win. Phillip expected to inherit, but his mother changed her will, leaving the bulk of her assets to Beth.'

'So if Phillip killed her, it was for nothing? What about Beth? Could she have killed her aunt?'

'Anything's possible, but I doubt it.'

Thomas had already made up his mind. Sir Reginald would get his way this one last time. Thomas would do so because of Cat. All he needed to do was convince her to go with him.

'What exactly do you want me to do? I have no standing, and surely the police are working the case.'

'I need your eyes, nothing more. This is strictly a watch-and-observe mission, with an eye towards interested parties who may try to influence the investigation or who show an unusual or inappropriate interest in things. There will be plenty of time for you to rest and take care of yourself. The country air will build your strength. The long walks in the woods will put the colour in your cheeks. I told the police you were coming as a favour to me. The DCI in charge, one Colin Kent, knows of Win's service in the last war. Kent's a good chap. He understands the lay of the land. He'll give you no trouble. You can speak freely to him. Mutual cooperation is the operative word here.'

Trust Sir Reginald to make it all sound innocuous.

'So am I correct in understanding you want me to observe the investigation, keep my eyes open in the village, and determine if anyone involved with Fifth Column operations murdered this woman as a vendetta killing? You'd think they'd have more pressing matters, like the war at hand, rather than the settling of scores from twenty years ago.'

'It is not as far-fetched as you think, old boy. Win was a dear friend, a brave operative who is – was – respected and admired by her colleagues. I need to know what her son has been up to, or if someone from her past tracked her down and killed her. If that's the case, other agents could be in danger. Some of Win's contacts in the last war are in play now. This is important, Thomas. I don't trust anyone but you to handle this one.'

'And Cat Carlisle? How is she to be involved in this? How do you suggest I make use of her?'

'You will simply start working on your next book. I was thinking a detailed study of monastic houses in Cumberland should keep you busy for a few years. Cat is a gregarious creature. Before long, she'll fall in with her childhood friends. You can accompany her to social functions and get a first-rate view of village life, get a sense for who belongs where.'

'I thought you didn't want her involved with our arrangement any longer. You said she – and I'm quoting now – was reckless, inconsistent, and too emotional for this sort of work.'

Cat had worked for Sir Reginald briefly in 1937, when it came to light that a member of her household was stealing her

8

husband's classified documents and passing them on to a German agent. The mission had ended in disaster, with her husband's murder and attention from the media.

'Do you have any idea how hard it was to keep that mess with her husband off the front page of the papers? Mrs Carlisle is like a ticking bomb. She bumps into something – correction, she simply takes a breath – and things start exploding.'

'That's a little exaggerated, don't you think?'

'Just follow the orders, Thomas. Please.'

'I haven't seen her nor spoken to her since April, Reginald. I left – dropped off the face of the earth – without an explanation. I don't suppose you took the time to let her know I've been in hospital recovering from a gunshot wound?' Thomas didn't wait for Sir Reginald's response. 'I didn't think so. She's probably furious with me. There's a very good chance she won't speak to me. If I were in her shoes, I wouldn't.'

'You've fallen in love with her, haven't you? My God, I can see it on your face. You've fallen in love with her, but the feeling isn't reciprocated.' The old man tipped his head back and laughed.

'My love life, or lack of, is none of your concern.'

'Ah, but it is. Everything you do is my business, Thomas, and it will be until the day I die. I admit to having a soft spot for Cat Carlisle. She did well for us. But there's no way she could operate without close supervision. Surely you can see that? And as for you falling in love with her, forgive me for being insensitive. I've watched women fall at your feet over the years, old boy, and you've been impervious to their charms. Now you find a woman who piques your interest … In any event, you should be glad she doesn't reciprocate. There's no room for romantic entanglements in this business.' He gave Thomas a stern look. 'She's not to be involved in this, Thomas. She is not to know about Win's activities, or why I have sent you to Rivenby. Do you understand me?'

'I'll do my best.'

'That's not good enough. Surely a man of your abilities can manage a woman, despite your feelings for her.'

'Cat's got a nose for subterfuge. She'll know I'm up to something, mark my words. When my investigation for you comes to light – and believe me it will – there will be hell to pay.'

'Handle it, Thomas. That's an order. Cat Carlisle's your problem, not mine. Bigger things are in play here than your affection for some woman.'

Thomas wanted to scream that Sir Reginald certainly didn't feel that way when he asked Cat to drug her husband and switch his papers. This parry between Reginald and him had been ongoing for years. They had both grown used to it, expected it. But Thomas didn't want Reginald issuing edicts where Cat was concerned. Because of Cat's involvement – and his desperation to be near her – he'd take the mission. Didn't he always?

'A few ground rules before you go,' Reginald said.

'I've been at this a bit too long for ground rules, don't you think?' Thomas picked up the folder and walked out of the shop.

***

An hour later, after a stifling bus ride and a somewhat circuitous cab ride in the gruelling sticky heat, Thomas stood in front of Cat's house in Bloomsbury, gathering his courage to walk up the steps and ring the buzzer. What if her attitude was ambivalent? Could he cope with her utter lack of caring? All he needed to do was lay his eyes on her and he would know how things stood between them. If she harboured the slightest affection for him, he would be able to see it on her face. And if he didn't see anything? It was time to level with Cat, and, if necessary, walk away, Reginald be damned. He wouldn't torture himself by continuing to work side by side with this woman. Unrequited love didn't suit Thomas, and he had no intention of suffering through it. No, if Cat didn't want him, he'd end the relationship. After they moved north and Cat and Annie were safely away from the impending disaster that would be London, Thomas would rescind his request for an easier job and let Reginald find him something all-consuming and dangerous, a job that would require all of his focus just to stay alive. Once he forgot Cat, he would end his relationship with Sir Reginald for good. If he survived.

He took a deep breath, hurried up the stairs and was met there by Annie and Aunt Lydia as they stumbled out the front door. Cat's aunt illustrated a popular children's book series. She claimed she did this to pay the bills, but that her still-lifes were her passion. An influential collector had become enamoured with Lydia's work last year, and now she was enjoying success. He watched the two women, surprised to find that he had missed them as well. Each of them carried a canvas under one arm, an easel under the other, along with matching tote bags slung over their shoulders. The box that held Annie's gas mask threatened to fall out of her tote. Lydia – as was her custom – wore a pair of men's dress trousers in a grey pinstripe, covered with a loose-fitting button-up shirt. At one time, the shirt was a fine custom-made affair, probably worn by a solicitor or banker. Thomas often wondered where Lydia obtained the fine men's clothing that she painted in. He had asked Cat about this once. Her comment had surprised him. 'Oh, from her lovers, probably. She's had her share of them.' He shouldn't have been surprised. Splotches of paint cascaded down the front of this particular shirt. Lydia's hair, as wild and curly as Cat's, was piled on top of her head and held in place by two criss-crossed paint brushes.

Annie Havers had started out as a maid in the Carlisle house before Cat's husband was murdered. After the case was solved, Cat had taken Annie with her, offering her a job as a paid companion. They had become close, and now Annie was Cat's ward. Cat confessed to Thomas that she wanted to adopt Annie, but Annie was loyal to her mother. The girl was 16 years old now and blossoming into a young woman. Thomas watched her fuss with her tote bag. Her movements held an acquired grace that Thomas recognized as a mimicry of Cat's easy elegance. Cat's influence was further reflected in the fine yet understated linen skirt and blouse Annie wore. The sight of Annie, the way she had grown stronger while under Cat's care, touched his heart.

'Hello, Annie.' He smiled at her.

Her face broke into a big smile. 'Oh, hello! You've come back. Miss Catherine will be ever so pleased. I'll just go and tell her.' She dropped the canvas and easel and ran into the house. Thomas just saw her duck down the staircase which led to the basement kitchen.

Thomas cast a sheepish glance at Lydia. 'How is she, Lydia?' Thomas had learned early on not to mince words with Cat's aunt. The woman had the intuition of a witch, coupled with a rapier wit and an equally sharp tongue.

'Lonely. Missing you,' Lydia said. 'And don't act so surprised. She's been out of her mind with worry. We read about the King's harrowing escape, being chased across Norway in the snow with Nazis on his trail. I assume you were involved in that?' Her eyes went to his shoulder.

'I got shot. Infection. Forced hospitalization.'

'You could have written,' Lydia said.

'May I come in?' Thomas asked. He wasn't in the mood for Lydia's diatribes. They had a tendency to be blunt, prescient, and to the point.

'Of course.' Cat's voice rang through the dark hallway. She appeared out of the dim gloom of the hallway, with Annie at her feet. His heart squeezed at the sight of her. 'Lydia, let the poor man in.'

She came towards him, hands outstretched, a smile on her face. 'Thomas—' She took one look at his shoulder and stopped in her tracks. 'What's happened?'

12

Lydia said, 'We're going. We'll be back later. It's too hot to eat dinner, so don't bother with it.' Lydia ushered Annie out the door, shoving the canvas and easel into her arms.

'Be careful,' Cat said.

'We will. Don't worry,' Annie said. She held up her gas mask, smiled at Thomas, and trotted after Lydia.

Cat and Thomas watched as they walked down the sidewalk.

'Come in. Let's go down to the kitchen. It's cooler down there.'

He followed her, noticing how the waist of the linen dress she wore was loose around her thin frame. Her hair was longer now. She wore it tied back with a scarf. A stray curl, a perfect curlicue, rested against the white of her neck. Thomas bit back the relentless yearning and followed her down the stairs.

Cat pulled a chair out for Thomas. While he sat down, she poured him a glass of lemonade from a crystal jug on the counter. She placed the glass in front of him and sat down across the table.

'Enjoy that. I'm told lemons will be in short supply before too long. We've actually planted vegetables to eat in Pete's back yard, if you can believe that. He and Lydia tilled up the grass, and we've got rows and rows of things growing. I don't know a thing about gardening ...'

She rambled about new friends and the projects they were undertaking, Annie's hard work under Lydia's tutelage, and the child's worry about things to come. The words kept coming, a feeble attempt to fill the empty space between them. Finally, she stopped speaking mid-sentence and stared at him, her eyes as green and clear as an emerald pool. He surrendered, met her eyes, unafraid to get lost in them.

'What happened, Thomas? Where did you go? How did you hurt yourself?'

He didn't want to talk about where he had been. He wanted to talk about where they were going. 'Norway. I got orders to leave immediately the day after – I'm sorry I couldn't let you

13

know I was leaving. I wasn't sure if you'd want to hear from me.'
Thomas ran a hand over his face. He was hot and tired. His
shoulder throbbed.

Cat nodded. 'I read the account in the papers. At least he didn't
abdicate.'

'He refused. He felt horrible about leaving his people. He's a
good chap, really, unassuming and fair minded. Good qualities
in a king. He's going to do his part from here.'

'We were worried about you,' Cat said. She picked at her cuticle
on her ring finger, caught herself doing so, and tucked her hands
under the table, out of sight.

'The wound got infected. I stayed in hospital until it was
resolved.'

She wrapped her hands around her untouched glass of
lemonade. 'Better now?'

'Much, actually. It still aches at night, but I am officially on
the mend.'

'Reginald must be pleased.' Cat got up and busied herself with
the tea things on the counter. Without thinking, Thomas got up
and went to her, stopping himself before he got too close.

'I am sorry things didn't work out with you and Reginald,'
Thomas said.

'There's no need to explain.' She busied herself with the stack
of cups in the sink.

'I think it was rather rotten of him,' Thomas said. 'This is a
brutal business, Cat. Consider it a blessing you are no longer
involved in it.'

'Admittedly, I feel a bit used,' Cat said. She didn't meet Thomas's
eyes. 'He expected me to do things without proper training,
promised me a job. It's not about the money. I wanted to do
something useful, something I was good at. I don't understand
what happened.'

'Me neither,' Thomas lied. He knew full well that Cat had
made a mess of things. Undercover operatives – at least those

14

who report to Sir Reginald Wright – never end up in the newspapers.

'I've found other ways to be useful. And I don't blame you, Thomas. Honestly.' She tossed the tea towel on the counter and refilled Thomas's lemonade. They sat back down at the table.

'What've you been up to?' He glanced at the two stacks of papers, which sat next to Cat's leather notebook and a fancy fountain pen with a gold nib. An inkwell rested on a small plate, small drops of blue ink spattered here and there. He smiled as he thought of all the times Cat had filled her pen and spilled ink everywhere. It had become a joke between them.

'I'm on some committees, trying to get people with no soil around their house access to garden space to grow vegetables. We're hoping to plant a garden in the square. I'm also working on a fundraiser for three new fire trucks. You'll be pleased to know I've nearly got enough money for one of them.' She flipped through the stack of papers, set them down, and folded her hands on top of them, as though in repose. Thomas's heart beat faster. He waited. She looked up at him with soft eyes and a trusting look which made Thomas lose his reason. God, he loved her. When she spoke her voice was soft and full of worry.

'We never talked about what happened before I left.'

He nearly groaned. The near kiss. The hint of a promise. The one thing that had kept Thomas going during his convalescence. He continued. 'We don't have to talk about it. It's in the past. If it makes you uncomfortable, and you don't want to work with me anymore—'

'Of course I want to work with you! Why would you think otherwise?' She put her hand on Thomas's arm. 'I owe you an explanation. I am afraid I was sending mixed signals.'

'You owe me nothing. Really. I came here with a plan to get you and Annie – and Lydia, if we can convince her – out of the city.'

She cocked her head. 'Out of the city?'

'It's not safe here. The bombs will come. I'm sure of it. And I would rest much easier if you weren't here when they did.' Thomas met her eyes, careful not to show his feelings. He knew Cat had yet to recover from the brutality of her marriage to Benton Carlisle. He understood her reluctance to open her heart. This small show of affection would have to do. For now.

She didn't look away. Instead, she took a deep breath, as if savouring the heat between them. They sat like that for a few moments, neither of them speaking. A small frisson of hope bloomed in Thomas's chest. Cat smiled as she leaned back in her chair and shook her head. 'I hadn't thought of actually leaving. It seems as though we're running away.'

Thomas shook his head. 'We're at war. London will come under fire. Why stay when there's no reason for you to? And I've got a commission, if you're still wanting to work with me.'

'I do! Let's hear your plan.'

Thomas resisted – for what seemed like the hundredth time today – the physical pull he felt towards Cat.

'I've been commissioned to write a series of books about monastic houses in Cumberland. I'd like you to take the pictures and help with layout, like you did last time. I'm going to move to Rivenby. There's a church nearby whose vicar apparently has a canon of research – his life's work actually – that he's offered to share with us. Do you want your job back? You'd spend the bulk of your time tromping around old churches taking pictures. I hope you don't think me forward for suggesting you leave, Cat. I'm not trying to tell you what to do. But I think you, Annie, and Lydia would be better off in the country.'

'I can't believe you're going to Rivenby. I grew up there.' She gazed dreamily over his shoulder. 'It's been years since I thought about home. I wonder if the house where I grew up is still standing. This is a wonderful idea, Thomas. Annie will be pleased. I've missed working with you.'

16

When she reached for a fresh piece of paper and her fountain pen – the sure sign that soon she would start making lists – he knew she was in agreement.

'I know of a house you could rent. But you'll have to call the agent today. Evacuees are going north in droves. Housing will be difficult to find.' He didn't tell her the house had already been arranged, and the phone call requirement was just a ruse to lend authenticity to Reginald's scheme to get Cat to move. Thomas reached into his pocket and pulled out a card. 'The house is called St Monica's. It's got five bedrooms, four baths, and a big kitchen with lots of light. There's five acres attached to it, so you can grow all the vegetables you want.'

'How ever did you stumble across St Monica's? I used to love that place as a child.' Her eyes danced. 'I used to daydream about living there. Beth – my childhood friend – and I would sit outside the property and gaze at the house, making up stories about our pretend husbands and servants.' She shook her head. 'I hadn't thought about Rivenby in a long time. I'm rather looking forward to going home.'

'I was looking for a place for myself, and the agent mentioned the house. I'll be staying at the inn.'

'The family who owned it back then had a daughter who used to hitch her goat up to a cart and ride through town. What was her name? Gwendolyn? They used to throw a Christmas do every year, with carolling and an old-fashioned Christmas tree with candles.' She shook her head. 'I know Lydia won't come with me. She's ordered a Morrison shelter for the basement. She wanted to get one for me, but I couldn't bear the thought of getting into it. It's nothing more than a small cage. This will do well for Annie. I wasn't sure what to do about her. We're so close to the police station, the sirens keep us up at night. Annie hasn't slept in ages. The poor thing's scared to death, and she feels guilty for it.' Her eyes took on that familiar softness that reduced him to adolescent longing. 'And in you come, with the perfect solution to this mess. Thank you, Thomas.' A look of worry passed over her face.

'What is it?'

'What about Annie's studies? Lydia has been giving her art lessons. The child's been working herself to the bone. And she's sold a few paintings. She's got talent, Thomas. I mean she's really good. I've never seen anyone work so hard. It seems cruel to take something she loves so much away from her.'

'There's a day school for her there. Surely Lydia can give her projects to do. They could communicate via the post.'

They made arrangements. Thomas waited while Cat called the agent and agreed to lease the house. He sipped his lemonade as Cat took notes about furnishings, linens, and other mundane household items. She hung up the phone, excited, focused, and busily making lists.

'I'll have to give away most of my clothes. I don't see how I can possibly take them all on the train.'

Thomas shook his head. 'Clothes will be rationed at some point.'

'Clothes? Surely not.'

'It's bad, Cat. All of the extra leather and fabric will go for shoes, uniforms, parachutes, you name it. Save your clothing. All of it.'

Their eyes met as the gravity of the situation sunk in.

'How will I get there? Surely I can't take all the trunks on the train.'

'I'll see to it. Pack all your clothes, linens and the like. I'll arrange a lorry. Can you be ready the day after tomorrow?'

'Yes,' Cat said, serious now.

'Thank you for agreeing to leave. I'll sleep better because of it.' Thomas stood. 'Can you and Annie see yourselves to the train? I've things to tend to here, but hope to leave within a few days. I'll send the lorry for your belongings the day after tomorrow and send word when I arrive in Rivenby.'

'Of course.' She capped her fountain pen and stood up. 'I'll show you out.'

They walked upstairs together, talking of Cat's childhood in the country. When they reached the door, she turned to him, rose up on her toes and kissed his cheek. It took every ounce of discipline not to wrap his arms around her.

'Thank you, Thomas. I should have known you would save the day.'

'Glad to be of service.' Thomas tipped his hat. 'Safe travels.'

'To you as well,' Cat said. 'See you in a few days.'

Thomas waited while Cat shut the door behind him and slid the bolts in place. Once he knew she was locked in the house, he headed towards the square where – if providence smiled on him – he would find a taxi. His heart swelled. He had seen the promise in Cat's green eyes. His question had been answered.

***

Cat leaned against the front door, weak-kneed, surprised at the physical reaction to seeing Thomas again. One look at him had opened the flood gates. The emotion she had so successfully been hiding rushed over her. She loved him. After her failed attempt at working with Sir Reginald, Thomas had championed her photographs and had used them in his books, ultimately lettering her serve as art director for the last book they had worked on together. Thomas's support had galvanized the bond between them. Their creative work had become a partnership. The sum of their whole – the books they produced – a marriage of Thomas's keen prose and Cat's pictures. One critic had said that the photos in the book had their own personality and evinced an emotional response. Cat would never forget Thomas's supportive friendship while she had dealt with the fallout of her husband's murder and his massive estate. She liked the work.

19

She liked her independence. She loved Thomas. And that had been the problem.

Thomas loved her. She knew it. By all methods of logic, they should be married right now. But they weren't. And it was all because of Cat, and the internal war that raged within her. If there had been any questions about her feelings for him, they were answered these past few months while he had been away. Her heart ached with longing for him, while her mind worried for his wellbeing. And yet – wasn't there always an 'and yet' – whenever Cat let the fantasy run its course, whenever she envisioned herself married to Thomas, sharing his house, his life, his bed, she was overcome with a sense of panic so strong it knocked her to her knees. Her heart loved Thomas Charles. Her mind was scared to death of committing to him. She simply wasn't ready to share a house with anyone – except Annie, of course.

Lydia – who could see the conflict of emotions and anxiety in her niece – suggested that Cat see a psychiatrist. But Cat resisted, trusting that her troubles would sort themselves out. And then she and Thomas had nearly kissed. For a brief moment, Cat had let herself go. One moment she had been swept away, weak-kneed as a school girl. Seconds later, she tasted bile. She had pulled away – ran away – like an adolescent. The next day, Thomas left without a word.

And now he's come home, so it's time to repair things between us. In truth, moving to Cumberland was the answer to everything. It would be best for Annie, and Cat could only hope it would provide an opportunity for her to make things right with Thomas. She had to manage this relationship somehow. Thomas deserved that.

With fresh resolve, Cat spent the entire afternoon calling the members of her various committees, handing off her responsibilities to any able-bodied soul who would take them. She explained her decision to take Annie to the country, as the

20

child was nervous and on edge. Most of her fellow members were supportive. Those who responded with irritation changed their ways when Cat promised a generous cheque in lieu of her hands-on efforts. With each call the idea of the move became more agreeable. How perfect it would be to return home, where the summers weren't so sweltering, where Hitler's bombs would be less likely to fall. How lovely of Thomas to arrange it all.

When the last call had been made and the papers filed away, Cat sat at the kitchen table for a moment, thinking of Rivenby, the place she had called home until her parents had been so tragically taken from her nearly twenty-two years ago.

That morning, she had gone walking on the moors. On her way back home, she had seen Beth kissing the boy who Cat thought was the love of her life. She hadn't confronted them. Instead, she had run home to her mum, hot tears running down her cheek. In her mind's eye, she conjured the kitchen of her childhood, with the flagstone floor, the warm Aga, and the curtains billowing in the afternoon breeze. How desperate she had been for her mother's comfort. But her mum wasn't there. Her Aunt Lydia sat at the table, crying into a handkerchief, a cold cup of tea before her on the table. 'It's your parents, pet ...'

Cat shook her head, tamping down the memories that threatened. Lydia had swept her away to London and had done her best to help Cat forge a new life.

Reaching for another piece of the thick linen paper she favoured, Cat started a new list of the things she had to do before she and Annie moved. Tomorrow she would start getting things sorted. She and Annie would need new coats, sweaters, Wellies, and other necessities for life in the country. By the time Annie and Lydia returned home, Cat had a plan in place.

Annie and Lydia found her in the darkened front room, the curtains drawn against the sun, drinking a large cup of tea. Lydia took one look at her and raised an eyebrow. She sent Annie off to wash up.

'So you've talked to him? Told him how you feel? Annie's been talking about the two of you all day. She's fantasized the wedding, the dress, and she hopes to be in the wedding party.'

'Whatever gave her that idea?' Cat set her cup down.

Her aunt gave her a knowing look. Cat ignored it. She patted the spot next to her on the sofa. 'Before Annie comes down, I need to talk to you.'

Lydia sat.

'Thomas has offered me my job back. He's been commissioned to write a series of books on monastic houses in Cumberland. I've decided to go with him. Annie will be safe there. The research should be interesting.'

Lydia snorted. Cat pushed on.

'You can come with us, if you'd like. I'd feel better if you were out of the city.'

'No. I'll stick it out. I'll have my cage in the basement to keep me safe from the bombs. I've lived in this house for over thirty years. I'll not be pushed out by the likes of Adolf Hitler.' Lydia put a cigarette in her mouth. 'The child is on edge. A motor-car backfired today. Annie dropped her paint brush and promptly burst into tears. She needs to get out of London. How perfect of Thomas to ride in on his white horse and save the day.'

'I'll pretend that I don't hear the undertone of sarcasm, darling,' Cat said. 'What about Annie's lessons? She won't be happy there without her art work.'

'I'll give her a list of projects that will take years. I'll come for a good long stay at Christmas. How about that?' Lydia said.

'Perfect. We'll have an old-fashioned country Christmas, like we used to do when my parents were alive. Maybe you'll like it so much, you'll stay.'

'Don't get your hopes up.' Lydia smiled to take the sting out of her words. 'Revisiting the past leads to inevitable disappointment.'

'Thanks, Lydia.'

She looked at Cat in surprise. 'For what?'

'For letting Annie and me stay here these past few years, for standing by me.' Cat would miss her aunt, their artsy friends, the hours of intellectual conversation with people who didn't judge her. She would miss London, but she had Annie to think about. 'I wish you'd come with us.'

Lydia patted Cat's hand. 'Don't be afraid of him. Thomas Charles is not Benton Carlisle. The man loves you. Take a chance, love. Follow your heart.'

'I can't,' she said.

'Why? Just tell me. I've watched you mope around this house since April. You love him. Why won't you let yourself be happy?'

'Because we'll go along fine for a while. Then, slowly but surely, he'll be telling me what I can and cannot do. Or he won't, and he'll ask me to marry him. Then what? I'll have to say no. I've grown accustomed to my freedom, Lydia. Do you realize that I have yet to live in my own house, with furniture and paint and curtains that I pick out for myself?' Cat shook her head. 'Surely you of all people can understand that.'

'That's not it, and you know it. What are you afraid of? He's a decent man, Cat. He's foolish over you.'

'What happens if he changes?'

'Thomas? Don't be absurd. He's solid as a rock, that one.'

'Ben changed.' Cat met Lydia's eyes. 'Ben seemed solid, too. Ben loved me. He was kind, and tender, and utterly devoted.'

'For how long, three years?' Lydia gave her head a tiny shake. 'He didn't change, love. I knew what he was made of when I first laid eyes on him. Tom isn't like Ben. I wish you'd just take my word for it. You're about to turn 40. You're lonely. I don't want you to look back on your life with regret of a chance not taken. Of course, you could always take him as a lover. Just think, you could sneak around some quaint country village, spending the night in each other's beds and creeping to your own house in the gloaming.' Lydia spoke before Cat reacted. 'Never mind. I know that's not your style.'

Cat giggled.

'In the end, you'll do what's best. Just keep your mind open. A solid relationship with a good man shouldn't feel like a prison sentence.' Lydia stood. She put her hands on her lower back and stretched. 'We'll leave it for now. At least he's back and that cloak of doom that's been hanging over you has lifted. You're working together again. That'll have to do for now.'

CHAPTER 2

Phillip Billings sat in his solicitor's office, waiting for his mother's will to be read, thinking of Lady Penelope Blythedale, the bitch who tried so hard to ruin his life. After today, he would be a man of independent means. Oh, how he wished he could travel to Edinburgh and flaunt his newfound wealth. He could just imagine the look on Lady Blythedale's face, as he drove by in a brand-new fancy car. He sighed out loud, not realizing that his cousin and her daughter – who also sat in the chairs opposite the solicitor's desk – looked at him strangely.

About time my luck has changed. Lady Fortune will now be sitting on my shoulder!

The past two years had been difficult. Granted, he did play a small role in the collapse of the life he had so carefully created. So what if he had taken his boss's wife as a lover? Lady Penelope had made the first move, after all. These were modern times. And women – especially women of means – took lovers just as frequently as men. In addition to being married to Phillip's employer, Lady Penelope Blythedale, a blond socialite with money and connections, had a voracious sexual appetite that nearly wore Phillip out. Nearly. Had Martha, Penelope's young maid, not been so eager, he would have been faithful to Penelope. Sleeping with

Martha – in his own bed, no less – had been a mistake. Phillip realized that. He would never forget the look on Penelope's face when she caught them in flagrante delicto.

Lady Blythedale – Phillip was only allowed to call her Penelope when they were in bed together – shopped and lunched with her lady friends on Wednesdays. In a natural series of circumstances, Martha and Phillip had started having their weekly trysts during this time. Soon the affair escalated, fuelled by delicious secrecy. Wednesday afternoon soon became a standing date. They would spend their afternoons in Phillip's opulent bedroom, tangled in the sheets, drinking expensive champagne – all paid for by Lady Blythedale. Someone must have told her about the affair. Why else would she have come home early and burst into the room? He cringed at the thought of the ensuing row, the crystal glasses thrown against the wall. Martha scarpering away, grabbing her clothes as she ran. Phillip spent about three seconds wondering what would become of poor Martha, sure in the knowledge that a reference would not be forthcoming.

After Martha had fled, Lady Blythedale had tossed a beautiful chair, covered in sky-blue silk, at a closed window. It crashed through and fell two storeys to the courtyard below. She surveyed the wreckage and cast a knowing glance at Phillip. The look in her eyes had chilled him to the bone. Without a word, she turned and walked out of the house. He thought about going after her, but changed his mind. She would come around. They always did. He would go to her house with champagne and a token of his affection – charged to her account, of course. Phillip had no money of his own and had become accustomed to the lifestyle that Lady Blythedale had provided him. She really had been very generous. He lived in the gatehouse on her vast property, had access to any number of her automobiles, and enjoyed a generous allowance which she deposited into his bank account every week like clockwork. They had too much invested in their affair to let it go. Surely this one indiscretion would be forgiven. He'd talk her around. Once he told her how things stood, Phillip felt certain she would forgive him.

Phillip had showered and dressed. After arranging for one-dozen long-stemmed red roses to be delivered to the big house – where Lady Blythedale resided – Phillip walked up the long curving driveway. No one seemed to be home. After knocking for a good fifteen minutes, he started to walk around the back of the house where a burly gardener intercepted him.

'She wants you off the property,' the man said.

'This is too ridiculous. It was a simple misunderstanding. Please go and tell her to at least speak to me. I can explain.'

'She doesn't want to see you. Doesn't want you here. Now get off the property before I throw you off.' The man's hands were clenched into ham-sized fists.

'What about my things?' Phillip had whined.

'They ain't yours. Paid for with her money, weren't they? The locks on the gatehouse are being changed right now.'

Given no other choice, Phillip had left. At the bank, he had tried to cash a cheque, only to discover that his account had been closed. Luckily, he had enough money to lodge for a night or two at a cheap hotel.

The next day, the police had come to question him about a diamond necklace that Penelope had claimed had been stolen. Not wanting trouble with the police, he left on the next train south, where he wound up at his mother's house two days later, with only the clothes on his back.

During his absence his cousin Beth and her daughter, Edythe, had moved in with his mother, Win. Beth's husband had died, leaving the woman alone with a daughter and little money. Phillip imagined that Win appreciated having Beth do the cooking and cleaning. She was a marvel in the kitchen. And although Beth was rather shy and quiet, his cousin was sweetly disposed. Edythe was another matter altogether. Headstrong, with fancy ideas of being a professional dancer, Edythe would have to be taken in hand.

His mother had not been overjoyed when he showed up at her door, his clothes rumpled, in need of a bath and a hot meal, not a penny to his name. Win Billings had never minced words. 'Beth's taken your old room. You can have the bed in the attic.' He had taken a hot bath, thinking that his mother would see to his clothes. She had begrudgingly found something for him to wear, old clothes of his father's that – by the smell of mothballs – must have come straight from the attic. A set of clean sheets lay folded on his bed.

'I'll not be your servant, Phillip, and neither will the girls. I'll give you a roof over your head and a place at the table. Nothing more. You'll need to find a job and support yourself for a change.'

'What about those?' He eyed the pile of dirty clothes that he had tossed on the floor.

'What about them?' His mother had turned on her heel and walked away.

Weeks later, his mother's frosty indifference still hadn't thawed. Phillip looked for work but couldn't find anything to suit him. Following his natural proclivities, he had started gambling. It didn't take long for him to accumulate a sizable debt, even though he had no way to pay it. And then, by some fortuitous stroke of circumstance, someone had tampered with his mother's brakes, had murdered her in cold blood. And all of Phillip Billings' problems had been solved.

He wondered if Edythe and Beth would stay on now that Win was dead and Phillip would inherit everything. He could pay his cousin a stipend and allow her to serve as his housekeeper. As for Edythe, she would respond to some proper discipline, of that Phillip was certain. If Edythe behaved properly, Phillip would consider paying for her schooling. Provided, of course, that Beth stayed on as housekeeper.

His cousin sat next to him, picking at her cuticle, lost in her own thoughts. When Beth met his gaze, he noticed the dark smudges under her eyes. She really was in desperate straits. He winked as he offered her his handkerchief. She grabbed it, careful not to let his fingers make contact with hers in the process.

The only light emanated from the solitary banker's lamp that sat on the solicitor's desk. In the shadows, old law books and stacks of files were arranged in bookcases against the walls. The desk, as big as a ship and made of dark wood, was covered in the clutter that accompanied a busy schedule. The chair behind the desk was empty. Mr Broadbent – the Billings family solicitor – was running late. When they had arrived, the secretary, Miss Hinch, had arranged three chairs in front of the desk – one for Beth, one for her daughter Edythe, and another for her cousin Phillip.

Phillip felt certain Broadbent was deliberately keeping them waiting. He sat in his chair, his hands clasping his knees, confident at his sudden change in circumstances. He moved into his mother's bedroom twenty-four hours after the police had arrived on the doorstep with the news of the car accident that had killed her. As was his god-given right, he demanded regimented meal times. When he had approached Beth with the proposition she pay him a small fee when she used the kitchen to bake the cakes she sold, she had recoiled. He bit back the irritation. How dare she? She had stepped into his family home and insinuated herself into his mother's good graces. Once the will was read, Phillip intended on setting things right. Beth and Edythe would be living in his home. As long as they remembered that, they were welcome. If not, other arrangements would need to be made.

Edythe sat with her head bowed, one lock of honey-gold hair coming untucked from her best hat, an expensive felt concoction – purchased on the last trip to London – fashioned in a shade of green that flattered the girl's complexion. He wondered how much his mother had paid for that hat. Surely Beth didn't have money for clothes like that.

Beth started to cry, gentle silent sobs.

'Mum, what's wrong?' Edythe put her arm around Beth.

29

'I can't believe she's dead. Who would want to kill her? Why would someone tamper with her brakes like that? I can see her lying there, mangled, wishing someone would come to save her.' Beth covered her face with her hands and sobbed like a baby. Phillip looked away, uncomfortable with the overt display of emotion. He had little time for female histrionics. His mother was dead. The police were investigating the murder. He had an inkling that he was a suspect, but he didn't care. The police couldn't prove anything. There was nothing else for them to do. Sobbing certainly wouldn't bring her back. He placed a large hand on Beth's thigh. She recoiled and flicked it off.

Phillip ignored the slight. 'I'm sure she didn't suffer. The impact – it would have been immediate. I'm sure of it. It will be all right, Beth. I'll help you get through it. I'll see you're provided for financially.'

Beth looked up at Phillip's words, feeling the heat as her pale cheeks flushed. 'We don't want your help, Phillip.'

'I know my mum gave you an allowance, and I know you depend on it. You won't go without. Neither will Edythe.'

'And what will we have to do in return? Will you make my mum your maid?' Edythe said. 'What about our house? Are you going to make us move?'

Phillip smiled at her. *So we've come to the truth of the matter. You greedy little bitch.* Edythe didn't care about his mother. She cared about money, and expensive hats from London. He pushed his anger aside. This was not the time.

'What do you expect me to do?' Phillip said. 'I need a place to live, and you know it. That's my childhood home. And although my mum has let you stay with her all this time, surely you couldn't expect the arrangement to be permanent.'

Beth didn't get a chance to respond. David Broadbent hurried into the room, a thick folder under his arm.

'Sorry to keep you waiting. A bit of an emergency.' His thatch of blond hair and smattering of freckles over his nose and cheeks gave him a somewhat childish air. But the lines on his forehead and the puffiness under his eyes bore witness to his age and – in all likelihood – the stress of a domineering wife and a headstrong daughter. Phillip had never liked David Broadbent, but he pushed his feelings aside as the solicitor sat at his desk.

'Would anyone like tea? No? Then let's get down to business.' He took an old document, the pages yellowed with age, out of an envelope and set it down on top of the folder. They waited while he took yet another envelope out of the file, this one newer, pristine and white. He took his time opening this envelope.

'What have you got there?' Phillip asked.

'Your mother made a new will,' he said. 'She just signed it last month. She wished to change the way her assets were distributed. She had grown very fond of Beth and Edythe, and wanted to make sure they were provided for.' He pushed his reading glasses up on top of his head and studied Phillip. 'I'll read the will and give you all the details. But I should tell you she's left the bulk of her estate, including the house, to Beth and Edythe.'

Phillip jumped to his feet and slammed his hands on the desk so hard Beth yelped. 'I don't believe it. Why would she do that? I'm her son. Did she think I didn't deserve …' He let his words trail off.

'Your mother said she vested you with your own money when you came of age, and – as I said – she wanted to make sure the girls were provided for. She was a forward thinker, your mum, and she didn't want Beth to marry someone she didn't love for financial security. She—'

'Are you saying I get nothing?'

'Of course not. If you'll sit down, I'll explain.'

'I just don't believe it,' Phillip said. 'My father would be furious if he knew what mother had done. Have you thought of that, Mr Broadbent?'

'Sit down, Phillip. I will explain once you've sat down.'

Edythe, eyes agog, stared at Phillip, whose face was now a

mottled shade of red. Out of the corner of Phillip's eye, he saw Beth open her mouth and close it again. As if she wanted to speak but couldn't find the words.

Phillip felt the room spin. This couldn't be happening. This was a joke, some sort of a sick joke.

'I didn't expect – she never said anything.' Beth turned to her cousin. 'I'm so sorry, Phillip. I had no idea.'

White hot fury flashed before Phillip's eyes as his rage boiled over. He didn't dare look at his cousin, for fear he would put his hands around her lily-white throat and choke the life out of her. She had ruined everything, ruined him. He should have known the lay of the land when he arrived home. He took a deep breath and wheeled around to face Beth. 'Really? No idea? You've been angling to inherit ever since you moved in. I have to give it to you, Beth, for being a quick worker. Well done.'

Beth's face – already pale – blanched. She wobbled on her chair as though she were about to faint.

'Mum,' Edythe cried out. She moved to her mother's side. 'How dare you speak to her that way?'

'Shut up, you little bitch. You should be ashamed of yourselves, taking what is rightfully mine.'

'Phillip, that's enough. Sit down right now,' David Broadbent said. 'Don't make me call the police.'

Phillip hadn't realized that he had sprung to his feet and was now towering over his cousin. Edythe rose too, and stood so close to Phillip their noses nearly touched.

'Keep away from her,' Edythe hissed.

'Or what? What will you do?'

Edythe didn't flinch. Phillip sat and plucked at a non-existent piece of lint on his trouser leg. He gave David Broadbent a forced smile. 'She needs discipline. And I apologize. I just wasn't expecting—'

'Never mind that,' Broadbent said. 'Phillip, you're to get a lump sum payment of one hundred pounds, along with a life income from a trust your father set up when you were born. With careful investing, you should be able to live quite well on that for the rest of your life. Your mother transferred the cottage off the high street into your name months ago. She's been collecting the rent on your behalf, and those funds will be made available to you immediately. The tenants moved out last week – death in the family, I'm told – and the cottage is available now.' He held up a set of keys.

'The cottage? The bloody cottage?' Phillip Billings grabbed the keys from David Broadbent's hand. 'She gets to live in my family home, and I get the rundown house that isn't fit for a gentleman?' He bit back his fury, doing his best not to rampage through Broadbent's office and break everything in sight. He stood and grabbed his hat.

'I am putting you on notice. I'll be hiring my own solicitor to look into my mother's estate.' He turned to Beth. 'I'd like to come to the house and go through my mother's desk, if you don't mind. Surely you have no objection to that? There are photographs of my father and other family papers that I would like to retrieve. Unless you've something to hide ...' He let the accusation hang heavy in the air.

'Of course not,' Beth said.

'I don't recommend that,' David Broadbent cautioned.

'You'd better hope your file is in order, Mr Broadbent.' Phillip nodded at Beth and Edythe. 'Good day.' He burst out of the office.

Emmeline Hinch waited for Phillip in the foyer, a worried expression on her face. 'Are you all right? I'm so sorry. He wouldn't let me see the new will.'

'Not your fault.' He pushed out the door and stepped onto the high street. Emmeline kept speaking. Phillip ignored her.

***

33

Some said the Dirty Duck had been around since Henry VIII's reign. Low ceilings crossed with thick dark beams, a fireplace large enough to roast a cow, and a bar made of ancient wood, gave credence to this. During the day, the Duck served a hearty lunch, drawing a crowd of pensioners and men without someone to cook for them, grateful for an affordable meal. Jemmy, who took pride in the ale he made and the food his wife cooked, could always be counted on to stand a pint to those short of funds. As a young man, Phillip had spent many a happy hour at the Duck, drinking with his mates, boasting about his future plans for fortune and fame. Now, as he downed one pint and ordered another, he longed for the type of clubs that he and Lady Blythedale would frequent, the places of high ceilings, Aubusson rugs, and the lush quiet that comes with unfettered opulence. They had travelled all over Scotland and England, under the name of Mr and Mrs Cyril Hammond, staying in posh hotels, ordering room service, and spending hours in bed. It didn't take long for Phillip to become accustomed to the lifestyle. It took even less time for him to feel entitled to it.

Phillip tucked himself into a quiet table in the back and gazed out the window at the high street. The table afforded a perfect view to the path that led to the tiny cottage that would now be his home. He would live in a three-room shack while Edythe and Beth would live in his childhood home. The injustice of it all made him want to scream. Instead he sipped at his pint, and let his anger towards his mother, Lady Blythedale, Beth, Edythe, and all the women of the world flow freely. Truth be told, all of Phillip's problems lay on Lady Blythedale's shoulders. If she hadn't been such a prude, he would not be in this position. How dare she bring him into her life, treat him as an equal, and then kick him out with nothing. She could have at the very least let him pack a trunk and take the suits that were custom-made for him. What was she going to do with them? And why had she told the police he had stolen her bloody diamonds? *Hell hath no fury.*

34

He sipped his beer, longing for the fine Scotch served in the heavy crystal glasses that he kept at his gatehouse. It wasn't his fault that in the throes of his despondency he turned to a gentlemanly game of cards. It wasn't his fault that he bet money that he didn't have, was it? Wasn't he used to having money? Wasn't he used to asking for anything he bloody wanted and getting it in spades? It wasn't his fault that the truth of what he possessed in his everyday life and what actually belonged to him could become blurred, was it?

And then there was Emmeline Hinch. Dear Emmeline and her unconditional love. He sighed. Love didn't pay the bills – or the gambling debts – and love certainly didn't put food on the table. Emmeline would be no help. Eventually the men would come for their money. It was just a matter of when. What Phillip needed was a miracle. Through the old warped glass Phillip watched Beth and Edythe as they stepped out of Broadbent's office and headed down the high street, arm in arm. Beth huddled over as though she were in pain. Edythe, tall and willowy, had her arm around her mum, as though holding her up. He bit back his rage. Once it was tucked away, the answer presented itself. The perfect solution to all of his troubles. He downed the rest of his pint and hurried after them.

'Beth, Edythe,' he called out. They stopped and turned to face him. Edythe stepped closer to her mother, in a protective stance. Phillip didn't let his emotion show on his face. Instead, he forced a smile and approached them with the charm that he had perfected over the years. 'I want to apologize for my outburst. It was horribly boorish of me. I'm grateful for what my mother gave me, so you don't have to worry about me bothering you.'

'You embarrassed Mum,' Edythe snapped.

'I know. That's why I am here, young lady. I'm apologizing. And you'd do better to learn respect for your elders.' He turned his gaze to Beth while Edythe continued to glare at him. 'I acted a fool and took it out on you. My mother loved you both. I had no right to say those things. It's time for me to see about getting a job somewhere. I'll have to move, probably. Sell the cottage.'

'Why don't you enlist?' Edythe asked.

'Why don't I treat you to tea?' Phillip ignored Edythe's question. He stepped between the women and offered each of them an arm. They had no choice but to take it and walk with him along the path to Gilly's. He needed to get rid of Edythe, so he could talk to Beth alone.

Edythe stopped walking and untangled her arm from Phillip's. 'Mum and I were just going to get some bread and butter and have some time alone together, Phillip.'

Phillip almost snapped at the young girl for her utter lack of manners. He stood silently by while Beth reached into her handbag and handed her ration books and some coins to her daughter. 'Why don't you head over to Gilly's and get the bread and butter if she has it, and anything else you fancy.'

'It'll be margarine, Mum. But I'll see if there are any tinned peaches or lemon curd.' Edythe glanced at Phillip – as though to make sure her mum would be safe with him alone – before she took the money and ration books, headed towards the café and the shops.

'What a graceful child,' Phillip said.

Beth gave him an irritated look. 'She's been working so hard. I worry she's not resting enough.' Beth sighed. 'She's set on going to London and dancing with a professional company.'

'We need to talk,' Phillip said.

'I'm sorry, Phillip. I don't want to talk. Not today. Please leave me alone.' Beth turned and headed towards Gilly's.

'Beth, wait. Please.' He stepped close, placing a gentle hand on her elbow. She froze under his touch but slowly turned to face him.

'That's better. What I want to say to you, and what I hope you'll agree to, is for us to get married.'

36

'Married? Us?' A bubble of hysterical laughter burbled out of Beth's throat. She covered her mouth and coughed.

'Please don't react like that. You know it's the right thing. You're a 39-year-old widow, with a young daughter. And this is not about the money. I don't care about that. You're my family.'

'You're my cousin, Phillip.'

'That doesn't matter.'

'But I don't love you.'

'You could learn to love me. Over time we would grow close.' He stepped close and tried to put an arm around Beth. 'Why don't you let me take care of you?'

Beth pushed away from him. Anger flashed in her otherwise passive eyes. 'I don't need taking care of. I've been widowed for six years, four months and eight days, and I've managed just fine—'

'You're being unreasonable. You need a man. All women do. What kind of an example are you setting for Edythe? She's head-strong already, and if someone doesn't take her in hand, she'll just get worse.'

Beth slapped Phillip across the face, just as two women came out of the fruiterer's. They hurried by, trying not to stare.

'Go to hell,' Beth said.

When Beth turned and walked away, he grabbed her arm in a vice grip, turning her to face him. 'Don't you dare walk away from me.' He squeezed her arm and pulled her close.

The two women who had passed them had stopped. Standing a few yards away, they watched the scene unfold before them.

'Beth, do you want us to get the police?' the younger of the two asked.

Phillip turned to face them, enraged. 'Mind your own damn business.'

The women stepped closer.

Beth looked down at Phillip's fingers as they dug into the soft flesh of her upper arm. Her voice shook. 'Let. Go. Of. Me.'

He let go of her and took a step back, holding both hands in the air as if to surrender. 'Beth—'

'I don't want you around my daughter,' Beth said. She didn't care who heard. 'You've got your cottage and your money. The house is mine now. I want you out, Phillip.'

Two other women had joined the group, one of them had a young girl in tow. 'Are they going to fight, Mummy? Is she going to hit him?' Her voice trembled.

'Beth, don't—' Phillip said.

'You moved in without any regard for us. You have treated me like your maid. You've abused my good will and Edythe's. The house is mine now. You are not welcome there. You can come and get your things this afternoon at four o'clock. After you get your personal items out, you are not to come back again unannounced or without permission. Do you understand? I've had it with you.'

She turned and, with a bowed head, hurried towards Gilly's. Phillip stood, humiliated, unable to do anything but watch her go.

'Serves you right,' one of the women said.

He stared at the lot of them. 'Show's over, ladies.'

So much for his *miracle*.

CHAPTER 3

Carmona Broadbent was no beauty. She knew this, just as she knew the sun would rise in the morning. A thick-ankled, thick-waisted girl, who had grown tall at an early age, Carmona lived her life with the awareness that no prince loomed on the horizon, waiting to ask her to the ball. This should have bothered Carmona, especially since her best friend in the world, Edythe Hargreaves, was blessed with the stunning good looks of a film star. But Carmona's lack of physical attributes did not bother her, for she had something even better than porcelain skin, a tiny waist, and long supple legs. Carmona Broadbent had brains.

She had spent her entire life watching the side effects of Edythe's beauty. Mothers stared, goggle-eyed, taken aback by Edythe's beauty as a child. As she got older and blossomed into womanhood, wives would stare, before they would search out their husbands, as if worrying Edythe would somehow lure the men away from their families. And poor Mrs Hargreaves worried and fretted, as though she were the custodian of a hothouse flower in need of continual tending. Carmona thought it all ridiculous. She knew, with that certain wisdom of hers, Edythe's beauty wouldn't last forever. Edythe would one day grow old, as that poet – Carmona could never recall his name, as she had little time for romantic notions – said, the proverbial bloom would eventually come off the rose. Carmona didn't wish her friend any ill will, she simply had seen into the future and knew what Edythe's life would be: she would meet someone of wealth and influence. Likely, he would see her dance and fall in love. They would properly court – or not, Carmona didn't care – marry, have many children, and live happily ever after in some big country house. By the time Edythe's looks had faded, she would be happily ensconced in her life on some anonymous manor somewhere. Her influential husband would have a mistress in a luxury flat in London. Carmona, on the other hand, would be using her fine mind to save humanity, one injured brain at a time. She was going to be a doctor, so busy saving people's lives, she wouldn't even miss the husband and children she would not have.

Carmona and Edythe were as opposite as night and day. Edythe, kind-hearted and good-natured, had done a fine job of balancing Carmona's irreverent sarcasm. Like only best friends can do, they had supported each other through the tragedies and upsets children experience on the road to adulthood. Carmona didn't resent Edythe's beauty. She believed each person had their own gifts to bring to the world.

Edythe's father was a farmer, who was lucky enough to own the land he used to grow vegetables and graze a sizable herd of sheep. Although they were financially comfortable, Edythe's family didn't have the wealth and influence – and all its accompanying responsibility – Carmona's family enjoyed. As a result of this, Edythe had developed a strong sense of purpose. When Carmona and Edythe were 10 years old, Carmona's mother had dressed them up in their fancy best and had taken them to London to see *The Nutcracker*. The girls enjoyed the train ride in the first-class car, staying in a hotel, and eating in the hotel restaurant without adult supervision. When Carmona's mother, Claris, had come down with a banging headache and had sent the girls to dinner unsupervised in the safety of the hotel dining room, the two girls had spent a happy hour watching all the well-dressed men and women, who moved so glamorously in this affluent world.

They had seen a matinee, and given Claris's influence, sat in the best seats. When the dancing started Edythe was mesmerized. She had not moved during the performance, rather she watched the show, her eyes riveted to the stage. Carmona had never seen such rapture on a human being's face. After the performance, Edythe asked question after question about the story, the dancers, how the dancers trained. She kept her programme with her on the train. After she had read it for the fourth time – Carmona had kept track – she poked Edythe's side and said, 'Why are you reading that over and over?'

Edythe had looked at her with bright eyes and said, 'I'm going to dance, Carm. Going to ask my mum for lessons. I'm going to be a ballerina.'

Carmona had watched Edythe set out to do that very thing. She had insisted on dance lessons. Her parents had given in. After a year or two, a room in her parents' home was converted to a small studio. Edythe practised, read every ballet book she could get her hands on, and practised some more. She dragged Carmona to every performance she could afford to attend. If a major company came through on tour and Edythe couldn't afford the tickets, Carmona would treat her to the cheap seats at the matinee. Ballet became the centre of Edythe's life. Driven by passion, Edythe was not afraid to work hard to get what she wanted. Carmona admired this trait in her friend. She wasn't afraid of hard work either. All Carmona needed was to find her passion. Luckily, things got much easier for Carmona when she discovered what her particular talent was.

She tried painting, writing, and dress designing. For a brief moment she entertained the idea of being an architect, motivated to some extent by her father's passion for Heart's Desire, the

41

historically significant country house that her grandfather had purchased after Carmona's grandmother died. But buildings bored her. She had all but given up the ghost and resolved herself to spending her adult life bored and unremarkable, when she stumbled across an ancient copy of *Gray's Anatomy* in her father's library. It was a rainy afternoon. Edythe was home practising. Tired of the murder mysteries she usually read and not in the mood for an historical biography, Carmona had picked up the book and thumbed through it, captivated by the drawings of body parts. With nothing better to do, she had taken the book to her room and spent the rest of the day lost in the interior workings of the human body and the diagrams which accompanied the writings. She read until her neck ached, surprised when she stood up to stretch that four hours had passed. Carmona had found her bestowed mission.

Carmona's mother, Claris Broadbent, had a very specific plan for her only child: Marriage, children, death. End of story. Carmona wasn't having it. Of her own volition, she stole a piece of her mother's stationery and wrote to the London School of Medicine for Women. She used Edythe's address – with permission of course – knowing her mother would not be happy with Carmona's newfound interest. The school wrote back, sending a packet of information setting out the type of course work a young woman could do to prepare herself for medical school, along with an application for admittance.

Carmona had always been a diligent student. Her grades were exemplary. She had a flair for maths and science. Since her studies kept her out of trouble, her parents arranged extra tutoring on the subjects she loved. By the time she turned 18, she had a firm grasp on anatomy, physiology, and all the other subjects required for medical school. Now that Edythe's mother had inherited money – the whole village knew of Phillip Billings' crushed expectations and the very public altercation on the high street – Carmona realized it was time to act. Edythe would be able to leave for

London in January. Carmona intended on going with her. The time had come for her to speak to her parents of her plan.

Carmona and Edythe met for a night at the cinema, but Edythe was so excited about her upcoming move, the two had forgone the movie, choosing instead to spend the evening at Edythe's making plans. The girls reckoned their parents would rest easier knowing they were together. They would find a flat together. They would look out for each other as they made their way in the big city. It seemed so easy when Carmona discussed the move with Edythe. Now all she had to do was tell her mother and father of their plans and convince them to let her go.

Making a point to be home promptly at a quarter to ten, fifteen minutes before her curfew, Carmona found her parents in the drawing room, sitting before the fire as they often did of an evening. Her father wrote something on a legal pad, while her mother thumbed through a magazine, turning the pages too quickly to read the words on the page.

'Hello, dear one.' Her father had smiled when she walked in the room. Her mother smiled at her before she went back to her magazine.

She stood before the fire and faced her parents. 'Mum, Dad, I want to speak to you about my future.'

Her mother looked up, surprised. Carmona had never allowed her mum and dad to see her serious side. She had kept that part of her psyche protected, secluded in her room with her medical books and studies. Her mother closed her magazine and tossed it in the basket at her feet. Her father put the cap on his pen while Carmona pulled up a vacant footstool, and sat before her parents, eager and expectant.

'I want to go to medical school.'

She remembered her father's eyebrows had flown upward and her mother had gasped.

After a moment's pause, her mother spoke first, taking command of the situation, like she always did. 'Don't be

43

ridiculous, Carmona. Do you know what you're saying? Do you have any idea what medical school entails?'

She glanced at her father, hoping for some help. 'Of course, I do, mother. Why do you think I've been studying so hard these past few years? I'm ready.' Encouraged now, she stood up before the fire. 'I'll go to the London School of Medicine for Women and do my clinical studies at the Royal Free Hospital. I'll have to move, but Edythe and I can share a flat or a room, if we have to. She's going to London as well. In January. That will give me a few months to get ready. I won't be in the city alone, so you won't have to worry about me. I'm 18 now. It's time for me to do something with my life. I want to be a doctor.'

If Carmona could have seen herself, passionately persuading her parents about her future, she would have been pleasantly surprised. Her thick brown hair glimmered in the dim firelight, and her cheeks glowed with passion. She spoke in a clear and concise way that showed her intelligence, education, and breeding. A shame she was too preoccupied to notice the tale-tell glimmer of a proud smile on her father's lips.

'Absolutely not.' The Broadbent family was not a democracy. Claris Churchwright Broadbent had long grown accustomed to running her family like a tight ship, handing down edicts she expected to be followed by her husband and her daughter alike.

'Why?' Carmona demanded. 'Tell me what you've got against me moving? There's nothing holding me here. I know you want me to marry, but all the eligible men are off fighting. Edythe's mother is letting her go. She cried when Edythe told her she wanted to go, but Mrs Hargreaves just hugged her and promised to help in any way she could.'

Carmona's father opened his mouth to speak, but her mother interrupted him.

'Carmona, darling, sit down.' When Carmona complied, her mother changed her tone. Carmona knew she was trying to sound reasonable, but to Carmona's ears her mother sounded condescending, bossy, and authoritarian.

'Edythe Hargreaves doesn't have the opportunities you have,
darling. She has no chance of securing a husband from a fine
family. While I'm glad that she and her mother are now financially
secure, the circumstances are completely different. I've gone along
with your educational whims because you are so passionate about
them. You should see yourself now, Carm, you look beautiful.
But no, dear. No medical school, no London, and no college.
You've a responsibility to this family, to your father and to me.
You must marry well and settle down to domestic life. Surely you
can see that?'

'Dad?' Carmona turned to her father for help. David Broadbent
didn't even look at his wife. He didn't dare go against her. If he
did, there would be hell to pay. Carmona would have felt sorry
for him if she weren't so angry. 'Dad, surely you're not going to
agree with her on this one issue? This is my future we are talking
about.' Carmona turned to face her mother. 'I won't get married.
I won't do as you say, and I won't be treated like chattel in a
medieval fiefdom. My God, who the hell do you think you are?'
Her rage, now released, sprung forth like a gusher. 'And don't
think you can stop me. I don't need your permission, Mum. I
am of age.'

'You'll not get a penny from me, Carmona. Nor your father.
Not one penny. So if you want to live on the streets—'

Carmona remembered the trust fund, set up long ago by her
grandfather. Surely there was enough in it to pay for her schooling.
A part of Carmona, the childish part that would have cherished
a moment of vengeance against the overbearing woman who had
ruled the family roost with an iron fist, wanted to tout her victory.
But Carmona kept quiet. The stakes were too high. Claris
Broadbent would seize the knowledge and use it to sabotage
Carmona's plan. Taking the high road, she stuffed her anger aside
and forced a congenial smile. The look on her father's face shifted

from surprise to curiosity. David Broadbent wasn't used to his headstrong daughter giving in so quickly. Carmona looked down at her feet, smoothed her skirt, and forced an acquiescent smile. 'Can't blame me for trying.' She kissed her father's cheek and then her mother's.

'I'm tired. Good night.' She turned and walked out of the room, leaving her parents in stunned silence. Had her parents not stared at each other in shock at Carmona's sudden change of emotion, had they happened to turn their glance to Carmona's reflection in the mirror over the fireplace, they would have seen the devious expression on her face. Had they seen the expression, they would have been very concerned indeed.

Carmona's room was at the back of the house, close to the library. She had chosen it because she loved the sunlight that flooded through the large window in the afternoon and because the room was big enough for her to have a fireplace with two comfortable chairs in front of it, along with a huge desk where she studied. She and Edythe had spent hours there, playing games as children, planning their lives as they grew older. There was no fire now. Her maid, Liddy, met her at the door.

Carmona had never wanted a maid. She didn't like being waited on. She liked Liddy, though. Over the years, the two of them had become trusted friends, had shared their dreams and secrets.

'I'm just leaving. How did it go? Did you talk to them?'

'I did. My mother said no.' Carmona stripped off her clothes and threw them on the bed. Liddy started to pick up the clothes. Carmona stopped her. 'Just leave them. I'll put them away when I get back.'

'So what will you do?'

Carmona pulled on a pair of her father's corduroy trousers and an old fisherman's sweater. She donned a dark coat and hat, along with warm gloves. 'I'm going out.' She raised the sash of her window and swung one leg out. She smiled at Liddy. 'Don't worry. I have a plan.'

'That's what I'm afraid of. You're going to get me fired,' Liddy called out just as Carmona swung her other leg out the window and disappeared into the frigid night air.

***

Phillip arrived at Beth's just as she and Edythe, along with Carmona, were sitting down to dinner. He didn't care that he was three hours late, all but ignoring Beth's four o'clock edict. The house smelled of onions and chicken. His stomach rumbled in response to the enticing smells, but he had no inclination to sit down to a meal with Beth or Edythe, not that they would ask. Dining with those women and their surly attitudes would do nothing for his digestion. He popped his head into the kitchen.

'You're late,' Beth said. The look on her face made it clear she wasn't glad to see him.

Edythe shot him a glance and slammed a serving plate piled high with meat and potatoes down on the table. Carmona Broadbent jumped at the sudden crash, her eyes moving from Beth to Edythe and, finally, to Phillip. Phillip had always liked Carmona. Although she was a bit chunky and thick-ankled, she wasn't half bad. The Broadbents were rolling in money, but Carmona didn't put on airs. Phillip knew Carmona fancied him. A wink from him would cause Carmona's pretty skin to blush a becoming shade of rose. Her eyes danced when she saw him.

'I'll just get down to it. Shouldn't take long.' He winked at Carmona and – satisfied with her response – headed towards the small room that held his mother's desk. Once he was certain no footsteps followed, he methodically took everything out of the desk, in search for any stray envelopes of cash. His mum was known for stuffing pound notes in envelopes and hiding them all over the office. A thorough search – including looking through all the books – netted him a few coins and an unopened pack of cigarettes. He cleared the papers out of his mother's desk – he would go through it all later – and stuffed them, along with the few clothes he had, in a carryall. He slipped out the front door without saying goodbye.

By the time he made it to the Dirty Duck, all the tables were taken and the bar was standing room only. Jem looked up when Phillip came into the pub, took one look at Phillip's face and poured him a pint and a shot of whisky. The whisky went down too easily. Phillip accepted the second one and took his drinks to the back of the room, waiting for the couple who sat at his favourite table to leave. Timing was a funny thing. Had the pub not been crowded, had Phillip been sitting at his table, he would have seen the two men loitering in the alley that led to his cottage. But Phillip's obsession with the unfairness of his life rendered him oblivious to the two men. When the couple who sat at his table tottered out of the pub on unsteady legs, leaning against each other for support, Phillip ordered another round and spent the next two hours drowning his sorrows and listening to the regulars sing their bawdy songs.

Rivenby was a small village, and the Dirty Duck its only pub. During the week, things got quiet around nine-thirty or ten. Most of the patrons were farmers, who had early chores in the morning. Soon Phillip was alone at his table. Jemmy came up with the bottle of whisky and two glasses, a rag hanging out of his back pocket. He poured a drink for Phillip and for himself.

'For luck,' Jemmy said.

'God knows I need it,' Phillip said, surprised that his words slurred. He sipped the drink. 'You've probably heard what's happened.'

'Yep,' Jemmy said. He busied himself wiping down the other tables around Phillip, polishing them to a high shine. 'It's a shame. But you've got a roof over your head and a wee bit of money. That's something.'

48

Phillip never ceased to be amazed at the way gossip travelled around a small village. 'It's complicated, Jemmy.'

'It always is.' Jemmy picked up the bottle, filled his glass, and waved it at Phillip. 'Another?'

'No. Better not.' Phillip stood. 'What do I owe?'

'On me tonight,' Jemmy said.

'Thanks, Jemmy.' Phillip grabbed his hat and headed towards the door.

'Mind how you go, mate.' Jemmy sprayed lemon oil on Phillip's table and started to rub it with sweeping circular motions.

Phillip stepped out into the clear night and shivered. Rivenby was a far cry from the warm seaside towns that he and Lady Blythedale had visited, places with azure seas, white sand, and golden sun. God, could matters get any worse? He ran the numbers in his head once again as he tried to find a different way to make the money he inherited from his mum and the money he could get from the sale of his cottage cover his debts and give him a fresh start. He would need a place to live, no matter where he went. No matter how he played it, there simply wasn't enough.

Phillip didn't notice the two men who blocked his way until he bumped into one of them.

'Excuse me,' he said.

'Not so fast, Mr Billings.' They wore dark suits and hats pulled down low over their heads. One of them was tall and rangy. The other short and thick, with a nose that resembled a mangled cauliflower. Phillip looked around. The street was deserted. No one would come to his rescue. His eyes darted, looking for an escape path.

'Don't even think about running, boyo.' The tall one spoke with a thick Irish lilt. 'You're piss drunk and you'd never get away.'

'I – I – I don't have your money yet,' he said. 'But I'll have it in a week or so. I've got an inheritance coming, and I'll pay. I owe ten pounds. You'll get it all. Just give me a week.'

'Oh, you'll pay all right, boyo, but the price has gone up. You'll pay fifteen pounds.'

'Hey, that's not what we agreed,' Phillip said.

'Keep talking and we'll make it twenty,' the tall one said. He nodded at the shorter man. Like a flash, his fist flew, landing a punch to Phillip's abdomen, that knocked the wind out of him. When he doubled over, the man kneed him in the face. Phillip felt his lip split, as the metallic tang of blood dribbled into his mouth. Unable to catch his breath, he gasped and fell to the ground in a heap.

'One week, boyo. Fifteen pounds. And don't even think about running. You can't hide from us.'

They stepped over him and slipped away into the dark night.

***

Carmona was used to taking late-night strolls. She liked the feeling of solitude under the stars. The night noises – nocturnal birds and animals – were a symphony to her. She landed on the loamy grass outside her window and headed by rote to the high street, which would lead her towards her grandfather's house. If she hurried, she could make it there in fifteen minutes. Grandfather may be asleep already, but she would wake him. She needed to tell him of her plans, confirm that she had his blessing. If Grandfather supported her decision, she wouldn't need anything from her parents. She wouldn't need their money and she wouldn't need permission. She'd wait until January – when Edythe was leaving – and move to London with her. The wind clipped at her cheeks. Carmona liked the feeling of the cold night air against her skin almost as much as she liked being alone under the bright stars.

Occupied with thoughts of the new life that awaited her in London, Carmona walked along the high street, making a mental inventory of all the things she would have to do to prepare for her trip without her mother being aware, enjoying the solitude of the quiet village. A man lay curled up in the foetal position on the walkway. He groaned.

'Phillip? What are you doing there?' Without thinking she hurried over to him. When he rolled over on his back, she took off her sweater and placed it under his head. 'What's happened to you?'

'Got mugged. Wind knocked out of me.'

Without thinking, Carmona smoothed back Phillip's hair. 'Just take a second and get your breath.' She tried to remember what she had read about people that couldn't breathe. 'Just stay calm. Don't force it.' His breath was heavy and laboured. While Phillip collected himself, Carmona did a visual inventory of his injuries. His lip had been bleeding. Trails of red clotted on his chin, with accompanying splatters down the front of his shirt. His arms and legs didn't look like they had been broken, but Carmona gently ran her hands over them, just to make sure. 'Can you bend your knees?'

'No broken bones,' he said. 'Just a split lip and a punch in the gut that knocked the wind out of me.'

'Can you sit up?' Carmona helped Phillip sit up. After a moment, he rose to his feet. Once standing, he wobbled. 'Put your arm around me. I'll try and hold you up.'

'You're a good girl, Carmona.' He reached into his pocket and handed Carmona a key. 'Let's go to my cottage.'

When Carmona was 10 years old, Harry Brewster had tried to look up her skirt. Carmona had given him a black eye for his trouble. That had been the only time that Carmona had been physical with a man. Her father hugged her on occasion, but Carmona had never felt the hard muscles of a male before. They stumbled up the steps to the cottage. Phillip unlocked the door with a shaking hand.

'Light switch is by the door,' Phillip mumbled. Carmona's

suspicions that Phillip had been drinking were confirmed when he put his head on her shoulder and she got a whiff of his breath. Carmona turned on the light. The kitchen was old, clean, and utterly bare save a kettle, a tin of tea, a tin of biscuits, half a loaf of bread, and an unopened jar of Bede Turner's raspberry preserves. Two plates, two chipped mugs, and one bowl were the only dishes on the shelf.

'Where are the rest of your dishes and things?' Carmona asked.

'Don't have any. Not yet, at least. Just moved in today.' While Phillip sat at the kitchen table, leaned his head back and closed his eyes, Carmona took a quick tour of the house. Two comfortable chairs and a table were in the small living room. The tiny bedroom at the back of the house had a single bed and a dresser, a utilitarian grey blanket folded at its foot. She opened the wardrobe and saw two shirts and a pullover sweater folded on the shelf. She took the sweater and brought it back to Phillip. 'Here, put this on.'

The bathroom was clean, but tiny, and – thankfully – stocked with towels. Carmona grabbed three of them, soaked one with hot water, one with cold water, and left one dry. Back in the kitchen, she found Phillip trying to stand.

'I need tea. And maybe something stronger.' He rose to his feet but sat back down. 'My head. Good God. Hurts.'

'Don't be an idiot, Phillip. Sit down and let me clean you up. After that, we'll give you some tea.' Carmona pulled the chair next to him. 'Tip your head back.' She folded the cold cloth into a square and placed it on his forehead.

'Oh, that's nice,' Phillip said. He remained still while Carmona wiped the blood off his face.

'I'm afraid your shirt is ruined, unless your laundress is a miracle worker.'

'I don't have a laundress,' Phillip said.

Carmona stopped, embarrassed. Of course he didn't. Everyone in the village knew Phillip Billings was a ne'er do well, always in financial difficulties. 'I'm so sorry, Phillip. I didn't mean anything by it.' When her eyes met his, she was startled by the warmth she saw there, warmth that was directed at her.

'You're a good girl, Carmona.' He stood, reached out, and ran a gentle finger over her cheek.

Unable to stop herself, Carmona moved closer to him. He smelled of lemon and cedar and cigarettes. She stared at his full lips, taken aback by her body's physical response to him.

'You're very beautiful. It's a different sort of beauty, one of good bones and character. I hope you know that.' He stood now, stable on his feet, moved to the stove, and put the kettle on. 'Forgive me for being forward.'

Emotions swirled in Carmona's mind, while newfound sensations awakened in her body. She wanted to press herself against Phillip Billings and feel the heat of his body again. She stared at her feet, as if her brown outdoor shoes and her father's corduroy trousers could bring her back to reality. They didn't. Something had come to life in Carmona, something physical and frighteningly wonderful. She met Phillip's gaze, caught his eyes and didn't look away. 'I should go.'

He stared at her for a moment, his eyes saying one thing, his words another. 'I understand. Thank you for you ministering to me tonight. You're like an angel.' When he smiled, Carmona's heart sang. 'Come back and see me?'

Carmona nodded. 'I'll come and check on you tomorrow.'

'Good night, Carmona Broadbent.' Phillip started to bow but stopped midway. 'Oh, my head. Not ready for that yet.'

'Get some rest.' Carmona stepped out in the night air, not caring that it was now too late to go to her grandfather's.

53

CHAPTER 4

The sun shone on Cat and Annie as they stood on the path before St Monica's. A gust of wind whipped around them. Annie's hat flew off. She grabbed it before it hit the ground, and tucked it under her arm. Cat saw the smile in her eyes and remembered when Annie had first come to her to work for the Carlisle family. She had been 13 at the time, and had lied her way into a job to escape an abusive stepfather. As far as Cat could remember, she hadn't heard Annie laugh since September of 1939. Now, with her cheeks red from the wind, and her hair loose from its pins, Annie looked like a carefree young girl. Her eyes still had the dark circles of exhaustion, but Cat remained hopeful the change of scenery would revive Annie Havers and wash away the fear which had kept her from sleeping these past few months.

'Is it always this cold in the summer?' she asked.

'We're more north now, darling. We do get our summer days, and then we get this. Let's go in.'

'It's an awfully big house.' Annie picked up her valise and the carryall that held her precious art supplies. 'Sprawling even. What are we going to do with all this room?' She headed up the path, which cut through two sloping lawns. Two raised beds had been placed in the sunniest spots. One held what Cat imagined was a picking garden. There were two rose bushes, delphiniums, foxgloves, and a myriad of other flowers Cat didn't recognize. The other held rich, black soil that looked freshly tilled and in need of planting. She followed Annie up the brick path, thinking about flowers and gardens, and how she had so much to learn about both of them.

The house was bigger than Cat remembered. Her childhood recollections were of a massive brick house, with large windows and lots of light. Now ivy grew up the sides. The brick that showed through the ivy had mellowed with age. The window frames glistened white with fresh paint, an acknowledgement someone had maintained the house, despite the shortage of workers. A woman wearing a black dress, white apron, and a severe look on her face opened the front door just as Cat and Annie approached. She took one look at them, and her severe expression broke into a lined smile, revealing even white teeth.

'Catherine Paxton,' the woman said. She stepped out of the house, wiping her hands on her apron as she came towards them. 'I used to watch you when you were just a wee thing. You were a handful. Inquisitive little thing. And those red curls. Pretty as a summer's day, you were.'

'It's Carlisle now, I'm afraid. Hello,' Cat said. 'You must be Bede Turner? Thanks for being here to greet us.'

'Let me take those bags.'

Cat looked at Annie, who smiled and shrugged her shoulders, as they stepped into the house. Memories flooded over Cat. She hadn't been in the house for more than thirty years. Back then, the sweeping staircase that wound around the wall up to the second floor had been cluttered with books, coats, knapsacks, and other childhood detritus waiting to be carried up and put away. Now the stairs lay empty. The bannister gleamed with a high shine. A long trestle table rested against one wall, a single brass lamp sat on top of it. That, along with a rug large enough

55

to cover a good part of the parquet floor, was the only furniture in the room. Cat liked the austerity of it.

'I've always liked this part of the house. You might want to add more furniture, a bigger table,' Bede said. 'Follow me. I'll just show you to your rooms.' Bede headed up the stairs, chattering all the while. 'If you don't like where I've put you, no worries. You've got five to choose from. Mrs Carlisle, I thought you'd want the biggest room. It's only proper.'

She stopped at the room. 'This is yours, miss.' Annie stepped into her room and gasped. 'It's beautiful.' She put her carryall down and rushed to the window. 'Look at the view. I'm going to paint this. Tomorrow. First thing.' A tall twin bed with a mahogany headboard was nestled against one wall. A vanity and mirror, along with a matching wardrobe had been placed opposite. The wardrobe had tall mirrors on its doors. They reflected the light from the windows. A small chaise had been tucked into the corner, a reading light next to it. Annie walked over to it. 'Would it be all right if we moved this?'

'Whatever for?' Bede said.

'I'm going to set up my studio here,' Annie said. 'I'm an artist.'

Cat laughed. 'Let's just wait and see the rest of the house, Annie. We've plenty of room. You shall have a studio, but let's get the lay of the land before we decide where it will be.'

'Okay.' Annie shrugged. 'Thanks for carrying my bags up, Bede. I like to cook, and will help you in the kitchen if you want me to.'

'Do you now?' Bede said. 'I'd welcome the company, miss. I'll just show Mrs Carlisle to her room, and then I'll be back to unpack for you. There's fresh towels in the bathroom down the hall.'

They left Annie unpacking her art supplies, a contented smile on her face.

'She has a hard time accepting help with domestic chores,' Cat whispered. 'Feels guilty being waited on.'

'She's a painter? An artist? She's just a girl.'

'I know,' Cat whispered back. 'But she's quite good. Even sold a couple of paintings. She wants to illustrate children's books.'

'Is she one of them child prodigies?'

'You know, Bede, I believe she is.' Cat stepped into her room. 'This is absolutely perfect.' The room was bigger than Annie's, but it was situated in the corner of the house and had the benefit of windows on two walls. The furniture was old, made of heavy wood. The bed looked comfortable, with clean linen sheets and a peach silk counterpane. She pushed open a window and took deep breaths of the country air. Green fields seemed to stretch for miles before they reached the woods. The side windows showed a view of the road that led to the village. Farther along the lane was a brick house with a large garden surrounded by tall hedges.

A sweep of memories came rushing back. In her mind's eye she saw herself as a child, her long red braids dangling down her back as Beth pushed her on the swing that used to hang from the old oak tree. Beth's family had their own house, but her parents travelled a lot, so Beth and Cat spent a lot of time at Beth's Aunt Win's. The tree had grown bigger in the twenty-plus years she had been gone. Its gnarled branches seemed to wave at her, as the memories came forth, unbidden. Cat closed her eyes and leaned against the windowsill. She saw her mum walking through the gate and up the path to Win's house, come to fetch Cat home. Cat shook her head and pushed those memories away. Now wasn't the time.

'Whatever happened to Win Billings? Does she still live there?'

Bede came to stand next to Cat. 'Winifred Billings. That's a sad story there. She had a car accident. Drove right off the Lea Road that leads to the village. Come to find out her brakes had been tampered with. She was murdered.' Bede said the words slow, with dramatic emphasis.

Cat turned to face Bede. 'Murdered? Are you sure?' This was

a small village. Gossip spread quickly and was often embellished in the process.

'It's true. There was an inquest. I heard it with my own ears. Cliff Swan got up on the witness stand – he's the village mechanic. Knows more about cars than anyone. I'm friends with his mum. He always had a talent for building things – has one of those mechanical minds. He testified under oath someone cut through some pipe with a hacksaw. Said it disabled the hydraulics, so the brakes couldn't stop the car.' Bede's eyes teared up. She wiped them with her apron. 'Excuse me, ma'am. Miss Win was a dear soul. I used to do for her on Tuesdays. Now I go in and do the rough for Beth and her daughter Edythe.'

'Beth married then?'

Bede looked at Cat. 'That's right. You two were mates. She's Beth Hargreaves now. She and her daughter Edythe live in the house now. She'll be right pleased to see you.' Bede moved to shut the window.

'Let's leave it open for a while,' Cat said. 'The fresh air is bracing.'

The women headed downstairs, Bede chattering all the while about the peculiarities of the house. Cat stopped in front of Annie's door and rapped. When Annie didn't answer, she pushed it open to find Annie on her bed, fast asleep.

'Poor thing,' Bede said. 'Exhausted. I noticed it when I laid eyes on her.'

'It's the sirens. Our house in London is near the police station. They go off all night. And they are so loud.'

'We don't have no sirens around here. We've got evacuees, a lot of women and children who aren't familiar with country ways, but we've got no sirens.'

They had buttered toast, apples, and biscuits still warm from the oven at the table in the kitchen. Cat insisted Bede eat with her.

'Tell me more about Beth,' Cat said.

'Inherited the house, Beth did. Win changed her will and left everything she owned to her niece. Well, not everything. Her scoundrel of a son got some money and a cottage off the high street. There are those who say Beth murdered Win for her money. But that's not true, miss. No how. Beth loved Win like her own mum. And she's a hard worker. Bakes cakes for fancy parties and weddings. Delicious cakes. I am a fairly decent baker myself, but my biscuits and cakes don't come close to Beth Hargreave's. She's got a gift for it. Anyway, her husband died, left her and the girl – Edythe, she's 18 now – short of funds. Win took them in. She enjoyed having them around. She was lonely. Husband died so young. He was the love of her life, so she never remarried. Miss Win had money, but she didn't put on airs. Used to eat the midday meal with me. Sometimes when I was busy cleaning, she'd get right in the kitchen and cook for us.' Bede shook her head. 'She was a great lady.'

'Are the police investigating the murder?'

'Now I don't say nothing about that. Best not to ask questions about them police. They have their own way of doing things. Beth didn't do nothing wrong. That's all I can say about it.' Bede refilled Cat's cup. 'Now, about them drapes ...'

After the tour of the house, Cat and Bede sat down together and spent a pleasant hour making arrangements for Bede's employment. They discussed meal times, menus, and provisions available with rationing. Bede knew many farmers, and as such was able to barter for eggs, butter, and milk. 'We'll get some vegetables planted in the garden outside. Once we've got some vegetables to trade, we may be able to get a bit of meat. We could keep our own chickens, so we can barter with eggs, too.' Cat agreed to all Bede's suggestions, glad to have someone so competent in her employ.

Bede pushed away from the table. 'I'll wash up and unpack your things. Why don't you walk over to Beth's house? I'm betting she'd be glad to see you after all this time. I'll see Miss Annie is tended to when she wakes up.'

'Thank you, Bede. Do we have secateurs in the garden shed? I may cut some of those flowers for Beth.'

Half an hour later, Cat headed down the lane, a bunch of lupines wrapped in newspaper under her arm. She would have to face Beth sometime and tell her that she had seen her best friend kissing her boyfriend. Although that particular tragedy diminished with news of her parents' death, Cat knew that she had to tell Beth what she had seen on that brutal day so long ago. Beth would have wondered why Cat hadn't responded to the myriad of letters she had sent. Best to get it over with now. The wind had died down. The air still held a chill, but the sun felt good between her shoulder blades. As she walked down the lane, the anxiety about Thomas, Annie, and the move evaporated. She had made the right decision for Annie and for her. All she needed was for Thomas to arrive. She missed him.

***

Beth's front door stood open. Cat's stomach growled in response to the smell of cinnamon, ginger, orange, and vanilla that wafted towards her. Cat rapped on it, and called out. 'Hello?'

'In here,' a voice responded. 'In the kitchen. Come in.'

If Beth's cakes were as good as they smelled, Bede was right. There was something inherently intoxicating about the scents. Cat stepped into the kitchen, a spacious room with a tile floor and a large work space in the middle. Copper pots and pans gleamed from shelves along the walls. In the centre of the work table lay three tiers of un-iced cake. Next to it on a cooling rack were several dark nutty loaves.

She found Beth sitting at the table, her blonde curls piled on top of her head and covered with a hairnet. Wisps had escaped and hung into her eyes.

'Cat! I meant to come to you as soon as I finished working.'

Beth stood up and hurried over to Cat. She wrapped her arms around her, as though the past hadn't happened, and pulled her tight. 'I heard you were taking St Monica's. Are you glad to be home? Please, have a seat. I'll make some tea.'

'These are for you,' Cat said.

Beth took the flowers. 'Thank you. They must be from your garden?'

'Yes,' Cat said. 'And there's plenty more where those came from, so feel free to pick a bouquet for yourself anytime. I'm about to get busy planting vegetables. Getting used to country life.'

Beth poured strong sweet tea into the same cups with the red peonies on them that she and Cat had used as young girls.

'I remember these cups,' Cat said.

'I knew you would.' Beth smiled. She took a cake from a tin, sliced two pieces and brought those to the table as well. 'I read about you in the papers. We all did. Your husband's murder, the police investigation. Was it terribly horrid?'

Cat nodded. 'I'm still picking up the pieces. Every now and then someone recognizes me on the street, or the newspapers run a story on Benton's death, trying to revive the sensation. At least they did before the war, and the fall of France. Safe to say I am no longer newsworthy. I'm hoping this move will give me – and Annie – a fresh start.'

'Who's Annie? Your daughter?'

Cat explained Annie's place in her life.

The buzzer dinged. Beth pushed away from the table and took two round cakes out of the oven. With professional expertise she took them out of the pan and placed them on cooling racks on the worktop. That finished, she topped up the cups with tea and sat back down.

'I take it you bake professionally?'

'I do, by necessity. Rationing makes things a bit difficult these days, but baking is the only thing I'm good at.'

Cat spoke, eager to clear the air between them. 'I'm sorry I didn't write back to you.'

61

Beth looked at Cat with sad eyes. 'Why didn't you? When your parents died, you left without saying goodbye. You were my best friend.'

'I saw you, Beth.'

Beth looked at Cat as though she didn't understand.

'With Bill. I was so angry at both of you, especially you.'

'Bill told me that when he spoke to you, you gave us your blessing. Then when you just upped and left—'

'Bill never told me about the two of you. I saw you heading into the woods together and followed. I saw him kiss you. Admittedly, the betrayal stung at the time. When you wrote, I just didn't have the courage to write back and confront you. My life was in a tailspin.' Cat shook her head. 'It's all so long ago.'

'I'm so sorry, Cat. We fell in love. I tried not to acknowledge my feelings, but there they were. Bill said he told you about us and that you were fine with it. And then your parents died, and you were gone. I hope you can find it in your heart to forgive me.'

'I forgave you ages ago. I'm ashamed for not reaching out. Bede mentioned that Bill died. I'm sorry.'

'Thank you. It's been six years, but I still ache for him. We had a child together, Edythe. She's just turned 18. We worked his parents' farm, and we were really happy together. And then he died, and I've got Edythe to think about ...' Beth sighed, holding her tea cup with both hands. 'Aunt Win took us in. Gave us this home. And then someone bloody murdered her and the police think it was me.' Tears welled in Beth's eyes. 'Sorry. I'm at my wits' end.'

'Surely they don't,' Cat said.

'I wouldn't be so sure. I have a motive, you see. Aunt Win changed her will and left all of her assets, with the exception of a small cottage and a settlement, to me. Her son, Phillip, isn't too pleased.'

Cat vaguely remembered stories about Phillip Billings as a child, but other than that she had no recollection of him.

'I've been advised not to leave town. Two of my best clients have cancelled their orders. I'm almost afraid to answer my telephone.'

'Oh, Beth, that's horrible for you.' After Cat's husband had been murdered, she had been under police scrutiny. She knew how unnerving it was to have your every move examined, to feel as though you were being watched all the time.

'Actually, I was hoping I could get you to help me,' Beth said. 'I want to hire you to find out who killed my aunt.'

'I'm not a detective,' Cat said. 'What could I do?'

'You solved your husband's murder. I read about it in the papers. You were the talk of the village, a local celebrity. I've got everything ever written about you.' Beth stood and took a folder out of a drawer in the kitchen. 'See. You solved your husband's murder. Now I need you to find out who killed my aunt. Everyone in the village knows that I'm a suspect – you remember how gossip travels here. What if the police can't find out who killed her? The nagging cloud of suspicion will hang over my head. I'll probably have to move. Thank goodness I don't have to worry about the money anymore, but there's Edythe to consider.' Beth wiped a tear. 'God, I feel so helpless.' She gave Cat a rueful smile. 'The police have had me in to answer questions – nothing direct, mind you, more like a gathering of historical data about my past, about my relationship with Win before my husband died.'

'Be honest with the police. Trust them to get to the truth.' Cat set her cup down and pulled the plate towards her.

'I have been honest with them. And cooperative. They still think I killed her.'

'Who do you think killed her? You must have some idea.'

Beth met Cat's eyes. 'I think my cousin killed his mum, thinking he was going to inherit. I cannot think of anyone else who would

63

want to harm her. She had so many friends. She was loved by so many people.'

'Do you think your cousin is capable of murder?'

Beth dabbed her eyes with a handkerchief. 'I have no idea. Nothing makes sense.'

Cat couldn't help but feel sorry for her. She had been in Beth's shoes not long ago. What harm could come of her doing a little digging into Phillip Billings? She would be discreet. And if she couldn't find out anything about Phillip, she could certainly see that Beth had proper legal representation, should she need it.

'I'll help you,' Cat said. 'I don't know how much actual investigating I can do, but we can dig around. I'll help you find a barrister, if the need arrives.'

'You mean if I'm arrested?' Beth said.

'Let's hope it doesn't come to that.'

Beth sighed. 'Thank you.'

'Don't tell anyone, please. We have to do this carefully. The police don't favour civilians meddling in their investigations.'

'I understand,' Beth said.

Cat poured them both more tea. 'Now, tell me everything about Phillip.'

***

That afternoon, Cat managed to carve out some time for herself. Annie was busy painting and Bede had gone into town. She donned a hat and gardening gloves, grabbed the secateurs, and headed outside to cut flowers for the myriad of vases that were placed around the house. St Monica's was the first home that Cat had taken of her own volition. It was hers, her responsibility. She could fill empty vases – or not – with whatever she wanted. Savouring the delicious feeling of independence, Cat thought of Thomas, realizing that she missed him.

64

'Mrs Carlisle.' Cat turned to see a young woman, blonde and willowy, walking towards her with the grace of a dancer. When the girl was close enough for Cat to see her face, there was no denying this was Bill Hargreaves' daughter. The young girl looked exactly like him. The familiar cord of sadness wove itself around her heart. For a fleeting moment, Cat thought of her own desperate need for a child, the ensuing miscarriages, Benton's infidelity. The fights and the ultimate failure.

'Mrs Carlisle, are you all right?'

'You must be Edythe,' Cat said. She took off her gloves and hat, and stuck out her hand. The girl took it, her grip strong.

'I'm sorry to barge in on you, but do you have a moment? I want to talk to you about something.'

'Of course,' Cat said. 'Would you like to go inside? I can offer you tea.'

'No, thank you.' Edythe looked towards the house. 'I need to speak to you in confidence.' Edythe licked her lips. 'Mrs Carlisle, I know who you are, how you solved your husband's murder.'

'I wouldn't say that—'

'I followed the investigation in the newspaper. My mum clipped all the articles.' Edythe shook her head. 'That doesn't matter. I want to hire you. I think David Broadbent killed my great-aunt.'

'Who's David Broadbent?' Cat asked.

'He's our solicitor. Before you dismiss me, hear me out. Would you do that, please?'

Cat didn't want to listen. She wanted to put her gardening gloves back on and hack away at the lush flowers that grew around her house. She wanted Thomas, and an uncomplicated, undemanding relationship with him. But she had always had a soft spot for teenage girls in need of help, so she forced a smile, and spoke as if she had all the time in the world. 'Of course I will listen. Do tell.'

Edythe sighed with relief. 'My dad died six years ago. Farming accident. It was the most horrible experience in my life. After my dad's estate was finalized, my mum discovered we barely had enough money to put food on the table. That's when we leased our farm out and moved in with Aunt Win. My mum never questioned anything. Dad didn't discuss finances with her, so she had no idea of our situation. Win helped us, and eventually Mum earned enough for us to live on. Of course, since Win left us well situated, we'll be fine now.'

'So what's the problem?' Cat asked.

Edythe gazed off into the distance. Cat realized Edythe Hargreaves was not an impetuous young lady. 'My dad never discussed our finances with my mum. She didn't understand nor care about them. But he discussed them with me. Quite often, actually. He didn't want me to wind up like Mum, totally stupid when it came to money. He had modern ideas, my dad. He wanted me to understand commerce and economics. He wanted me to make my way in the world before I married and settled down.'

'Edythe, what in the world does this have to do with David Broadbent?'

'You cannot repeat what I'm about to tell you. If you do, I'll know. You especially cannot repeat this to my mum. Understood?'

'Understood.'

'My dad told me he had money set aside for me, enough to go to school or move to London and study ballet, maybe set up my own ballet school if I didn't get on with a reputable company. He wanted me to be independent. I asked Mr Broadbent about that, and he just dismissed me, told me I was mistaken.' Edythe's eyes blazed with anger. 'He said my dad would have never left money directly to me. If he had wanted to, Broadbent would have advised him against it. That's not true. I know it.'

'David Broadbent sounds like an idiot,' Cat said. 'But that doesn't mean he's murdered anyone.'

'I've been suspicious for a couple of years now, so I started doing a little digging into Mr Broadbent's past. His father lost their family's dairy farm in a card game, so he doesn't have any money of his own. Carmona Broadbent – that's his daughter – is my best friend. We practically live at each other's houses. I know for a fact Carmona and her mum have money from James Churchwright. That's Carmona's grandfather. He's an industrialist of some sort. Credited with the Midas touch or something. Anyway, Mr Broadbent doesn't have access to Carmona or her mother's trust funds.'

'That's not unusual. But still that doesn't prove—'

'They live a very rich life. Big house, servants, Carmona has a car her father bought her. How much money does a country solicitor make? Rivenby is a small village to support someone in such an opulent lifestyle. I told Aunt Win about my suspicions. She believed me. I think she was looking into it.' Edythe looked side to side, as if to make sure no one listened. She stepped close to Cat and whispered. 'I think she found something out. I saw Miss Hinch come to our house. She gave Aunt Win an envelope. Aunt Win spent the evening locked in her room. I peered through the keyhole and saw her reading. The next morning, I overheard her on the telephone with someone. She said, "I know what you've been up to. We need to talk. And you should know that I plan on telling James. You need to make this right."'

'Who's James?'

'Carmona's grandfather. He and Aunt Win are – were – very close. I think everyone in the village expected them to marry but they didn't. Never mind that. It's not important. What if David Broadbent was embezzling and Aunt Win found out? That would give him a motive to kill her. And it made me wonder, if he's embezzled from my dad, maybe he's embezzled from other people too.' She glared at Cat, irritated. 'You don't believe me, do you? You think I'm a fatuous young woman with ideas …'

Cat considered Edythe. She chose her words carefully. 'I will tell you that I don't *not* believe you, if that makes sense. You make a very persuasive argument against Mr Broadbent.'

Edythe sighed with relief. 'Do you have any idea how difficult this has been for me? Carmona is my best friend. I can hardly be around her. I'm about to burst with a helpless desperation to do something. But I just don't know how to proceed. Will you help me?'

'This is an awful lot to take in, Edythe. Let me think about things. It's important we not do anything rash. We need to be very careful. I am not happy about going behind your mum's back. If I decide to help you sort this out, we will have to take her into our confidence.'

'She'll never condone it. She thinks David Broadbent walks on water.'

'Let me do a little digging and see what I can find out. If we go to your mum with some evidence of his guilt, I feel certain she can be made to see reason.'

'That's brilliant.' Edythe smiled at Cat. 'I can't tell you what a relief it is to get this off my chest. I've been dying to tell Carmona, but she'd never believe me. Not that I blame her. It's her dad, after all. Will you contact me if you find anything out?'

'I will,' Cat said. 'Will you promise not to do anything without talking to me first? We don't want Mr Broadbent to know we are investigating him.'

'I promise.' Edythe crossed her heart. 'I better get back. Mum will wonder where I've gone. Thank you, Mrs Carlisle.'

Cat watched for a moment as Edythe turned and headed back to the cottage she shared with her mum. Their conversation ran through Cat's mind. She took the various facts and rearranged them like pieces of a puzzle as she turned back to the flowers. She wondered what Thomas would make of Edythe's accusations. Her curiosity had been piqued. Cat was eager to get a look at this Mr Broadbent. The idea of an investigation excited her. She'd enlist Thomas to help her.

Thomas. He couldn't arrive fast enough.

CHAPTER 5

Armed with way too many petrol coupons, Thomas left London early in the morning and headed north towards Rivenby. Feeling guilty for the privilege of driving his treasured Wolseley coupe, he vowed to park the car once he reached Rivenby and walk as much as possible. His mood lightened with each mile, despite the grey skies that hung in the summer sky. Rain was coming. He didn't care. He had grown weary of London, the tension among the citizens, and the speculation about what would happen next. Thomas didn't need to speculate. He knew what was coming. Bombs. A litany of terror similar to that which the poor citizens of Guernica had experienced in April of 1937, similar to what the Norwegians had experienced in Nybergsund. This war was going to get brutal. He thanked God he had been able to convince Cat to leave.

He pulled his car off the side of the road in Penrith and put the top down, not caring about the threat of rain. It wouldn't be the first time the rain had soaked him in his car. He longed to feel the wind in his hair. He stretched his legs and rubbed his shoulder. His doctor had cautioned him against the long drive to Rivenby, but Thomas had ignored the admonitions. He would no more leave his beloved car in London than he would leave a beloved child. *No more likely than I would leave Cat.* Just the thought of her threw him into an emotional muddle, like that of an adolescent school boy.

Under the shade of a rowan tree – a perennial favourite, thanks to the faerie stories his grandmother had told him as a young boy – he took his time over the sandwiches and Thermos of tea Mrs Barrows had prepared for his journey. Together, they had stowed half a dozen bottles of claret and two bottles of brandy in the boot of his car. If the food in Rivenby was lacking, at least he had an ample supply of spirits. His shoulder ached a bit, but he ignored it as he got back in the car and continued north.

Four hours later, Thomas turned off onto the narrow country lanes that would lead to Rivenby. The road climbed steadily uphill. Following the written directions Sir Reginald had given him, he looked for an old folly, and soon saw the sign that said 'Rivenby – 11 miles'. This road was dirt and gravel. He drove slowly so as not to stir up dust. The hedges grew high in places, but the road was straight and just wide enough for two vehicles to pass. He gauged how far he had travelled, ready for the sharp turn where Win's car had gone off the road.

He found it easily, a hairpin curve with a wooden fence that had been smashed to bits. He slowed his car, coming to rest on a grassy layby. He parked and listened for other vehicles approaching. When he didn't hear anything, he got out of the car and walked over to the place where Win Billings' car had gone off the road. Splintered beams littered the ground. He peered over at the precipice below him, surprised at how steep the drop was. The cliff wall was composed of jagged rocks, the valley below green and lush. He felt a moment of terror as he realized what it must have been like to approach this dangerous curve and discover the brakes didn't work. *Poor woman.*

Thomas took in the sweeping view of Rivenby, the lush green fields, the grazing sheep, along with the dense woods even further beyond. He wasn't fooled by the bucolic setting before him.

He had grown up in a village similar to this one. Greed and subterfuge was the same, city or country. With one last look at the gorgeous view, he turned towards his car. With determination he started the engine and eased his way around the bend, as he wound down into the village proper.

Fifteen minutes later, he turned onto the high street and drove to the hotel where Reginald had arranged a suite of rooms for him. Three buses crowded the streets, blocking Thomas's way as a never-ending stream of women and children exited, carrying tattered suitcases. When one of the buses pulled away, Thomas drove behind it. The hotel – a three-storey stone structure with gleaming windows – lay further down the street, a parking place near the front at the ready. Stretching out the kinks from his long journey, he had moved to put the convertible in place, when an authoritative woman with a clipboard came out of the hotel and approached his car.

'Excuse me,' she said. 'Are you by chance Mr Thomas Charles, come from London?'

Thomas wondered whether Reginald had made changes to their arrangement and hadn't bothered to tell him. He decided to answer this officious woman with a question of his own. 'And you are?'

'Do forgive me. Bit frazzled.' She tucked the clipboard under her arm and stuck out her free hand. 'Mrs Broadbent, Claris Broadbent. Call me Claris. Everyone does. I'm so sorry to tell you this, but I've cancelled your reservation at the hotel. We've a shortage of space and my father won't have just anyone to stay with him.'

'Forgive me, madam. But I've no idea what you're talking about. I've been on the road since early morning. I am tired.'

'Of course you are, Mr Charles. Let me assure you the accommodations are far better at Heart's Desire, my father's home. My organization has commandeered all of the rooms in the hotel. We are bringing in bunk beds, as we need to fit as many people in the rooms as possible. We've evacuees from London, you see, families with young children that can't be separated. We are rather short of space. It's really a mess.'

Thomas watched as a harried-looking mum with a young boy holding one hand and a sleepy-eyed baby cradled in the other arm approached Claris. The boy wriggled out of the woman's grasp and tried to run back down the path towards the buses.

'William,' the mother cried.

'Excuse me,' Claris said to Thomas. She took the baby out of the woman's arms. 'Go and fetch him, dear. Your room's all ready for you. I'll hold the baby.' The baby started to fuss. 'Be still. Go back to sleep,' Claris commanded. To Thomas's utter surprise, the infant did as she asked. He laid his head on her shoulder and closed his eyes.

'As I was saying, my father has a nice house with a few extra rooms, but he hasn't been very cooperative in allowing me to use any of them. He's made up for it by giving me the money to rent the hotel for our newcomers. I'm so desperate I can't afford to let one person stay in a room. Alone, not when there are so many families who need lodging. When I explained who you were, my father was more than happy to have you.'

'Who I am?' Thomas felt his heart beat. What did this woman know about his trip here? How did she find out? Surely the police wouldn't disclose confidential information about Thomas's visit.

'Don't be shy, Mr Charles. My father has read all of your books. He's got a passion for historical houses and churches. He's read everything you've ever written.'

Thomas found he was tired all of a sudden. His shoulder throbbed. He wanted a good meal and a hot bath.

The woman came back, having subdued the errant William. He clung to his mother's hand, fresh tears wet on his cheeks. 'You'll stay by my side,' she said to the boy.

'Yes, Mum.' William whispered his response.

The woman took the baby. 'Will someone see to my bags?'

'Yes,' Claris said. 'Just give your name to the front desk.'

'Thank you,' the woman said. 'Come, William.'

Once the woman was out of earshot, Claris turned to Thomas. 'You'll like my father. He has a splendid cook, a good wine cellar, and plenty of room for you to spread out and work. He won't bother you during the day. He's rather busy actually.'

Thunder boomed. The sky darkened. Thomas half expected Claris Broadbent to raise her hand to the heavens and command it to stop.

'Better put the top up,' she said. 'My car's just there. Follow me?'

Thomas pulled the convertible onto the road behind Claris Broadbent's Vauxhall. He followed Claris as she drove down to the end of the high street and turned into a narrow lane flanked by hawthorn hedges in desperate need of a trim. They wound upwards for two miles, when Claris turned into what looked like a layby. Two brick pillars which where almost hidden by brambles and bushes marked a driveway of sorts. Thomas followed Claris's car down a winding wooded drive, surprised to see the charming cottage sequestered in the trees. Heart's Desire exemplified the traditional modest gentleman's home. He had read about houses such as this, but had never seen one in person, and had certainly never stayed in one. Thomas got out of his car and stretched his legs.

'I'll just go and tell him you're here,' Claris said. 'Enjoy the view. Back in a moment.' She knocked on the front door – a garish green thing polished to a high shine – and let herself in. Thomas studied the house. Guessed it to be mid-nineteenth century. Before he could walk around and get a proper look, Claris came back out.

'He's just finishing up a telephone call.' She came to the car. 'Let me help you with your bags.'

'That's not necessary,' Thomas said.

'Nonsense. Forgive me for being forward, Mr Charles, but you favour that arm and you look like you're in a fair amount of pain. Let me help you with your bags. Really. I displaced you from your accommodations without your permission. The least I can do is carry a bag into the house.' She picked up the heaviest bag with ease and carried it in through the open door. Thomas followed.

Claris set the bag on the floor at the bottom of the staircase just as an elderly man with a thick shock of grey hair entered the room. 'Ah, Beck. Good. Here's Mr Charles. He's exhausted from his trip, so if you could carry up his bags and have Mrs Beck send something up on a tray?'

'Very well.' When the man turned, Thomas saw he was missing a good section of his right ear. 'How do you do, sir. We hope to make you comfortable here.' Beck picked up both of Thomas's bags and headed up the stairs.

'I've a typewriting machine and some wine in the car.'

'I'll see to it, sir,' Beck said. He disappeared up the stairs carrying Thomas's bag.

Claris turned to Thomas. 'My father's household seems impervious to rationing. If Beck needs your ration book, he'll ask for it. My father eats dinner at 8 p.m. He'll expect you at 7 p.m. for drinks in the drawing room. There.' She pointed to a room near the front door. 'The house isn't too big, so you'll be comfortable here. Your rooms are up the stairs at the end of the hall. My father has one of the bedrooms set up as an office for you. There's a telephone and plenty of light. If you need anything, Beck will see to it. Must be off.' She started to head to the front door, but stopped at the last minute and gave Thomas a bright smile. 'Thank you for being so understanding, Mr Charles. I really appreciate it.'

Thomas headed up the stairs, reeling from the whirlwind that was Claris Broadbent. He wondered whether she and Cat would be friends. He wondered what Cat would make of Claris's domineering ways.

He entered the room that was to be his for the duration, taking in the high bed, the large mullioned windows, and the ornate chimney piece. He shut the windows, glad for the heavy drapes that blocked the light. As he unbuttoned his shirt, he felt a moment's pity for Claris Broadbent's husband. God help the poor man. After a few minutes, there was a quiet knock on the door. Thomas opened it to Beck, carrying a tray with a large pot of tea, a decanter of Scotch with a soda syphon, and what looked like a ham sandwich on thick bread.

'My wife thought you might want a drink after your journey.' He made quick work of setting the tray on the table.

'Thank you,' Thomas said. He ate the sandwich, kicked off his shoes, and lay down on the bed in the darkened room. It started to rain. Thomas's eyelids grew heavy. The steady rhythm of the drops against the window lulled him to sleep.

The rain had tapered off to a gentle shimmer when Beck knocked on Thomas's door. He carried Thomas's dinner suit, freshly pressed and brushed over his arm. Beck didn't speak to Thomas as he hung the suit in the wardrobe, while Thomas lay in the bed, watching the stealthily moving butler with one eye.

'Mr Churchwright will see you for drinks in half an hour, sir. I've run you a bath.' He didn't wait for Thomas to answer or acknowledge his presence. He simply slipped out of the room as quietly as he had come in.

Thomas sat up, surprisingly refreshed. He opened the window and took the clean fresh air into his lungs. During his nap, his clothing had been unpacked and his toiletries stowed in the large bathroom. He opened the door to the room adjoining his, where his typewriter had been unpacked and placed atop a large table which would serve as his desk. The table had been arranged under one of the windows which overlooked the moor, the view sweepingly beautiful, but just desolate enough to not be distracting. As he stripped off his clothes and headed into the bath, he decided he could get very used to country living.

Half an hour later, Thomas headed downstairs to meet his host. He found James Churchwright standing before the fireplace, tall and statuesque, dressed in an impeccable dinner suit. He wore his hair closely shaved, which only accentuated his thick neck and bulbous nose. Thomas imagined him as a young man playing rugby with an aggressive but fair manner that had probably carried into his business affairs.

'So very pleased to make your acquaintance.' James Churchwright approached Thomas, hand extended. 'James Churchwright. Call me James.' He nodded at the drinks trolley. 'What's your pleasure?'

'Scotch, if you've got it.'

James put ice cubes into a crystal glass and doused it with Scotch. After he handed the glass to Thomas, the two men drank in silence.

'Let's sit. Dinner will be ready in a few minutes.'

'Thank you for having me,' Thomas said.

'Your arrival was rather fortuitous. Had you not shown up when you did, my daughter would have finagled the use of my house for her pet charity. She's committed to providing a positive experience for the children from London. She's rather tireless about it.'

'She's certainly very …' Thomas paused, searching for the right word. 'Convincing.'

'That she is. Tell me, Mr Charles, what do you think of my house?' Mr Churchwright didn't wait for a reply. 'At first I found the florid embellishments a bit much. I prefer simple things, but the house is solidly built, eighteenth century. It's what's called a gentleman's house, not too big, but enough room to entertain. It's made of stone rubble, lime-rendered, and washed in the local tradition. That's all I know about it. I like the size and layout of it. Bought it when my wife died, back in 1933. Turned over the big house to my daughter.'

'It is very comfortable,' Thomas said. 'Elegant without pretence. I like it.'

Mr Churchwright nodded approval, as though Thomas had passed some unspoken test and was now accepted into the fold. They sipped their drinks and chatted about the war, Hitler, the bombs which would surely come to London. Thomas found his host very informed about the war effort, so much so he wondered whether James had connections to Whitehall. They had finished a second drink when Beck came to announce dinner. He led the men into a dining room big enough to comfortably seat twelve people. Mullioned windows filled the room with natural light, the rain danced against them. A sumptuous feast awaited.

They ate a rack of lamb, potatoes with rosemary, and a soufflé so sublime Thomas didn't hesitate to take a second helping. Mr Churchwright ate heartily and slowly. Beck kept the wine glasses full. Neither one of them felt compelled to fill the silence with chatter. Thomas appreciated the quiet and enjoyed his meal all the more because of it. When they had finished eating, James announced they would retreat back to the drawing room for coffee and brandy. Mrs Beck brought them in an assortment of brandy, port, and cheeses. Once they were comfortably situated, James showed his hand.

'I know you're here about Win's murder.' At Thomas's surprised look, he said, 'Reginald and I go back a long time. I know what he's up to in London. I know of his concerns about her death.' James leaned back in his chair, crossed his leg over his knee. 'Win wasn't murdered because of her past life. I'm sure of it.'

'Do you know who murdered her?'

'I believe I do. It's a touchy situation.'

'Forgive me for being blunt, but don't you think you should go to the police?'

'Oh, I plan to. It's just not so straightforward. There are others involved who will be affected by the whole situation, innocents. I must keep them out of harm's way. Surely you understand?'

'Unfortunately, I do.' Thomas wanted to ask about Phillip and Beth Hargreaves. He wondered whether either of them had been involved in Win's death. A feeling of uneasiness distracted him from the food, wine, and good conversation. He didn't like the idea of this man knowing who had murdered Win Billings, despite his honourable intentions. He felt a pang of worry. 'I still don't like it. I'm not disputing your ability to take care of yourself. It's just not safe.'

James Churchwright levelled his gaze at Thomas. He wasn't deterred by the stubborn determination he saw there. 'I am not here to make an arrest, James. You can trust me. I think it would be better for you if you would tell me what you know.'

The man shook his head. 'Sorry, old boy. Can't do that.' He set his brandy glass on the table next to his chair. 'I'm going to London tomorrow to get things sorted. I'll be back in a few days and promise to tell you everything then. If you'd like, you can come to the police with me. I'll be gone early, so I won't be joining you for breakfast.' James stood. 'Help yourself to anything you like. My house is your house.' And with a nod, James Churchwright walked out of the room, leaving Thomas alone with his worries.

CHAPTER 6

Carmona woke up to grey skies and the promise of summer rain. Today she and Edythe were planning on going to the cinema, but Edythe had called last minute and cancelled. When Carmona asked why, Edythe had become short with her. Something was wrong with her friend. Carmona made a mental note to ask her about it. Before Phillip, Carmona would have showed more concern about Edythe's change of temperament. Now neither Edythe nor this gloomy weather could spoil Carmona's mood. Ever since the night she had helped Phillip, and felt his body next to hers, something had changed in her. She felt like a flower coming into bloom, but shook that notion off as too romantic. *It's an awakening,* she thought.

Images of Phillip's stunningly handsome face and his electric blue eyes swirled around the tangle of emotions that pulsed through her. She was giddy and excited and utterly distracted. Yesterday morning, her mother had accused her of daydreaming, something so out of character for Carmona, Claris had suggested they call the doctor. It had been three days since she had found him in a bloody heap. How she had enjoyed administering to him. Desperate to see him again, she planned and schemed to get a glimpse of him. After about ten walks through the high street – no luck there – she gave up on the casual encounter. A plan was in order. Carmona needed an excuse to call, so Phillip wouldn't think she was pursuing him. This morning, out of the blue, the perfect plan presented itself.

Carmona chose a simple tweed skirt, a silk blouse in a shade of rich ruby that flattered her skin, and a matching cashmere jumper. She spent extra time on her hair and even went so far as to brush some powder over her nose. Once she was sure her mother had left for the day, she checked her appearance in the mirror, turning this way and that, pleased with her efforts to look nice. Satisfied, she hurried to the kitchen, grabbed a wicker basket from the larder and generously filled it with tinned meat, bread, a small wedge of cheese, six eggs, three carrots, a bunch of green beans, and a fresh tin of biscuits. She scooped some loose tea into an empty jam jar and stuffed that into the basket too. She topped off her load with four cloth napkins, two plates and two teacups from a China pattern that her mother had all but forgotten, along with two knives, forks, and spoons.

Once her basket was full, she loaded it onto her bike and set out for Phillip's house. The damp morning air smelled sweet to Carmona. The high street was empty as Carmona passed her father's office and headed towards the haberdasher's. Thank goodness. No prying eyes to report to Claris about Carmona's early morning, unchaperoned tryst. She turned into the alley which was full of pot holes and overgrown hawthorn shrubs, and hid her bike well out of sight. Laden with her basket, she hurried to Phillip's backdoor, heart pounding. What if he didn't want to see her? What if she was imagining the attraction between them? He opened it before she had a chance to knock. Carmona was at once struck by his good looks.

'Good morning! I see my angel has come to save me again. What've you got there?'

'I thought you could use a little civilizing, so I've brought you some food and other supplies.'

80

He took her basket and stepped aside. 'Brains, beauty, and a kind heart. Please, come in. I was just making tea.'

Carmona stepped past him, heart pounding. 'There're a couple of eggs in there and some bread. I wasn't sure if you had any pots and pans.'

'I do.' He held up a small cast-iron skillet. 'One lone pan, but it'll do.' The kettle boiled. Phillip took the last two tea bags out of a glass jar, placed them in the chipped mugs and took them to the table. Carmona followed him. She cradled the warm mug of tea in her hands, savouring its heat.

'There are new teacups in the basket, along with a couple of plates and utensils …' She let her voice trail off. Phillip had a strange look on his face. He stared at her, his head cocked sideways, studying her through squinted eyes.

'Why have you come, Carmona? Why does a beautiful young woman such as yourself care about a reckless reprobate like me?' He reached out his hand. Without thinking, she took it. The electricity of Phillip's touch travelled through Carmona's body. Every nerve ending sang in response to his touch.

'I mainly came because you needed help. I also came because I like you.'

'How old are you? Eighteen? I'm seventeen years older than you. Surely you're aware of that.'

Not trusting herself to form a cohesive sentence while Phillip touched her, Carmona pulled her hand away. 'Phillip, you've known me for a long time, seen me with Edythe, eaten your share of meals with me. We've talked about things over the years. Correct?'

'Well, yes.' He lit a cigarette and watched her through plumes of smoke.

'Can you honestly see me befriending any of the boys in the village – or anywhere else for that matter – that are my age?'

He laughed, but stopped himself. His lip started to bleed. He winced as he took a handkerchief out of his pocket and dabbed

81

at the blood. When he spoke his voice was soft and sweet as honey. 'Point taken. But have you given any thought to what your mother's friends would say if they knew you were visiting me, unchaperoned, before 10 a.m.?'

'They won't know. I hid my bike. No one was on the high street when I arrived.'

'Care to place a bet on that? I am glad you're here, really. But I want you to be careful. I'll not be the one to sully your otherwise stellar reputation.'

When he smiled, Carmona's heart clenched. How she longed for his well-muscled arms to encircle her. He took her hand once again. This time, he turned it over and ran his fingers over the soft pink skin of her palm in long, sensuous strokes. For a moment, Carmona thought she would pass out from the pleasure of it.

'I can't seem to get you off my mind, Carmona Broadbent.'

'I know. Me neither,' Carmona said. Embarrassed yet enthralled by the level of intimacy, Carmona felt the heat seep into her cheeks. She pulled her hand away and stood up. 'And you're right. My mother would have an apoplectic fit if she knew I was here. But I don't care. Are you hungry? How about I cook some eggs.'

'Great. I'll make the toast.'

While Carmona fried the eggs, Phillip sliced the bread and put it in the cooker.

'What are you going to do with yourself, Carmona? Surely you're not going to stay in this godforsaken village for the rest of your life. I'm sure your mother expects you to settle down and marry, but somehow I don't see you doing what's expected of you.'

'I'm going to medical school,' she blurted out. 'Please don't tell anyone. My mum doesn't know. I've applied and am waiting for an acceptance letter. I'll be moving to London next January.'

'Brains and beauty,' Phillip said. 'I'm impressed.'

'I've been studying for this for a couple of years, anatomy, things of that nature. My parents paid for extra lessons.'

'You're not worried about invasion?'

'Not at all. Hitler needs to be stopped. If there's an invasion – and my grandfather is certain there will be one – I'm ready to do my part. We'll need more doctors,' she said with conviction.

'You'll do great,' Phillip said. 'If I were in the hospital, the sight of you would immediately alleviate all my symptoms.'

'Don't be ridiculous,' Carmona said. She flipped the eggs without breaking the yolks and turned to face Phillip. 'Why did those men attack you?'

A spark of anger – brief and short-lived – flashed behind his eyes.

'I didn't mean to make you angry. It's just …' She hesitated, afraid her questions were too forward. 'I'll help you if I can.'

At Carmona's offer to help, the look in Phillip's eyes had changed to surprise. When the surprise morphed into desire, he pulled Carmona to her feet and enfolded her into his warm grasp. Carmona had never been held like this before. The sensation was overwhelmingly pleasurable. *I could stay like this forever.* Shyly, she wrapped her arms around Phillip's narrow waist and rested her head on his chest. The feeling was so pure and real, she could have wept. Instead, she savoured the feel of his arms around her, the beat of his heart against her cheek, the scent of him.

'You're too good for me, Carmona.' His voice was a whisper, but even Carmona – so naive and inexperienced – could sense the desire behind the words.

She tipped her face to him, wanting the inevitable kiss like she had never wanted anything in her life. But Phillip shook his head, once again stepping away from her.

'Let's tread carefully here, my love. Best take this slowly.'

He touched her chin and tilted her face up to him. Carmona felt certain that everything she felt was reflected in her eyes. She wanted Phillip to see her love, to accept the gift of it.

He nuzzled her neck before he let her go. 'Breakfast is ready, I think.' He turned back to the cooker and took out four pieces of bread. Carmona slipped the eggs onto plates, and they sat at Phillip's wobbly kitchen table, eating breakfast like an old married couple. When they were finished, Carmona did the dishes, while Phillip dried and put things up on the shelf.

'What are you up to today?' Carmona asked. She wanted to spend the day with Phillip, go somewhere where they wouldn't have to worry about anyone from the village seeing them and reporting back to Claris. She envisioned them going for long walks together, followed by lunch at some obscure pub.

'Business to tend to, I'm afraid.' He spread the dish towel out on the cooker so it would dry. When he turned to face Carmona, his face grew serious. 'Thank you, Carmona. For all this.' He gestured at the kitchen, the new dishes, the food. 'It's been a while since someone's been kind to me.' He smiled at her, his blue eyes danced as they crinkled at the corners. 'You'd better go before someone sees your bike.'

His hand felt hot on the small of her back as he walked her to the door. On a whim, she stood on her tiptoes and kissed his cheek.

'Goodbye,' she said.

'I'll see you soon, my love.'

Careful to remain unseen, Carmona pulled her bike out of its hiding place, avoiding the high street on her way home. All the while, Phillip's words sang in her mind. *My love. My love.* He had called her *my love.* Carmona memorized the timbre of this voice and the look in his eyes, replaying the moment in her mind. What a perfect morning.

***

Carmona took the back roads all the way to her house, smiling the whole way. She thanked providence that she didn't see anyone who would wonder why she was out on this beautiful morning, dressed up in silk and cashmere. She longed for exercise, anything to dispel this pent-up energy. Surprised to see smoke coming out of her bedroom chimney, Carmona leaned her bike against the front of the house and let herself in the front door. Who would light a fire? Not Liddy. Her brother had sent a note saying she had come down with a sore throat and would be home for the next couple of days.

Noises came from Carmona's room as she headed down the hall. Her heartbeat quickened. Someone was in there, and from the sound of it they were rifling through Carmona's bookcase. Kicking off her shoes so as not to make any noise, she hurried back down the hallway to the drawing room and grabbed the brass poker from its spot by the fireplace. Without thinking of her own safety, she crept back to her room, kicked the door all the way open, and brandishing the fire poker shouted, 'What do you think—'

The words froze. Carmona stood, mouth agape, blinking her eyes, not quite able to take in the scene before her. Her mother – dressed like a maid in old clothes with a scarf tied around her head – had lit a fire and stoked it until it roared. Carmona's medical books lay in stacks on the hearth. Her mother took a book, perused the title, and tossed it into the flames. She must have been at it for a while, for only eight or nine books were left. Carmona's bookcase was now empty, save two murder mysteries that didn't even belong to her.

'Mother!' Carmona hurried into the room. Claris ignored her. She kept on with her task. 'Mother!' Carmona put her hands on her mother's shoulders. She could have shaken her. God knows she wanted to hurt her.

Claris pushed Carmona's hands away. She faced her daughter, eyes flashing with indignation.

'You've applied for medical school behind my back?' Claris gestured at Carmona's desk. On top of it was an envelope from the London School of Medicine addressed to Carmona. The

85

envelope had been ripped open, the letter read. The invasion of privacy, the indignity of her mother's violation caused Carmona's blood to boil. She started to shake.

'I'm leaving in January. You can't stop me.' Carmona's voice came out sharp and shrill.

'This is my home. You live under my roof. You will follow my rules.'

'No,' Carmona said. She opened her mouth to tell her mother that she was independent, that she had her own money.

'I know what you're going to say, Carmona. You're going to tell me you can do whatever you want because you have your own money from your grandfather. You don't get a penny from him until you're 21. He didn't tell you that little nugget of useful information, did he? You see, my father is an intelligent man. He knows little girls do stupid things. Like move to London and allow themselves to be taken in by Phillip Billings.'

Carmona felt the will leave her body in a rush. Her spine softened. Her knees became weak. Her entire world came crashing down around her.

'Ah, I see I have your attention. Has he asked you for money?'

Carmona stared at her mother.

'Has he?'

'Of course not,' Carmona said.

'Don't worry. He will. Surely you didn't think you could go to his cottage after the pub closes and take him food of a morning in a village this size and not be seen by someone. I thought you had more sense. This is partially my fault and your father's. We've given you way too much freedom, indulged you too much.' Her mother tossed Carmona's treasured copy of *Gray's Anatomy* into the blaze.

Utterly taken aback by her mother's behaviour, Carmona watched, mute, as the blue flames engulfed the book. She sat down on her bed and watched as her mother destroyed all the things that Carmona held dear. When the final book had been

86

consumed by the fire and all that remained were burning embers, Claris came and sat down next to Carmona. She put an arm around her daughter's shoulders and pulled her close.

'I'm your mother, dear. I know what's best. I always have. Forget medical school. You'll marry someone from a good family. Phillip Billings is a scoundrel. He's not nearly good enough for you. You, my dear, have means. He knows it. I know this sounds harsh, but please don't believe for one minute Phillip Billings is in love with you.' Her mother walked over to Carmona's desk. She picked up the acceptance letter and tore it in two.

'Let's put this nonsense behind us, shall we?'

Carmona's anger blossomed afresh, a shimmering wave of red which caused her to lose all reason. The heat of it ravaged her. She had no control over it or over herself. In one fluid motion she moved over to her desk and swept the contents to the floor. She watched her inkbottle – a birthday gift from Edythe – go sailing towards the carpet, as if in slow motion. The lid came off in flight and the ink spilled into a blue puddle on her mother's antique rug.

'You think you can stop me?' She turned on her mother, eyes blazing and shouted, 'You cannot! I'll do as I please. And you can just go to hell.' She didn't wait to see her mother's reaction. She hurried out of the house, slammed the front door, grabbed her bike and rode to Edythe's, pedalling furiously, like she had done hundreds of times before when she had clashed with her mother. Never before had she been so angry. Never before had she felt so utterly defeated. She felt the tears on her cheeks, hot and stinging, as she rode like the wind, faster and faster until her lungs threatened to burst. Numb to her surroundings, she hadn't realized she had reached Edythe's until she stopped near the hedges that surrounded the front of the house. Now she tucked her bike out of the way and wiped her eyes with her sleeve before she headed up the path to the front door, knowing that Edythe would talk her through her anger.

Taking comfort in this knowledge, Carmona took a deep breath as she headed towards the house, but stopped when she heard voices. She peered around the hedge to see Edythe – dressed in the leotard and long skirt she wore when she practised – with a towel around her neck. She approached the table where a pitcher of lemonade and two glasses rested on their usual tray. Edythe poured herself a glass and drank thirstily.

She spoke to someone out of Carmona's line of sight. Carmona crept closer, careful not to make any noise. A girl stood before an easel. She looked to be about 16-years-old. Wisps of brown hair escaped from the straw hat she wore. In one hand she held a palette, in the other a paint brush. The hand that held the brush danced across the canvas. Carmona watched as Edythe stood next to the girl and surveyed her work.

'That's really good,' Edythe said.

The girl said something in response, but Carmona couldn't hear her.

'I'd better get back to it. Carry on.'

Edythe went back into the house and soon Carmona could hear the faint strain of a Chopin piano etude. She imagined Edythe slowly bending and flowing across the floor, like a willow in the wind. Who was Edythe's new friend? She wondered for a fleeting moment if Edythe had cancelled plans with her so she could spend time with this girl. She wanted to be angry at Edythe, but she couldn't. Carmona hadn't told Edythe about her relationship with Phillip. Edythe would have tried to talk her out of getting involved with him. Now she wondered if the growing chasm between them was somehow her fault.

'To hell with her,' Carmona said aloud. She jumped back on her bike. She had adult problems now. She needed an adult to help her. She needed Phillip.

***

Carmona didn't bother taking the back lanes. What was the point? Her mother had eyes everywhere. For all she knew, the whole village was abuzz with news of Phillip and her. She didn't care. She tucked into the alley behind his house. Phillip stood in the window, smoking a cigarette and staring out onto the alley. His eyes opened in surprise when he saw her. Seconds later, he opened the door for her. Still raging, she stepped inside. For a second, she thought she heard the front door close and wondered who could be visiting Phillip. Those thoughts were quickly subsumed in the relentless anger towards her mother.

'What's wrong?' Phillip put a hand on her shoulder.

Try as she might, Carmona couldn't stop shaking. Phillip handed her a glass of water. She sipped it.

'Come and sit down,' Phillip said. 'You really need to be careful or someone will see you.'

'I don't care,' Carmona said.

'Of course you do—'

'She knows,' Carmona said.

'Who knows?' Phillip's voice had an edge to it. For the first time since she arrived Carmona looked at him and noticed the hollows in his cheeks, the dark half-moons under his eyes. 'Who knows?'

'My mum.' Carmona felt the tears threaten. She willed them back. 'She knows of my plans to go to medical school, knows that I've come here.'

'Tell me what happened.' Phillip stood and started to pace across the tiny kitchen.

'When I got home, I found her in my room burning my books.' She looked up at him, still horrified by the memory of her mother throwing her precious books in the fire.

Phillip put his arms around her. She buried her head in his chest and let the tears come.

'Poor thing,' Phillip crooned. When the tears stopped, he led Carmona to the table and poured a shot of brandy in the teacup she had brought earlier. 'How many books did she burn?'

'I don't know. Does it matter?'

'Listen, love, I'm getting money from my inheritance in about ten days. We'll buy you some new books, okay?'

The love that had been building inside Carmona burst forth in a fresh wave of emotion. For the first time in her life, Carmona understood what the poets went on about. What a blessing to share one's burdens.

'Thank you,' Carmona said. He loved her. She knew that now.

'Until my inheritance comes through, I'm in a bit of a bind. I need money, and I need it now. I don't suppose you could see your way through to a loan?'

'How much?'

He looked sheepish. 'Fifteen pounds?'

'Fifteen pounds?' Carmona had twenty-five pounds and some change in an account that she had started on her eighth birthday.

'Never mind,' he said. 'I shouldn't have asked. I'm so embarrassed. I drank too much and played cards with some chums.'

'Is that why those men beat you up?' Carmona asked.

He nodded. 'Please don't look so disappointed. This is a one-time problem, I promise. And when I get the money from my mum's estate, I'll pay you back, with interest. And I'll buy you as many books as you need.'

Phillip needed her help. And – Carmona rationalized – her mother was wrong. Phillip wasn't asking her to *give* him money. He was asking for a loan, coupled with an offer to replace the books her mother had burned. People that loved each other supported each other in times of need, emotionally and financially.

'I'll loan you the money,' she said.

He threw his arms around her and kissed her. 'Your books. The first thing we'll do when I get my money is replace your books.'

How lucky she was to have this man in her life. How nice it

was to have someone who cared about her, treated her as an adult, and – most importantly – supported her dreams.

'I'll try to go to the bank this afternoon.'

'Come to me tomorrow morning. I'll make us breakfast. Thank you, my angel. You've once again saved me.'

Carmona put her arms around Phillip's neck and kissed him.

***

Carmona hopped on her bike and hurried home, the taste of her first kiss still lingering. It had felt so right, so natural. Despite the succour Phillip had provided, Carmona felt as though she had been emotionally beaten. She needed a bath. Her silk blouse would be stained with perspiration, but she didn't care. Phillip loved her. He had kissed her. Together they had overcome what could have been a tragedy. She would never forgive her mother for the invasion of her privacy and destruction of her property. She longed to storm into the house and declare her mother a fool for judging Phillip as she had. But she wouldn't. Claris was so busy with WI business and dealing with the evacuees who flooded into Rivenby by the dozens, it wouldn't take much effort on Carmona's behalf to avoid seeing her mother altogether.

As she rode home, she surveyed her parents' relationship through the new perspective of her own relationship with Phillip and felt a stab of pity for her gentle father. He didn't stand a chance against Claris. Carmona knew her mother brought considerable wealth to her marriage. Over the years she had overheard snippets of conversation and realized her mother hadn't relinquished control of her money, as so many women did. All the financial decisions in the Broadbent household had been discussed between her mother and father, with her mother having the final say-so, regardless of her father's feelings.

She wondered what her father had been like as a young man,

in love with the daughter of a wealthy and influential man. Her father had no siblings. His parents had owned a dairy but had lost it when a competitor with more money had moved into the area and set out to take over the business. Carmona turned her bike onto the winding drive that led to her house, taking the twists and turns without thinking. Had her father always been cowed by Claris? Had he resisted her domineering ways at first? She could see her mother chipping away at her father's strength bit by bit, wearing him down over the years, until finally he had no will at all. She vowed never to treat Phillip like that. He would be her equal, her partner in all things.

She arrived at the house. In the distance thunder boomed. Smoke curled out of the chimney. Her mother's Vauxhall, an ancient thing that had belonged to her grandfather, was gone, much to Carmona's relief. Her mother would have kittens if she knew Carmona was going to take money from her bank account to help Phillip. She thought of her precious books, engulfed in flames. *Damn Mother and damn her bloody kittens.* She leaned her bike against the fence and slipped in through the kitchen door. With just a bit of luck, she could grab her bank book and be out of the house without being seen. After she'd taken the money out of the bank, she would come home, take a hot bath, and spend the rest of her day locked in her room.

Thinking she was alone in the house, she crept down the hall towards her room, surprised to see her father in his study. She paused for a moment and watched him. Now she knew what it was like to share a life with someone on an intimate basis, she saw her father in a new light, saw the results of her mother's aggressive domineering ways. David Broadbent had been beaten by his wife – if not physically, then certainly emotionally – until he had no will of his own. Carmona felt a moment's pity for him. *Dear old thing,* she thought.

No lamps had been lit. The curtains were drawn. The fire that burned in her father's study cast the only light. Shadows danced across her father's face, as he stood before the fire, staring at the portrait of Claris as a young woman that hung above it. Carmona opened her mouth to speak, but stopped as her father reached into his coat pocket and removed a piece of paper. With trembling hands, he unfolded it. She remained silent, watching as he read, his lips moving as his eyes roved the page. When he finished, he crumpled the paper in his fist, closed his eyes, and sighed. With a sure hand, he threw the wadded-up paper in the fireplace. Carmona stepped into the room.

'What are you doing?'

He yelped and turned to face her. 'Carmona. What are you doing here?'

She smiled at him. 'I live here. Remember?'

He gave her a sardonic look and smiled. 'You startled me.' He moved over to his desk and picked up a stack of papers. He carried them over to the fire and started feeding them to the flames, one by one. 'I'm just burning some of this office rubbish. It's confidential, so I don't want to put it in the bins.' He put the last of the papers in and turned to face his daughter. 'Your mother's not home. I wanted to talk to you about what happened. With your books.'

Carmona waited. As if he could do anything to ameliorate the situation. As if his utter lack of courage wasn't part of the problem.

'Please don't look at me like that.' His voice had a pleading to it that made Carmona take a step back. She knew her father was a weak man, but she had never seen him display this personality trait so blatantly. He stared at Claris's portrait as he spoke, his hands clasped before him, as if in reverence to this bleak state of affairs. 'We didn't start out this way, with your mother leading me around like a dog on a leash. It happened slowly over the years. The dynamic of the relationship shifted bit by bit, and here I am. In any event, I'm sorry about your books. I know you are going to leave home at some point, whether your mother approves or not.'

'Dad—'

'No, it's to be expected. God knows, I'd do the same thing in your position. Once you get settled, I'll replace your books. Every last one of them. She had no right to do what she did today. If I could have stopped her, I would. But I couldn't. All I can do is make things right.'

'Thank you,' Carmona said.

'I'm so sorry, Carmona. I should have been able to protect you from her. Can you ever forgive me?'

Her heart broke then. Her father reminded her of the damaged teddy bear of childhood, one eye hanging, fur matted, but so full of love. Despite his flaws, he had always been in her corner, quick with the consoling words after Claris had pinned Carmona under her iron fist, trying to break her spirit as she had done her husband's. He opened his arms. Carmona went to him. He pulled her against his chest.

She wept.

CHAPTER 7

Cat sat in her bedroom, dressed in old trousers and a thick sweater. The lights were off to better view the darkness outside. She had a pair of binoculars trained on Beth Hargreaves' house. The rain against the windows made it difficult for her to see, but she was committed to her vigil. Thankfully Bede and Annie were tucked in their beds. She didn't relish having to explain her actions to either one of them.

Earlier Cat had been dressing for dinner – Bede really was a wonderful cook – when she saw a man with a hat walking up the lane. Nothing suspicious there. Many villagers and walkers from out of town walked by the house to get to the turnstile that led to the myriad of footpaths in the area. But ten minutes later, this man came by again. Cat peered out of the window as he hid behind an old tree across the lane and stared at Beth's house. He must have stood that way for fifteen minutes. When Beth came riding up on her bicycle, he had disappeared into the woods.

Something didn't feel right, so Cat – out of concern for Beth – kept watching for the man, anxious to discover what he was up to. She started just after Bede and Annie got ready for bed. Hours had gone by. Cat hadn't seen a soul near the house, nor in the lane that led to the high street. Ready to give up for the evening, she stood and stretched her neck and back, when she saw movement in the bushes by Edythe's window. Edythe had her curtains closed, but she neglected to shut them all the way. A narrow sliver of light pierced the darkness. Cat pressed her forehead against the glass and watched as the figure covered his eyes with his hands and peered into Edythe's room.

Cat bolted. She grabbed a coat, frantically struggled to put it on, but soon gave up in frustration. She tossed the coat to the floor and flew down the stairs. She passed Bede in the entry hall, dressed in a long robe, her grey hair hanging down her back in a thick braid.

'Wherever are you going at this hour? It's pouring outside!' Cat just heard the words as she slammed the door shut.

She took off running, impervious to the rain that soaked her hair and clothes. She slowed when she reached Beth's house. The man was still there. He wore a coat with a hood of some sort. As Cat crept closer, she realized he was tall, well over six feet, by her estimation. He moved along the house, peering in the windows, searching for someone or something. She moved closer, never taking her eyes off him. The rain stopped. Cat called out. 'What are you doing? You tell me right this instant, or I shall call the police.'

The man stiffened for a quick second before he took off at a run.

Wishing she could get a glimpse at his face, Cat gave chase, running until a sharp cramp in her side nearly brought her to her knees. She bent over, waiting for it to pass, helpless to do anything as the man receded into the night.

'I'll get you next time,' she shouted.

***

Cat slept fitfully. At 4.48 a.m. she stood at the window watching the sun creep into the sky over Beth Hargreaves' house. Eager to see Beth and explain what she had seen the previous night, Cat had watched as Beth left early on her bicycle, the basket full of baking tins. Cat had a bad feeling about the events she witnessed last night. Thomas had called to explain his change of residence, with a promise to call her this morning. Someone was spying on her friend. Thomas would help her find out who and why. What if the man Cat saw last night came back and broke into the house? She shivered, afraid for Beth and Edythe. Something had to be done. Thomas was the only person she trusted to help her. Dressing quickly in trousers and an old work shirt, Cat hurried downstairs.

Annie and Bede were in the kitchen in front of the Aga drinking tea out of cups, whispering. When Cat came into the room they stopped talking.

'Good morning,' Cat said.

Bede and Annie turned to face her, a knowing look on both of their faces.

'I see you've been discussing my late-night outing with Annie,' Cat said. She poured herself a cup of tea and took two pieces of toast out of the rack.

'A lady of your position has no business being out of the house on a stormy night. You came back soaked through. You could have caught a deathly cold.' Bede shook her head.

'Where did you go?' Annie asked. 'Is everything okay?'

Cat took her plate to the table. She smiled at Annie, glad to see a bit of colour coming back into the girl's cheeks. Now if they could just get rid of that frightened look and the dark circles under Annie's eyes. 'I thought I saw someone who looked suspicious walking down the lane.' She bit into her toast, careful not to meet Bede or Annie's eyes.

'And so you decided to chase him? And if you caught him, then what?' Bede shook her head and pushed away from the table.

'I've never heard of such a thing. A lady, a right proper lady, chasing after a man in the middle of the night. As I live and breathe, I have never—'

'But she does things like this, Bede. She's a curious lady. That's how she discovered who murdered her husband—' Annie clasped her hand over her mouth. Her cheeks flushed a deep flush of crimson. 'I shouldn't have said that. Oh, I'm so sorry.'

'Annie, dearest, please don't worry about it. It's time Bede knew the truth.' Cat turned to Bede. 'Come sit. I've decided to take you into my confidence, Bede.'

'I think a fresh pot of tea is called for,' Bede said.

Once the tea was made and Bede was seated, Cat spoke. 'You may as well hear it from me. You've probably heard rumours about me, about why I'm here. You might not like what you hear, Bede. If you don't, I understand. You can leave my employment. I'll give you a month's wages and a reference.

'What Annie says is true. I did help discover who murdered my husband. Our household was horrible. Ben – my husband's name was Benton – and his sister both had terrible tempers. My husband and I were in love for the first four or five years of marriage. But I couldn't carry a child to term and we drifted apart. My husband soon took a mistress, led his own life. He started to hate me. The hatred grew into abuse. I suffered for years. After his murder, my sister-in-law did her best to cast me as a suspect. Of course I didn't kill him, but unless I found out who did, people would always look at me with suspicion. I couldn't bear that.'

'And did you?' Bede asked.

'Yes. It was her, my sister-in-law.'

Bede gasped. 'Good lord. Did she go to prison?'

'She did. She hung herself last year.' Cat met Bede's eyes. 'I've just told you a very personal story, Bede. I'm trusting you with it and I'm hoping you'll keep it to yourself. Since you will be living here, you should know that I may have reason to help other

98

people who need it. My husband left me a legacy. I'm going to use it in service to others. But secrecy is a must.'

'I can hold my tongue,' Bede said. 'As I live and breathe, I can hold my tongue. Alfred – that's my husband, God rest his soul – always did say I was a woman of honourable character. Now I may chit-chat with the ladies, but never about personal matters. So you rest easy, Mrs Carlisle.'

'Very well.' Cat took two more pieces of toast. 'I'm glad we've got that all cleared up.'

'I thought I would make lamb stew for our supper. If I can't get any meat – the butcher promised to hold me some back, but he's broken his promise before – it'll have to be vegetable.'

'I love vegetable stew,' Annie said. 'My mum used to make it.'

As Annie and Bede discussed the trick to making decent vegetable stew, Cat slipped out of the house and headed over to the Hargreaves'.

The greenery that provided cover for Beth's intruder glistened with the shimmer of last night's rain drops. By the light of day, the whole thing seemed surreal. But Cat knew what she saw. Someone had been outside Beth's house. Beth had to be warned. Cat knocked on the front door, but there was no answer. She tried the knob, found the door unlocked, and let herself in the house thinking she would leave Beth a note. The house smelled of scones and pound cake. Cat's stomach rumbled, even though she had eaten a sizable breakfast an hour ago.

A pile of clean baking racks were stacked on the draining board. A notepad lay on the work space in the middle of the kitchen. Cat saw a list: *two dozen scones, one pound cake to Claris Broadbent by 10.30 a.m.* Cat saw it was just 10.30 now. Beth must have baked this morning and was out on deliveries. Cat tore a sheet of paper from the pad and left Beth a note asking her to call or come by as soon as she was able. Cat almost wrote it was urgent, but decided not to frighten her friend.

Back home, the lorry with their trunks had arrived. Two

delivery men were methodically unloading them into neat stacks in the foyer. All the windows had been opened and a summer breeze, made sweet by last night's rain, circulated through the house. Cat found Bede in the kitchen rolling out a pie crust, a pile of diced vegetables on the workspace next to her.

'Anything I can do to help?' Cat knew Bede would say no, but she asked anyway.

'Oh, no. Annie's chopped all the vegetables. Did a good job of it, and did it quickly.' Bede stopped rolling for a moment. 'Was the child really in service at your home?'

'She was.'

'She said you saved her,' Bede said.

'We saved each other.'

Bede turned her focus once again to the dough in front of her. 'I understand.'

Cat spent the next hour unpacking her trunks. She sorted her clothes into three piles – one to be hung up immediately, one for ironing and/or repairing, and one to donate to Claris Broadbent's ever increasing need for clothing for the evacuees from London. As she hung the clothes she was keeping on hangers and tucked them away into the wardrobe, she realized how wasteful she had been during her marriage. How many party dresses did one need? How many dress coats, day coats, evening wraps? How many pairs of silken slippers for dancing? She had spent a good part of her marriage filling her time with mindless things, like shopping and society luncheons. Until Isobel murdered her husband and Thomas had come into her life.

Sir Reginald had given Cat a purpose when her world had come crashing down around her. Although he had hinted at a permanent arrangement, that never came to fruition. Sir Reginald had never given her a proper reason, and she resented him for that. Instead, she had gone to work for Thomas as a research assistant/photographer. They had travelled all over England and eventually Europe prior to the war, researching and writing about historic houses and cemeteries. She had needed to be busy, craved something to keep her mind occupied while the chaos around her sorted itself out. The work she had done for Thomas had given her a sense of purpose. She tossed a moth-eaten sweater aside. She had missed him these past few months. She loved Thomas, she admitted that. But she loved her freedom more.

'Miss Catherine?' Annie knocked before she opened the door. 'Bede says to tell you lunch is in ten minutes. And Mr Charles is here. Bede asked him to stay and eat with us.'

Cat smiled. 'Very well. I'll be right down.' She changed into a new dress, dabbed on lipstick, and re-pinned her hair. Downstairs, she found Thomas sitting at the kitchen table peeling potatoes while Bede chopped onions, sniffing and wiping her eyes every few seconds. The vegetable pie cooled on the rack next to a fresh loaf of bread.

'Hello, Thomas,' Cat said. She knew her face was flushed, her eyes were bright, and anyone with half a mind could see the very sight of Thomas Charles lifted her spirits beyond measure. She wanted to kiss him, to run into his arms.

'Hello, Cat.' He stood, started to open his arms, thought better of it and extended both of his hands. She took them and rose up on her toes, offering her cheek to be kissed. Like old friends.

'I see Bede's got you working,' Cat said.

'No, I offered. I used to enjoy peeling potatoes. It's a fond childhood memory.' He rose and took the potatoes to Bede and tossed the peels in the rubbish bin.

'Thank you for that,' Bede said. 'It's nice to see a man in the kitchen. My husband didn't like kitchen work. He used to keep me company while I cooked, but claimed the kitchen duties were women's work.' She wiped the onion tears from her eyes. 'Go on through, if you please. I'll serve you in the dining room.'

'Where's Annie?' Cat asked.

'Took off for the moors with her sketchbook,' Bede replied. 'I sent her with a snack. She should be home in an hour or two.'

'Very well. I'll serve, Bede,' Cat said. She picked up the vegetable pie.

Two places had already been set. Thomas poured tea while Cat served. Bede brought out the loaf of bread, along with a crock of butter. Thomas and Cat tucked into their food. The pie was excellent, creamy and made rich by cheese from the local dairy.

'How've you been settling in?' Thomas asked.

Without asking, Cat refilled both of their plates.

'It's good to be back. I've spent the day going through clothes and hanging drapes. Thank you, by the way, for arranging transport for my things. You were right. I am glad to have brought them.' She looked around the spacious room, filled with light. 'I love the house. It's too big for us, of course. As soon as I get settled, I'll offer to take in a family from London. Maybe a young mother with a child Annie's age.'

'How is she doing? Has she made friends?'

'Of sorts,' Cat said. 'My next-door neighbour has an 18-year-old daughter, Edythe. She is a good girl, studying ballet with her heart set on going to London. She says she's not afraid of Hitler or of bombs. She's taken Annie under her wing a bit. When the child isn't with Edythe, she's taking long walks. Her appetite has returned. We made the right decision. Thank you, Thomas. How about you?'

'I'm enjoying Mr Churchwright. Interesting man. Seen the world a bit. Has an excellent cook. His daughter knows you. Seems you were childhood friends.' Thomas sliced two more pieces of bread.

'I remember Claris. She was the girl in school who liked to boss everyone around. She always managed to have a group of minions around her, all ready to do her bidding.'

'Not you, of course,' Thomas said.

'No. I managed to escape.' She gave Thomas a worried look. 'Something's happened, Thomas. I need you to help me figure out what to do.'

Thomas set the bread knife down. 'What's wrong?'

'My childhood friend, Beth Hargreaves – her aunt was recently murdered. She needs my help – our help.'

'What sort of help?'

Cat heard the worry in Thomas's voice. 'Beth and I were best friends growing up. We lost touch after I moved to London. Yesterday, I went to visit her. She told me the police suspect her of murdering her aunt. She knew of my involvement with Benton's murder. This is a small village, Thomas. I was in the papers. Everyone here – apparently – knows what I did. Believe me when I tell you I made it very clear to Beth that I couldn't interfere with the police. But she needs help. She's worried the police suspect her. She didn't do it. If the police arrest her, I'm going to help her. I can tell by the look on your face you don't agree with my getting involved. Too late. I am involved.'

'Cat, you can't—'

'—meddle in a police investigation. I know. I'm not. But there's more.'

Thomas didn't speak. Instead, he leaned back in his chair and waited for Cat's explanation.

Cat refilled her tea. 'Last night I saw someone spying on her house.'

'What?'

'Just as I was about to go to bed, I saw a figure – an extremely tall man, taller than you, I reckon – creep up to a window and try to peer in.'

'And what did you do next?' Thomas didn't bother hiding the irritation. 'Give chase? My God, you did.'

'He ran away. Nothing happened. I came home soaked. That's it.'

'And what would have happened if he hadn't run away? What would have happened if he had turned around and come after you?' Thomas closed his eyes and took a deep breath.

'I can look after myself, Thomas. My friend's in trouble. I couldn't stand by and do nothing.'

'Laudable but not well thought out. You can't look after yourself if a man twice your size attacks you. What would you have done? Did you even give that any thought?'

'But nothing happened.'

'This time.' Thomas shook his head. 'I'm sorry, Cat. I know you think I'm fussing, but you have this uncanny ability to put yourself in the middle of things.'

'She's a friend, Thomas. Someone was outside her house.'

'Have you told her what you saw?'

'No. I went over this morning, but she wasn't home. I'm going to speak with her this afternoon, see if I can get her to stay here with me. But I can't help but wonder if the person who was watching her house has something to do with her aunt's murder.'

Cat watched the familiar planes of Thomas's face, the lines around the corners of his eyes, the set of his mouth. He was keeping something from her.

'I'll talk to the police,' he said.

'I'll go with you.'

'No,' he said too quickly. 'Leave it with me. You just got here. If you go to the police, the gossip will start. I can slip in and speak to them under some other pretext. I think that would be the best course of action. Don't you agree?'

Cat knew he was asking the question to placate her. As much as she hated to admit it, he was right.

'Do you want to keep watch with me tonight?'

'Let's leave the watching to the police. If they don't take any action, yes, we will watch together. We will help your friend. Together. Agreed?'

Cat nodded. She decided in the end not to tell him about Edythe's suspicion of David Broadbent. For now, anyway.

'Will you promise me to be careful? I worry about you acting recklessly, Cat. Surely you can see that chasing after a strange man in the middle of the night is problematic.'

The concern in Thomas's eyes was far beyond that of a caring friend. She smiled. 'You're right. I admit it. I promise to be more careful. Now that I know you're going to help me, I will save my chasing until I've got you with me. How's that?'

He lifted a sardonic eyebrow. 'I suppose it will have to do.'

After lunch they cleared the dining table. Thomas spread out a large map of the area. He gave Cat a list of monastic houses that could potentially make it into their book. 'Do you think you could sort out a route for us? Save us from dashing all over the place. If you've got time, you could start with taking some photos of the local church.' They made a loose plan of how they would move forward. Cat would plan a route, Thomas would start the actual research. Soon they would start taking day trips and exploring new places, working together as they had in the past.

'And now I must go. I'm meeting with the retired vicar I told you about. Take a couple of days to finishing unpacking. We'll start visiting the churches next week. Does that suit?'

'It does.'

They both stood. Cat wove her arm through Thomas's as she walked him to the door.

'I believe the country air is doing you good, Mr Charles.'

At the door, Thomas turned to face her. 'No more chasing after strangers. Please?'

'Okay,' Cat said.

Thomas stepped outside. He tipped his hat before he placed it on his head. 'Until tomorrow.' She watched while he walked into the lane and turned towards the high street, his step sure and steady.

CHAPTER 8

For the past twenty-four hours, Carmona – with Liddy's help – had done a fine job of avoiding her mother. She managed this by leaving the house before her mother awoke, staying away during the day, and taking her meals in her room. By tacit agreement, her mother had left her alone. Carmona woke to the cool morning air. Her bedside clock said 7.30. She'd overslept. If she wanted to slip out unseen, she would have to hurry. Where was Liddy with her tea?

As if on cue, Liddy knocked on the door and came into Carmona's room. Worry lines were etched on her face. The apron Claris insisted she wear hung crooked over her shoulder. The usual sunny smile had been replaced by a scowl.

'Good morning,' Carmona said. 'Tea?'

'Sorry, Carm. Your mum said no way. She expects you at the table, and she sent me to fetch you.' Liddy sat down on the bed next to Carmona. 'You're going to have to deal with her at some point, so don't you even think about slipping out the window.'

Carmona put her feet on the cold floor, taking the dressing gown Liddy held out for her.

'Your mum is angry at me. She must think I've been a bad influence on you. She's given me a list of things to do that will keep me here all night.'

Carmona patted Liddy's shoulder. 'I'll talk to her for you, make her see it's not your fault.' While she bathed, Liddy had laid out a pleated skirt and white blouse, Carmona's usual attire. Carmona reached for the skirt, but changed her mind. She moved to the wardrobe and took out a straight skirt, navy blue with tiny white lines woven through, along with a white linen blouse she had bought on a trip to London with Edythe. She opened a package of silk stockings and slipped into a pair of navy kid skin shoes, also purchased in London, but never worn. She surveyed herself in the mirror, pleased with her newfound maturity.

'Did Edythe call?'

'Not that I know of. You look very polished, Carmona. Well done.' Liddy hoisted Carmona's laundry basket onto her hip. 'Good luck with your mum.'

When Carmona stepped into the dining room, her mother gave her the familiar *what are you up to now* look. But when she met Carmona's eyes, her expression became serious. She set her fork down and leaned back in her chair. 'Where are you going today? Why are you dressed like that?'

Carmona spooned scrambled eggs onto her plate, took two pieces of toast from the rack, and poured herself a cup of tea. She took her time about it. 'I'm going to visit Edythe. She hasn't called, has she?'

Claris didn't answer. 'Why are you dressed like that, Carmona?'

Carmona ignored her mother as she sat down at the table. She felt the power of her position and found she rather enjoyed having the upper hand with this woman who expected everyone to kowtow to her. 'I have some things I need to take care of today, and – as I said – I planned on visiting Edythe.'

'You're rather overdressed.'

'No more than you are, Mother,' Carmona said.

'Yes, but I'm a—'

'What? A woman? Well, Mother, so am I. I've just decided to dress the part. You of all people should understand that.'

'Carmona, please. I need to talk to you.'

'Okay.'

'I know you took money out of the bank. I demand to know why. Did you give it to him? Did you give it to Phillip? Tell me this instant.'

Careful not to lose her temper, Carmona finished chewing and dabbed at her mouth with the white linen napkin. She gave her mother a condescending look. 'Did you ever think I needed the money to replace my books?'

'You did. I can see it by the look on your face. Carmona, can't you see he is using you?' Claris stared at Carmona's face. 'Carmona. Please. Won't you listen to reason? Do not trust him. Phillip Billings is too handsome for his own good. He's a scoundrel. You need to see.'

'If you'll excuse me.' Carmona stood. She wanted to scream at her mother and run out of the room. She didn't. She put her shoulders back and walked out, slowly and with great deliberation. Victory was hers. At least for this round. She knew the battle between them was far from over.

'I just don't want you to get hurt,' her mother called out. She heard the break in her mother's voice, as if she were about to sob. She almost stopped. Almost turned around. Almost gave her mother a chance at destroying the only thing in her life that made her happy. Refusing to be tricked by her mother's insincere concern, Carmona didn't return to her mother. The chasm between them was too great now. Her relationship with her mother didn't matter anymore. She had Phillip now. He was her family. It took every ounce of discipline she possessed to not break into a run. Mature women didn't go bolting out into the street. She walked with purpose, with the maturity and – one could hope – grace befitting a lady.

***

108

The sun crept out, shining bright on the trees and grass, washed clean by last night's rain. Carmona thought about taking her car, but she decided to save the precious petrol. Rather than ride her bike and get mud on her good skirt, Carmona headed off on foot to Edythe's house. It wasn't like Edythe to stay away so long. Even when she was busy with her dancing, they always managed a few minutes or a cup of tea at the shop in town.

As the sun got brighter, Carmona's anger faded. The time would come when Carmona and her mother would no longer live in the same house. When she and Phillip were married and living happily in their new home, Claris would see just how wrong she was about Phillip. Phillip hadn't asked Carmona to marry him yet. It was much too soon, but she was certain a proposal would be forthcoming. She wondered if Phillip would ask her father for her hand. As for her mother, the old adage – embroidered in needlepoint in her grandmother's hallway – *this too shall pass*, came to mind. She would leave in January no matter what. She'd get a job if she had to. As for Phillip, she assumed he'd be coming with her. What did he have to keep him in Rivenby?

The warmth of the sun warmed Carmona's shoulders. She paused outside the gate at Edythe's house, smoothed her skirt, and pushed a stray lock of hair – fixed in a new, more grown-up style today – behind her ear. She heard Edythe's voice. Something about the very sound of it flooded Carmona with relief. *Thank God for Edythe*, she thought as she fiddled with the latch as she had done hundreds of times before. Edythe stopped talking and another voice answered her. She stepped back into the safety of the hedge and crept along for a better view, eavesdropping for a second time on her best friend.

Edythe, dressed in a flowing skirt over her leotard and a sweater to stave off the morning chill, and the girl who painted were arranging themselves out on the patio. Edythe carried a tray laden with a teapot and tea cups. The girl carried a functional carryall made of white canvas but splattered with splotches of paint. Today

Carmona noticed the girl's clothes were well made, but they hung on her frame as though she had undergone a difficult time and had lost weight. Carmona crept closer, careful not to step on an errant twig, as Edythe poured two cups of tea, handed one to the girl, and sat down at the table.

'Let's see that one,' Edythe said. She pointed to one of the sketch pads the girl had set before her.

The girl handed it to Edythe, who skimmed through it.

'These are very good. Is that Mrs Carlisle? And who is this? He looks like a pirate.'

The girl's voice didn't carry as well as Edythe's. Careful not to step on any branches or twigs, Carmona crept closer to better hear, captivated now by this girl.

'That's Mr Charles. He's in love with Miss Catherine. He is ever so handsome, even though he's a bit old. He went away to Norway. Got shot while helping the King escape. Now he's coming here to rest. He writes books about churches. Miss Catherine takes the pictures. They work side by side ...' The girl's voice lowered. Carmona strained to hear.

'Were you in the house when her husband was murdered?'

The girl looked up at Edythe, surprised by the question. For the first time, Carmona got a good look at her face. The paleness looked as though it came from a long illness. Her cheeks were gaunt. Her eyes had a haunted look. Carmona wondered if this girl had suffered some sort of trauma, or if her frightened malnourished look was a result of living in the city. Carmona had read about the sirens and the blackouts of London, about the frantic need to get the children off to safety. She wasn't put off by the warnings of the dangers of city life. Hitler wasn't going to stop Carmona's plans.

'Forgive me for being nosy, but I just can't imagine what it must have been like for you.' Edythe poured more tea for both of them.

'I found the body,' the girl said. 'His head was bashed in. Mr

110

Carlisle was so handsome, like a film star. But he was mean.' She picked up the sketch pad and pencil and started to draw, her hand moving with fury across the page. 'I ran away from home and lied my way into a service job at the house. One of Mr Carlisle's friends—' She stopped drawing for a moment and stared off into space. Afraid of being discovered spying in the bushes, Carmona didn't dare breathe until the girl continued. 'One of Mr Carlisle's friends cornered me on the staircase. He tried to – he trapped me.' The girl took a deep breath and shook her head. 'Mrs Carlisle saved me from him. She's been my protector.'

'Did she adopt you?'

'Not officially. We've talked about it, but my mum would be heartbroken. Mrs Carlisle likes to help people, no matter where they come from. She's got a kind heart. She doesn't want to hurt my mum.'

Carmona felt sorry for the little thing as she imagined there was more intrigue to her story than she was sharing with Edythe. Carmona remembered the scuttlebutt around Cat Carlisle's murder case, too. Her mother had studied the newspapers and reported the events at the breakfast table. In fact, Claris and her minions had been obsessed with the woman who solved her husband's murder. Was there mention of a ring of spies?

'Who else lived in the house with you? Just Mrs Carlisle and her husband?'

'Miss Isobel – that's Mr Carlisle's sister, who hired me to work – she tried to get the police to think Miss Catherine had murdered Mr Carlisle. In the end, it turned out she had done it in a fit of rage. She had a temper, Miss Isobel. So did Mr Carlisle. He was nice to servants, generous with money, but when he got angry, it was horrible. Miss Isobel always tried to boss Miss Catherine. She would bark out orders, but Miss Catherine would just smile and ignore her. When Mr Carlisle died, Miss Isobel was inconsolable. She blamed Miss Catherine for the murder, swore up and down Miss Catherine did it. Tried to get the police to arrest her.

And all the time it was her that done it.' The girl put her pencil down and sipped her tea before she continued.

'Mr Charles worked on the investigation with the police. That's how he and Miss Catherine met. And when everything was finished, Miss Catherine took me to live with her. Only she said I wasn't to be a servant.'

'Is Mr Charles a policeman?'

'I'm not sure. But he's so kind. He's in love with Miss Catherine. You can see it in his eyes when he looks at her. It's so romantic. If they get married, maybe I'll be in the wedding party. I've always wanted to be in a wedding. There's a church near our house in Bloomsbury. Sometimes when the bells ring, I go and watch the bride come out in her beautiful dress, so radiant and happy.'

Edythe laughed. 'You'll have your own wedding someday. Tell me about your parents.'

Carmona watched the walls come up around this girl. She was finished with confidences.

'Hold still,' she said. 'The light is hitting you in the just the right way.'

Edythe left her hands on the table and continued to hold her head in the position the girl favoured.

'I hope you can get used to country life. We don't have the excitement you're used to in London.'

'I don't mind.'

The girl's pencil flew across the sketch pad. Every now and then she would glance up at Edythe. Carmona recognized the joy. She had seen it on Edythe's face at the ballet.

'Okay. You can rest.' The girl tucked a pencil behind her ear. She sipped from her cup of tea. 'The sirens are awful. They go all night. I would lie in my bed, wondering when the bomb would hit us. Do you think it's painful to die from a bomb?'

'Don't worry about that. You'll be safe here,' Edythe said. 'Is Mr Charles as handsome in person as he is in your drawing? I understand he's coming here.'

112

'He's here already. Apparently, he is staying with a man named Mr Churchwright. He says he's writing but he's probably working on one of his investigations.' The girl continued to speak, but she dropped her voice. Carmona dared not risk getting closer. How would she explain herself if Edythe – and this girl – caught her eavesdropping in the bushes? But her curiosity had been aroused. Lucky for her she didn't need to spy in the bushes to learn about this Mr Charles. She could go right to the source.

***

Carmona loved her grandfather's house. Not because of its beauty or historical significance. The house – probably because her mother didn't have any controlling influence – always felt welcoming to her. Grandfather didn't judge her or expect her to adhere to social decorum every second. Grandfather, Beck, and the missus, liked her to be herself. They didn't think twice when she kicked off her shoes, untucked her blouse and curled up in a chair with one of the many books in her grandfather's well-stocked library. No one tut-tutted her when she ate buttered toast and licked her fingers afterwards. Grandfather didn't bother about the fastidious social nonsense that consumed Carmona's mother. He had given up the big house, along with the full accompaniment of servants, to his daughter. He preferred this smaller house, which he shared with his Beck and the missus, who were more like family.

Heart's Desire was quiet as Carmona let herself in the front door and stood in the foyer for a few seconds. Good. Better for snooping. Careful not to make any noise, she slipped up the stairs.

Her grandfather had put Mr Charles in the large bedroom with an adjoining suite and its own bathroom. Carmona knocked before letting herself into the room, taking in the tightly made bed, the perfectly tucked corners. She ventured over to the wardrobe and opened it, surprised by the orderly method with which Mr Charles hung his clothes. His shirt collars were organized, right alongside his ties. Two hats – one chocolate brown and one navy – were in their place on the hat shelf. Four crisp white shirts hung in perfect symmetry. Next to them was Mr Charles' dinner suit. A quick rifling through the drawers of the highboy dresser revealed nothing unusual. A stack of books sat on the bedside table. There was a well-worn volume about medieval architecture, along with a treatise on financial forecasting, which would have put Carmona to sleep had she taken the time to read it, and an old and well-used Latin dictionary.

She moved through the door that adjoined the bedroom to the small office next to it. Carmona had always liked this room. During one of her horrible rows with her mother, Carmona had come crying to her grandfather, begging to move in. Her grandfather had told her no. He explained she needed to sort things out with her mother. 'Don't live your life with anger towards your family, Carmona. It makes for a miserable existence. Your mum loves you. You must make peace with her and do your best to keep it. She's the only mum you've got, and despite her shortcomings, she's a good woman.' That conversation had been over ten years ago. Carmona wondered what her grandfather would say once he knew the current state of affairs between her mother and her. How would he feel when he found out her mother had burned her books?

The room occupied a corner, so it had the benefit of windows on two walls. It was bright and clean. Her grandfather had gone to the trouble of moving his old writing desk into the room, along with a gentleman's wing chair and ottoman. A large globe her grandfather had been given as a boy and the tall bookcases which lined one wall finished off the room, giving it the feeling of cosiness without too much clutter.

The top of the writing desk was empty, save a ceramic lamp and a typewriter Carmona reckoned belonged to Mr Charles. A tattered leather document case sat under the desk. Carmona picked it up and set it on the ottoman. She half expected the brass hasp to be locked, but when she pushed the button it popped open. Papers overflowed. She sat down on the chair, took the whole stack out and set it down on the ottoman before her. The first stack of papers – Carmona guessed there was upward of two hundred pages – looked like a manuscript about a church somewhere in Bournemouth. It was covered in red squiggles and dashes, probably proofreading marks. Carmona read the first three pages, decided the premise of the manuscript was boring, and set it aside. Next came two notebooks, all filled with what must have been Mr Charles' admirably clean handwriting. Nothing of interest there.

She carried on this way, snooping into Mr Charles' personal documents without the least amount of guilt until she came across a thick brown envelope which had at one time been closed with thick red sealing wax. Careful not to disturb the other files in the case, Carmona lifted this particular file out. The front was stamped with more red wax, but this seal had an imposing shield and an unreadable motto. Her heart beat faster. Not with guilt, but with anticipation.

Childish Carmona, who needed to know what was in the envelope, waged a mini-battle with mature Carmona, who would never condone the indignity of snooping. The battle was short-lived, with mature Carmona the victor. She stuffed the file back in the envelope, placed the envelope back into the stack with the other papers, and placed everything back in the document case. Once the document case was tucked back under the desk, Carmona walked to the door, proud that she had resisted temptation. Almost.

She rationalized curiosity wasn't a characteristic reserved for children. After all, wasn't curiosity the backbone of invention? If scientists didn't ask *what if* nothing would ever have been invented. So what if she wanted to see what was in Mr Charles' document case? He was, after all, her grandfather's guest. What if Mr Charles was working on a dangerous investigation? What if he was putting her beloved grandfather in harm's way? Curiosity won. Her newfound sophistication didn't stand a chance. Like a flash, Carmona flew back to the satchel, tore open the document case, and made quick work of pulling out the file. For a moment she clutched it to her chest, the thrill of the snooping nearly as captivating as the revelation. With shaking hands, she sat down on the ottoman, and opened Mr Charles' secret file.

A large picture of Phillip's handsome face stared back at her. He was smiling in the picture, his eyes crinkled at the corners. His tousled hair hung down over one eye, as though he had just come in from the outdoors.

'Oh, no,' her voice came out a whisper.

Carmona lifted the page that held Phillip's picture and read what lay behind it. She felt sick all of a sudden, discomfited at this surprise. She was so shocked by the file and Phillip's picture, she didn't see Thomas Charles as he stood in the door, his eyes blazing with anger.

'Can I help you?'

Carmona yelped, turned to face Mr Charles, and sent the file she held onto the floor. Its contents came to rest in a fan at her feet.

'I'm so sorry,' Carmona said.

She bent to retrieve the folder, but Mr Charles swooped in, and with his one good arm picked up the papers. He shoved them into the folder and stuffed the disorganized stack into the carryall that lay gaping at Carmona's feet. He snapped it shut and set it out of Carmona's way. She sat back down on the ottoman, her heart hammering in her chest. Mr Charles remained standing, his face still as etched marble. There was a quietude about him Carmona found frightening.

He positioned himself near the door. One step to the left and he would block her way. Carmona was trapped.

'What do you have to say for yourself?' His voice was calm and well modulated.

He reminded Carmona of a pile of kindling with petrol doused over it. One touch of the slightest flame and an explosion would ensue. She weighed her words carefully, opting for a skewed version of the truth.

'I'm Carmona Broadbent, your host's granddaughter.' Uttering her name gave Carmona strength. Her position wasn't so tenuous after all. This was her grandfather's house. By that rationale, Carmona had more of a right to be in this room than this man.

'I overheard my friend Edythe and Mrs Carlisle's ward speaking of you in the garden. She said you were staying with Grandfather and you were probably involved in some sort of investigation. I wanted to make sure you weren't putting him in danger. He seems like he's in good health—'

'Stop.' Mr Charles shook his head. 'I may be a lot of things, but I'm not stupid. Please, do not speak. Listen. Are you capable of that?'

Carmona swallowed the lump that had formed in her throat. She nodded.

'I am here on an investigation. You have just read a confidential file. I could have you taken in and questioned by the police. I could have you taken to London and questioned by authority that far exceeds your local police or Scotland Yard for that matter.' Mr Charles winced in pain and rubbed his shoulder. 'But I'm not going to. I'm going to let this one incident go by, provided you promise not to discuss this with anyone. Agreed?'

Carmona wasn't making any promises to this stranger until she found out why he had a file on Phillip. 'Why are you investigating Phillip Billings?'

'I cannot tell you that.' Thomas cocked his head and squinted his eyes. 'Are you involved with Mr Billings?'

'We're in love.'

117

'In love?' Thomas ran his hand through his hair. When he had finished, it stood straight up. Carmona bit back a smile.

'Do your parents know of your relationship with Mr Billings?'

'That's none of your business, Mr Charles.'

'You made it my business when you snooped through my papers. You cannot speak of this to anyone. Do you understand? I don't know you. I'm taking a risk by offering to accept your word, but I have no choice about that. Once your grandfather returns, I'll tell him of the situation and trust that he will reinforce the importance of keeping your mouth shut.' Thomas stepped away from Carmona. 'So, young lady, do we have a deal? You'll keep silent?'

'No deals until you tell me why you're investigating Phillip,' Carmona said.

'Very well. I'll just make that phone call.' Thomas walked over to the desk. He picked up the telephone and spoke to the exchange. 'Police, please.'

Carmona jumped up. 'Fine. I'll not tell anyone.'

'Good choice,' Thomas said.

'I won't speak to anyone but Mr Billings. He has a right to know you are investigating him. Is this to do with his mother's murder? Of course it is. I will promise you Mr Billings will speak to you directly. You can question him and clear up any misunderstanding. I won't let him be pushed around by the likes of you.' Carmona didn't wait for Thomas Charles' protestation.

'Good day, Mr Charles.' And with that, she fled the room.

CHAPTER 9

Carmona stormed down the street, each indignant step taking her farther and farther away from Thomas Charles and his stupid file on Phillip. She was sweating through her linen blouse, the silk stockings were sticking to her legs. The skirt was too tight around her middle, and she just wanted to pull the pearl necklace off her throat and send the white orbs flying. Tears streamed down her face, leaving a shiny trail through the face powder she put on that morning. She didn't care about how she looked. She had to get to Phillip, to find out what sort of trouble he was in. A cramp formed in the pit of her belly, the symptom of a sense of foreboding, the likes of which she had never experienced before.

Carmona didn't believe in superstitions, premonitions, or psychic ability. She believed in science, logic, thought, and reason. She shivered. Something was very wrong. The swirling emotions that had propelled her out of her grandfather's house and into the village were replaced by fear. Fear for Phillip, fear for herself.

'Dear? Are you listening to me?'

A claw-like hand clutched at Carmona's arm. Startled, she jumped. Bede Turner, her head swathed in a garish scarf, shopping basket tucked under her arm, gazed up at Carmona. She cocked her head, like an inquisitive chicken. 'I say, are you quite all right?' She pulled Carmona into the tiny alley next to the stationers and handed her a handkerchief. 'Here you go, dear. Your make-up is a bit smudged.'

'Thank you, Bede.' Carmona wiped her face.

'Now you shouldn't be too hard on your mum. She loves you and is doing the best she can.' Bede gave Carmona an encouraging smile. 'She seems to be overworking herself a wee bit, don't you think?'

'What are you talking about?'

'I just assumed that's why you're so upset. Your mum.' Bede nodded, as if encouraging Carmona to agree with her.

'This isn't about my mum, Bede. This is something entirely different.' She should have been angry at Bede Turner for her meddlesome ways, but she felt a kind affection for the old woman. Carmona remembered when she was a wee girl and Claris had slapped her face in public after some minor transgression. Carmona had run out of her mother's reach, and had cowered, humiliated, while her mother's friend had looked on, a bemused expression on her face. She was just a child, but she recalled the indignation she felt like it was yesterday. No one had been there to champion her. Her mother's friends would never question Claris's actions, even if they were cruel.

Carmona could still hear Bede's voice.

'Now, Claris, there's no cause to treat the child like that in public. You've embarrassed the poor thing.'

'She needed slapping. Mind your own business, Bede,' Claris said. She turned her back on Bede and continued her conversation with one of her minions.

Carmona had never seen anyone defy her mother before. Tears and shame forgotten, she watched as Bede had tapped Claris on the shoulder. When her mother had turned around, Bede said, 'You've no right to speak to me – or anyone – in that way. You've bullied her in public, embarrassed the little mite. She's done nothing wrong.'

'This is no concern of yours. Now, if you'll excuse me.' Her mother started to walk away. But Bede Turner had grabbed her mother's arm – much like she had grabbed Carmona's just now. She'd leaned close and whispered something in Claris's ear. Something in Bede's words gave her mother pause. She gasped. The colour drained from her mother's face. She closed her eyes, and for a moment, Carmona thought her mother was going to faint. When she recovered herself, she came over to Carmona and held her out her hand. 'Mummy's sorry, dear. Let's get you an ice cream.'

As they were walking away, Carmona ventured a look back at the woman who had saved her from her mother's bullying. Bede Turner winked, as if it was all a big joke. Years had gone by. Although Carmona and Bede didn't go on outings together, there was a bond between them. Carmona owed Bede a debt of gratitude. When Bede's husband had passed, Carmona had made a pot of soup by herself and taken it over. She had offered money, but had discovered Bede's husband had left her well situated. Carmona still felt loyal to the woman who had stood up for her so long ago.

She started to hand the handkerchief back to Bede, but pulled it back at the last moment. 'I'll wash this and return it.'

'Thanks, love. You look very pretty today. Grown-up.'

Her words reminded Carmona of her new attitude, her new, grown-up way of being in the world. She called up this strength and lied with ease. 'I'm going to dash home. I'm a mess. Thanks for the handkerchief.'

Before Bede could say anything, Carmona was off, leaving Bede staring after her. As soon as she could, Carmona ducked into an alley and backtracked down a side street to Phillip's cottage. She crept up to the back door and knocked, careful not to disturb Phillip's nosy neighbour. Phillip opened the door, took one look at Carmona and said, 'What are you doing here?'

Carmona pushed past him and went into the kitchen. Phillip

had finished lunch. The kitchen smelled of onions. The can of tinned meat lay empty on the drain board. Two dirty plates and forks sat in the sink. 'Who's been here?'

'Just an old mate. Stopped by for lunch.' He pulled Carmona close to him and kissed her cheek. 'Which I was able to feed him, thanks to you. Now, tell me why you are upset.' He pulled a chair out for her.

'There is an investigator of some sort staying at my grandfather's.' Carmona kept her eyes riveted on Phillip as she spoke, admiring the way his blond hair shone in the sun that came through the window. 'He has a file on you.'

'What?' Phillip's expression hardened as he met Carmona's eyes. The blood slowly drained from his face.

'I didn't get a chance to see what was in it. He caught me snooping. Threatened to call the police. I just opened it and saw a picture of you.'

A silver cigarette case sat on the counter. Phillip took a cigarette out. He lit it, blowing a plume of smoke in the air. 'Tell me about this bloke. What sort of file? Is he a copper?'

Carmona shook her head. 'I don't think he's a real policeman. He does investigations of some sort.'

'Tell me about the file. What did it look like?'

'I hardly see how that matters—'

'Tell me about the damn file,' Phillip shouted. He jumped up from the chair and walked over to the wall which separated the kitchen and the living room. He punched it. *So this is what it feels like to be bullied by someone you love.* The thought, which came out of nowhere, surprised Carmona.

Phillip came to her. He knelt before her. Her eyes flooded with tears. She vowed not to shed them. Her heart nearly split with love for this man.

'I'm sorry. Please, forgive me. I promise never to speak to you like that again. I'm worried, Carmona. Am I a suspect in my mother's murder?'

'Why else would he be here? And you didn't do it. I know that. You just need to talk to him.'

'Talk to him?' Phillip jumped to his feet. He ground out his cigarette in the ashtray on the table.

'Why not?' Carmona said. 'You didn't do anything. You certainly didn't murder your mum. Why can't you just cooperate? Let him investigate you. That will convince this Mr Charles you've got nothing to hide.'

'I've got debts. I needed the money. They'll think I killed her for it.'

'But you didn't. Don't you see? It doesn't matter what they think. You didn't do it. And the way to convince them of your innocence is to cooperate with their investigation.' Carmona got up from her chair and walked over to Phillip. She put both hands on his shoulders and stared into his eyes. 'Did you do it?'

'What?'

'Did you kill her?'

'God, no.' Phillip leaned against the counter. He crossed his arms over his chest, closed his eyes, and took a deep breath. Carmona waited.

'I told him you were innocent. I told him you would talk to him.'

'Surely you didn't tell him about me. Did you?'

'Of course I did. I'll not stand idly by and watch you persecuted for something you didn't do.'

'You had no right to speak for me, Carmona.' Phillip met her eyes. She saw something hard there, something far removed from the man she had found lying in a heap after the pub had closed. 'I'll talk to him, but not until I'm ready.' He came over to her and led her to the door. 'I need to be alone, so I can figure things out.'

'I think it is time for us to tell my parents about our relationship. You're going to need help. When my parents realize what we mean to each other, they'll want to help you. They are in a

123

position to help you. You want to be left alone to think about it? Fine. But don't be stupid, Phillip. You might be older than me, seen a bit more of the world, but I will not stand by and let you do something stupid, not when it affects both of us.' Carmona stormed out the back door, slamming it in her wake. She heard Phillip cuss, followed by the sound of breaking glass as he threw something against the wall.

***

Phillip stood amid the shattered glass on his kitchen floor. He stooped to pick up the bigger pieces, cut his finger, and cursed as the blood dripped on his last clean shirt. Stepping over the shards, he moved into the front room and peered out between the drapes. It had been five days since the debt collectors had roughed him up and issued their warning. Carmona had given him money. He wanted to pay them and be done with it, but Carmona's news about the dossier and the mysterious copper had taken him by surprise. He thought of Lady Blythedale's accusation of stolen jewels as he checked the street again. There was no doubting that Lady Blythedale could truly ruin Phillip, if she was so inclined. Ruthless, she wouldn't think twice about manufacturing evidence and sending him to prison for a crime he didn't commit. That's why he had fled Edinburgh. And DCI Kent would be glad to see him go down, even though Phillip was innocent.

The whole village probably thought he had killed Win. No one would meet his eyes. Yesterday, conversation had stopped and all eyes had turned towards him when he walked into the post office. DCI Kent's questioning at the police station hadn't helped matters. He had spent a good hour answering a barrage of questions about his time in Scotland, his relationship with his mother, all seemingly innocuous. In the end, DCI Kent had let him go, with an admonition not to leave town.

Phillip had stood, fixed his tie, and given DCI Kent a broad smile. 'Give my regards to Pamela.' Although he knew his words wouldn't endear him to DCI Kent, he couldn't resist the temptation to strike a blow. Admittedly, he took pleasure in DCI Kent's flashing eyes and the angry vein on his forehead that started to throb. Colin Kent hadn't been happy when he had caught his sister kissing Phillip, so many years ago. Phillip didn't like coppers. He especially didn't like DCI Kent.

Now he had another copper to deal with. Certain Lady Blythedale had finally caught up with him to get revenge, much like Pamela Kent had done all those years ago, Phillip decided the best course of action was to leave Rivenby.

Despite the early hour, he poured himself a tall brandy. He took the bottle and his mother's papers to the kitchen table and started sorting through them. Not sure what he was looking for, he spent thirty minutes with insurance documents, receipts, tax papers, and lists. An envelope labelled 'correspondence' caught his eye. He pulled a stack of letters out, some of them written to his mother, some of them carbon copies of business correspondence she had sent herself. Phillip was ready to call it quits, when he stumbled upon a carbon copy of a letter his mother had written to James Churchwright.

He skimmed it, then read it again, more slowly this time, heart pounding as a plan clicked into place. He had found his miracle.

***

Cat donned her new hat and gloves – which matched her dress perfectly – and headed into the village. The day was sunny, with just enough chill in the air to make the walk pleasant. She smiled at those she passed. Many greeted her with a smile. Others couldn't place her. Cat felt their stares as she walked past.

She found the garage at the end of an alley just off the high street. A gentleman in a well-worn suit was showing a car to a young couple. Cat hurried past them, around the corner to the garage, where she found the mechanic hunched over a motor. Cat had never been in a car repair shop before and was surprised at how clean and organized this one was. There was not one drop of oil on the floor. All the tools were hung by order of size along one wall.

'Can I help you, miss?' A voice said. Cat turned to face the man who was bent over the engine, surprised to recognize her childhood friend. 'Cat Paxton?' He squinted before he pulled a pair of spectacles out of his pocket and put them on.

'Cliff.' Cat extended her hand and moved towards him.

'I'll not shake your hand. Not until I've had a wash. How are you? It's been a long time.'

'Twenty-two years,' Cat said. 'And you haven't changed a bit. I see you still like to tinker with engines.'

'I do. Turned into a right livelihood. I've got a wife and three kiddies now. Well, they're not kiddies anymore. My oldest just turned 18.' Cliff had a thatch of dark curls, electric blue eyes, and the biggest ears Cat had ever seen. But he was a dear soul and had been a loyal friend during Cat's childhood. He smiled at her now. 'I remember climbing trees with you. Almost fell out of one. Remember?'

'Of course. Your poor mum. She never forgave me for that.' As a young girl, Cat made it a point of pride never to be upstaged by a boy. One summer day, she and Cliff had raced up the old oak tree in his front yard. Cliff had climbed nearly to the top. Not wanting to be upstaged by a boy, Cat had shimmied even higher. Cliff's mother came out of the house, saw Cat in the highest bough, and nearly had a heart attack. Cat smiled at the memory.

A young boy in dirty overalls and a cap came into the shop carrying a broom and dust pan.

'There you go, lad. Sweep the back room. When you've finished, I'll have a coin and a bite to eat for you.'

The boy touched the brim of his cap and hurried off.

'Poor kids from London. Don't know what to do with themselves. That one has a mum who pays him no mind. Trying to keep him out of trouble. This war is going to change village life for good, I'm afraid.'

'You've always had a soft spot for those in need, Cliff,' Cat said.

Cliff moved over to a sink, rolled up his sleeves, and set about washing his hands. 'I was sorry to hear about your parents. Didn't get a chance to tell you. Your aunt took you to London so fast. And now look at you. You've turned into a proper lady.'

'It's the clothes. I'm still the same person I always was, although I have lost my taste for climbing trees.'

'What brings you back to Rivenby?' Cliff dried his hands.

She stepped closer to Cliff and spoke in a low voice. 'I actually want to talk to you about Win Billings' murder.'

'Do you now?' Cliff looked around the shop. 'Meet me at the Dirty Duck in ten minutes. We should have some privacy there.'

***

Cat had never been into the Dirty Duck, although she had vague memories of her father going there of an evening to have a pint. Her mother never went to the pub. Back in those days, ladies didn't frequent establishments like the Duck. But times had changed, and – based on the tables covered in dirty plates – the Dirty Duck now did a good luncheon business. A tall man with kind eyes and a nice smile busied himself clearing off the tables and taking them into a back room. Cat caught a peek of a woman with ample hips, who took the dirty plates and put them in a large sink. Unsure what to do, she glanced nervously at the door, wishing Cliff would hurry up.

127

The man came out of the kitchen. He wiped his hands on a clean white towel and smiled at Cat.

'Mrs Carlisle? Cliff called and said to make you comfortable. I've got a table for you back here.' Cat was grateful that Cliff had the foresight to warn the publican she was coming. The dark beamed ceilings were so low, the man had to duck. He stopped before a table in a back corner.

'Thank you,' Cat said.

'Call me Jemmy. Tea? My wife does a good ploughman's, if you're interested.'

'Tea would be fine,' Cat said.

Jemmy nodded and hurried off just as Cliff walked in the door.

'Thanks for agreeing to meet me here,' Cliff said. 'Too many ears at the garage. I had to testify about the murder. Reporters have been coming to my house – the wife's not happy about it, I can tell you.'

Jemmy returned with a large pot of tea, milk, sugar, and two mugs. He poured out for them. 'Help yourself to cream and sugar.'

'Thanks, Jem,' Cliff said. He took his time about his cream and sugar, not speaking until he set the spoon on the table and took a sip. 'Jemmy does make a good strong pot of tea. Now, Cat, what are you up to?'

In an instant, Cat decided to trust Cliff. 'Beth Hargreaves thinks she's a suspect in her aunt's murder. She's asked me to help her. Who do you think did it?'

He gave her a surprised look. 'You certainly jump right in, don't you?'

'Come on, Cliff. I haven't forgotten what life in a village like Rivenby is like. Surely you have some idea.'

'I know what happened to you in London, how you helped solve your husband's murder. Everyone in the village read those newspapers backwards and forwards for news of you. But how do you think you can help Beth? I guess the better question is why. What's she thinking, asking you to get involved?' He shook

128

his head. 'I don't like it. Not one bit. It ain't right her involving you like that, and you just back here after all these years. People will start talking. Surely she considered that.'

'It's because of Edythe. If Beth doesn't find out who really killed her aunt, suspicion will hang over her. Do you think Phillip Billings had anything to do with his mum's murder?'

Cliff stared at his tea. He had always been a contemplative soul, a perfect balance to Cat's impulsive nature. That's why they had been such good friends.

'I'm going to tell you some things about Phillip Billings, but you can't breathe a word of this to anyone. I'm trusting you, Cat. If this gets out, I'll know it's you.'

Cat didn't speak. She gave her childhood friend the room to tell his story in his own words.

'Phillip was involved with an extremely wealthy woman in Edinburgh. She was married, but she set him up in her gatehouse and made no efforts to hide her affair with him. True to form, Phillip played the field. The short and long is that the woman caught him in bed with her maid, kicked him out of the house with nothing but the clothes on his back, and accused him of stealing some valuable diamonds.' Cliff finished his tea and refilled his cup. 'When he arrived back in Rivenby – road weary and penniless, I've heard on good authority – his mother put him in a cot in the attic. Soon the Edinburgh police came and questioned Phillip, probably about the stolen jewels. Nothing came of it. They left. Last week, two thugs came at Phillip and roughed him up pretty good. Carmona Broadbent found him in the alley. She's been helping him a bit. I've heard her mother isn't too pleased. Anyway, just after Phillip returned, some bastard sawed through the cable on Win Billings' brakes. She hit the turn on the Lea Road, and her brakes – you can imagine the rest.'

'That's horrible,' Cat said. She imagined the accident.

'It was a terrible tragedy.'

'Could Beth have done that? Or any woman for that matter? Do you need to be strong to cut through a brake cable?'

'I will tell you that Beth Hargreaves did not kill her aunt. She loved Win. Whoever tampered with those brakes would have had to know where the cable is. They would have to be handy with a saw. As for strength? Not sure.'

Cat shook her head. 'Changing the subject now if you don't mind.'

'Aren't you just the professional sleuth?' He smirked a little before his face became serious again. 'Go ahead.'

'What do you think of David Broadbent?'

'Now don't you go stirring up trouble about him.' Cliff's voice boomed. Jemmy stopped wiping the tables and looked in their direction. Cliff leaned closer to Cat and whispered. 'I'm sorry, but you'd best be careful. David Broadbent is a powerful man in the community, and that wife of his won't stand for any nonsense, not where her family is concerned.'

'No one is going to know I've asked about him,' Cat said.

Cliff shook his head. 'This is Rivenby. These walls have ears. I promise you, the fact that you've uttered his name is enough for word to get out. You need to be careful with him. There's those that like him, but there's plenty that don't.'

'Why don't you like him? What's he done to you?' Cat asked.

'Did I say he'd done something?'

'You didn't have to. I can see it in your eyes.'

Cliff shook his head. 'I always said you was one of them psychics. Again, this is confidential.'

'Of course,' Cat said. She leaned closer and whispered, 'I won't say anything, promise.'

'He cheated me once. Didn't pay me for work I did on his daughter's car, quite a bit of money, too. I asked him about it – more than once, if you get my meaning – but he told me that I was mistaken and that he had paid. I went to a solicitor in the next village. The man said I could bring a suit, but I thought better of it. A man like David Broadbent could use his influence to start a rumour about my work.' Cliff lowered his voice to a whisper. 'My wife told me that he took a mortgage on his wife's home without her knowing it. My wife's friend works in the banker's office. He likes money, does Mr Broadbent.'

'So you're saying he's dishonest?' *So Edythe was onto something after all.*

'I'm saying you'd do well to stay away from him,' Cliff said. 'And now, Cat, I've got to get back to work.'

Cat stood. 'Thanks, Cliff. It's good to see you.'

'Next time, I'll bring you to meet the wife and kids. You'll like Sybil. She's a fine lady. As for Mum, she's forgotten about our childhood mischief. She'd love to see you.' He gave Cat a worried look. 'What are you going to do?'

'I'm thinking of updating my will. I'm going to make an appointment with the village solicitor.'

'Be careful, Cat.'

'Don't worry. I will,' Cat said.

***

David Broadbent's office was situated between the stationer's and the land agent's shop. Cat opened the door and stepped into a spacious front office filled with ample light from the large windows that faced the high street. A mahogany desk kitted out with a typewriting machine, a basket full of files, and a half-drunk cup of tea rested between two doors. Sofas and chairs were arranged under the windows. In the corner of the room was a toy box. Cat thought how clever to provide entertainment for the children who were forced to accompany their parents. One of the doors had been left ajar. Cat almost called out, but heard voices coming from one of the offices, so she waited, quiet, eaves-dropping without shame.

'I need to leave,' a man's voice said.

'But that's blackmail, Phillip.' The woman's voice sounded frantic.

'Your boss will pay, Emmeline. Surely you can see that.' There was silence.

'Phillip, you're not thinking things through. I question your judgement. Carmona? If Claris gets wind of that—'

'She already has, and it doesn't matter. There's no involvement with Carmona. She's a silly child with a schoolgirl crush. Trust me. We need money to leave. Together. Come with me. We'll go to America. I'll take care of you, I promise.'

'But blackmail is a crime,' the woman's voice said.

'Blackmail is such an ugly word. And what you are up to is not better …' The man lowered his voice. Cat moved closer, hoping to hear more of the conversation. She didn't see the hat rack until it toppled to the ground with a clatter.

A frumpy-looking woman with thick calves and mousy hair hurried out of the office. 'Can I help you?'

'I wanted to make an appointment.'

The man hurried out of the office, stuffing his hat low over his face. Cat caught a quick glance of blond hair, a chiselled chin, and a flash of blue eyes.

The woman recovered herself. She tossed Cat an irritated glance. 'I'll have those documents to you by the end of the week, Mr Billings.'

'Of course.' Phillip pushed past Cat and hurried out the front door.

The secretary closed the office door and came back to the desk. Cat noticed the woman's clothes were well made. A good set of pearls circled her neck. *He pays her well.* She wasn't an oil painting, but she had clear skin and intelligent eyes.

'How can I help you?'

'Actually,' Cat said, 'maybe I can help you.'

'Help me?'

Cat took a calculated risk with her words. She knew what she'd heard and decided to use this knowledge to her benefit. 'I know that your boyfriend is going to blackmail someone.' The woman's face blanched. When she sat down in the chair, Cat knew her assumptions were correct. 'You look like an intelligent woman. I'm telling you that blackmail will lead you down a road from which there is no return.'

The woman gave Cat an inscrutable glance.

'You'd best speak to me now. I might be able to help you,' Cat cajoled. She waited, not daring to breathe.

'Get out.' The woman – fully recovered now – stood at her desk, eyes blazing. 'Get out now, or I'll call the police.'

The woman remained standing, but her eyes now had a troubled look.

'Whatever you're involved in – blackmail, for instance – will eventually catch up with you. You are going to need help. When you are ready, come to me. I will help you. Do you understand? I've taken St Monica's. You can come to me anytime, day or night.'

Cat had guessed and goaded, guided by the intuition Thomas had scoffed at. It had paid off. At some point, this woman would come to her. Of this Cat was certain.

133

CHAPTER 10

Carmona took the side street back to the lane that led home. She felt the wet heat of tears on her cheeks and dabbed at them with Bede's handkerchief. She passed the old rowan tree. When they were younger, Edythe would make up stories about its magical properties. She said an entire world of faeries lived in its roots. They had roads and horses and courts of law. The faeries only came out at night when no humans could see them. 'But if you ever have a problem that needs solving, all you have to do is touch the tree and ask your question. If you ask with love in your heart, the tree will guide you.' Although Carmona had been charmed by the story, she had laughed it off as absurd romanticism.

Desperate, Carmona looked to make sure no one watched. She reached out a hand and touched the tree. 'I love him. Show me how to help him.' She kept her palm pressed to the trunk. Eyes closed, she let the whispered hush of the wind in the leaves soothe her. After a couple of seconds, she pushed away. 'Well, that was utterly stupid.' She wiped her hand on her skirt and made her way home.

A murmur of voices coming from the drawing room greeted her. Carmona had forgotten that her mother was hosting a committee meeting today. She met Liddy in the foyer, pushing an overloaded tea trolley towards the drawing room. It was stacked with plates of sandwiches, biscuits, and a precariously positioned pile of cups and saucers.

'Can't you do this in two trips?' Carmona dashed over and righted the cups and saucers before they went crashing to the floor.

'No. Your mother loaded it this way. Wouldn't let me take anything off, and told me I would replace any broken items out of my wages.' A stray lock of hair fell in front of Liddy's eyes. She pushed it out of the way. 'I've half a mind to quit right now. But I need the money.'

'You can take the rest of the day off, Liddy. I'll see you're paid.' Carmona took the cups and saucers from the trolley and set them on the library table.

'Carmona, don't make trouble. Your mum is lecturing about the evacuee situation. Half the village is here. They are expecting me to serve tea right now.'

'You'd better leave before things get ugly.' Carmona heaved the heavy trolley into the drawing room. Her mother stood before the mantle, addressing a group of women who sat in strategically placed chairs.

'I think they will be okay through summer, but half of them don't have proper coats—' Claris forced a smile. 'Carmona, darling.'

Claris had a rotating circle of women whom she kept at the ready to do her bidding. She cajoled them with flattery. She exploited their desire to climb socially until she used them or angered them or until they realized the lay of the land. When that happened, the minion currently in play would retire from charity work and a new minion would take her place. Alice Gladwell, a harried-looking woman with too many children and badly tailored clothing, jumped up to help with the tea. Her white slip hung lower than the hem of her dress. Carmona watched her mother take notice of this. *Poor Alice. She'll be out of favour by tomorrow morning.*

Oblivious to the tension between Carmona and her mother, Alice gave Carmona a shy smile. 'I'll take the tray.'

'Thank you, Alice,' Claris said. 'Would you mind handing out the cakes? Ladies, if you'll excuse me while I have a quick word with my daughter.' She put a hand under Carmona's elbow and attempted to usher her away from the gawking crowd of women. Carmona moved out of her mother's grasp. 'Don't push me, Mother.'

Claris's cheeks blazed with red. Sparks of anger flew from her eyes. 'Don't make a scene.'

Carmona walked down the hall to her father's study, her mother at her heels. Carmona shut the door. She spoke before her mother had a chance. 'You're to leave Liddy alone. She has nothing to do with this thing between you and me. You've been working her like a draught horse. I've sent her home. You can do your own serving and you can wash your own dishes. And you'll pay her for today.'

They had done this dance a million times. Carmona anticipated Claris's raised hand, the impending stinging slap. This time she grabbed her mother's wrist, holding it tight as her mother tried to pull out of her grasp.

'I'm so tired of being bullied by you, Mother,' Carmona said.

Claris stood wide-eyed and open-mouthed. Her face paled. Carmona thought for a moment that her mother would faint.

'No more, Mother. No more slaps across the face. No more telling me what to do.'

'Carmona ...' her mother whispered. She put her hand to her throat.

Carmona sat behind her father's desk, beckoning to the chair across from it. 'Sit down, Mother. There's something we are going to discuss, something you need to know.'

As expected, Claris recovered. She ignored Carmona's request to sit. Instead she paced before the desk. 'You're just set on destroying this family's reputation, aren't you? Making a fool of yourself in front of our friends. How dare you tell me what to do. What am I to do with you, Carmona?' On and on her mother went, ranting and threatening. Carmona tuned her out. She watched her mother's lips move, watched her mother wave her arms like a circus clown. When Claris paused to take a breath, Carmona spoke.

'I'm in love with Phillip Billings,' she blurted out. 'He's in love with me. I am going to continue to see him. There is nothing you can do to stop me.'

Her mother froze, her mouth agape, her arms akimbo.

'He needs our help. If you don't cooperate, I'll make sure all of your friends know I'm in love with a man who may be a suspect in a murder investigation.'

Claris clutched her stomach and made her way to the chair on the 'visitor's' side of the desk. Carmona knew her mother wasn't in any physical pain. She had been dealt a blow. She had lost control of the situation.

'I'm going to ask Dad to help him—'

There was a quiet knock on the door. Alice Gladwell stepped into the room. She was followed by DCI Kent and another officer.

'These gentlemen need to speak to you,' Alice said. 'They're police.'

Carmona looked to her mother, expecting her to take charge of the situation. Her mother sat in the winged chair, clutching the arm rest in a white-knuckled grip.

'Thank you, Alice,' Carmona said. 'You can leave us.' She rose and walked over to the policemen.

Claris rose from her chair and joined Carmona.

'What's happened?' Claris whispered, her voice barely a whisper. 'Something's happened.'

Carmona looked from the policemen to her mother. Her heart sank in her chest. *They've arrested Phillip.*

DCI Kent pointed to the sofa and two chairs. 'I think we should sit, please.'

Claris sat for a moment, open-mouthed, her eyes darting from Carmona, to DCI Kent, to the other officer whose name Carmona couldn't remember.

'I'm afraid there's been an accident on the Lea Road,' DCI Kent said. 'Mrs Broadbent, I'm afraid your father – he didn't survive.'

Claris seemed to shrink before Carmona's eyes. In all her life, Carmona had never seen her mother in a weakened state. She had always thought Claris Broadbent would be running the world from her deathbed. Now she could barely stand. She put a hand on her mother's arm and led her to the couch. When the two women sat, Claris grabbed Carmona's hand. She squeezed it so tight Carmona nearly cried out.

'I don't believe it,' Claris said. 'There must be some mistake. How dare you—'

'Mother,' Carmona snapped. All heads turned to her. Her mother had the expression of a lost child. A wall of grief, black and smothering, threatened Carmona. She held it in abeyance. She had to be the strong one now.

DCI Kent broke the silence. 'I'm sorry for your loss, but I need to ask you some questions.'

'Can't this wait?' Carmona said.

'I'm afraid not,' DCI Kent said. 'Your grandfather's brakes were tampered with.'

'What?' Carmona said.

'I'm afraid he's been murdered, in the exact same fashion as Win Billings.'

CHAPTER 11

The sun dropped in the sky just as Thomas drove down the Lea Road into the village, slowing instinctively when he hit the hairpin turn where Win Billings drove off the cliff. He was surprised to see a lorry parked near the spot and several men standing around in a huddle. He thought about stopping to see if he could help, but his day had been long, and he was ready for a hot bath and a brandy.

Steven Templeton, a retired vicar who had a detailed and meticulously catalogued collection of books, writings, and diaries of all the churches and monastic houses in England had been generous with his time and resources. Thomas had spent the day engrossed in research, reading until his eyes ached, taking copious notes all the while. A portly housekeeper in a dress better suited to Victorian times and a respectable moustache had brought him a lunch of apples and cheese and a pot of strong tea. At 3 p.m. Mr Templeton had interrupted his work and asked if he would like to take a drive and see an old church that dated to Anglo-Saxon times.

The two of them had spent an hour walking around the grounds of Escomb Church, which had somehow survived through the ages. Mr Templeton had stopped to say hello to a friend and Thomas had proceeded to walk the grounds alone. He stood in front of the ancient stone chapel, and for a brief moment felt utter peace. In the quiet he could almost hear the whispers of the people who had worshipped here in the past. He thought of bringing Cat here, of the joy on her face when she saw the quaint medieval church. In his mind's eye, he saw her snapping photos, exclaiming while she circled the ancient stones.

Now he pulled his car into Mr Churchwright's home, surprised to see a black saloon parked in the drive. Mr Churchwright hadn't mentioned house guests. Thomas parked the car, got the box of papers and books Mr Templeton lent him, and trudged up to the house. He was hoping for a tray in his room, where he could read while he ate without the need for conversation.

Beck opened the door just as Thomas approached, his face ashen, and his eyes red as though he had been crying.

'Sir,' Beck spoke with a wavering voice. The man, usually so hale and hearty, seemed to have shrunken in on himself. His eyes looked vacant and haunted. The skin on his face seemed to sag. He reached for Thomas's box.

'I can get this, Beck. You look like you don't feel well. Can I do something for you?'

Beck shook his head. 'It's not me, sir. It's Mr James. There's been an accident. The police are in the study and would like to speak to you. You'd best go. They've been waiting for well over an hour.'

'What's happened?' Thomas whispered.

Beck shook his head. 'He's been killed.'

A spark exploded at the back of Thomas's neck and thrummed through his entire body. 'How?'

'His car. He drove off the cliff at the hairpin curve on the Lea Road.' Beck's voice broke as he spoke.

'I'm sorry for your loss, Beck. I know you were close to Mr Churchwright.' Thomas felt a moment's pity for Beck and his wife. Despite his short time at the house, he knew the Becks were devoted to Mr Churchwright. From what he could tell, Mr Churchwright treated them as though they were friends more than servants.

'Can I bring you brandy?' Beck asked.

'Yes. A large one, if you don't mind. And I hate to be a bother, but I'm rather famished.'

'The missus has a tray prepared already, sir. She's been trying to keep herself busy, you see.'

'Thank you,' Thomas said.

He waited until Beck's footsteps faded away before he pushed open the door and stepped into the study. Two men awaited him. One of them was perched on a chair, notebook in hand. The older one stood and walked towards Thomas, hand outstretched.

'DCI Colin Kent.'

'How do you do?' Thomas shook the man's hand, not the least bit surprised at the strong, sure grip.

'This is DS Wallace. We are here about an unfortunate accident.' DCI Kent had the build of a man who played sports to win. His dark hair was heavily laced with silver and cut short, military style. 'I'm afraid that Mr Churchwright's car went off the Lea Road. He didn't survive. It seems that his brakes were tampered with.'

'What? Are you sure about the brakes?'

'Yes. There's no doubt.'

'What can I do to help?'

DCI Kent nodded. 'Very good. I was worried you wouldn't want to cooperate. Let's sit, shall we?'

The men had just sat down when Beck came in carrying a tray with a pot of tea, a crystal decanter of brandy, and a plate of sandwiches.

'Thank you, Beck. You are a godsend.' They waited while Beck set the tray on the table. 'Shall I do the honours, sir?'

'No, thank you, Beck.'

After he left, Thomas motioned at the brandy.

141

DCI Kent said, 'Don't mind if I do. DS Wallace, come and sit over here. We're going to conduct this informally.'

Thomas poured a glass of brandy for himself and for DS Kent. He held the decanter over the third glass.

'No. DS Wallace is still on duty.' DCI Kent picked up the glass Thomas had placed before him. 'I, on the other hand, am not.'

DS Wallace took the slight with good grace. He helped himself to tea before he sat back in his chair.

'I assume you believe this has to do with Win Billings' murder?' Thomas asked.

DCI Kent nodded. He swirled it in the glass before he took a sip. 'I know why you're here, Mr Charles. Sir Reginald Wright told me you would be observing my investigation into Win Billings' murder from a distance, just to make sure no characters from her mysterious past are in the picture.'

'That's correct.'

'Have you actually discovered anything?'

'Not really. I found Carmona Broadbent snooping in my desk. I have a file on Phillip Billings. Reginald gave it to me, a dossier of sorts. I was to keep an eye on him. He's done something to attract Reginald's attention, but from what I gather, it mostly has to do with a clandestine love affair in Scotland and gambling debts. I know Phillip has money troubles. But I don't know if he is desperate enough to commit murder. In any event, Carmona Broadbent claims she is in love with Phillip, that they are courting.'

DS Wallace snorted.

'What is it, Wallace?'

'It's just not true, sir. You know as well as I do Claris Broadbent would never in a million years let her daughter be seen with someone like Phillip Billings. But I can't help but wonder what he's up to. She won't be the first girl – woman – he's conned for money. Wonder how much she's given him.'

'There's more,' Thomas said. 'After a dinner last night, we sat

142

in this very room drinking brandy. James confided he knew who murdered Win Billings.'

'He knew?' DCI Kent set his glass down.

'I'm afraid he did. I encouraged him to go to the police.' Mellowed by the brandy, Thomas recalled the chat he and James had the previous night. 'He said he needed to "protect the innocents". Yes, those were his exact words. He said it was a touchy situation. I tried to get him to share his suspicion with me, pointed out the dangers of carrying that type of knowledge. But he refused.'

They sat silent, waiting while DS Wallace completed his note taking. When the young man had finished writing, he nodded to DCI Kent.

'Anything else?'

'Yes. But this may not be important. My friend from London, Catherine Carlisle – she used to be Catherine Paxton – lives next door to Beth Hargreaves. Cat – Mrs Carlisle – actually saw someone outside the house peering in the window during the night. She's rather impetuous. Gave chase but the man ran away.'

'Did she see the person's face?'

'No.'

'Pity,' DS Wallace said.

DCI Kent sipped his brandy. 'I wonder if Phillip Billings' creditors followed him here.'

'It's possible,' Thomas said. 'Might make him a bit desperate.'

'Maybe Phillip Billings discovered that James Churchwright knew what he had done, so he killed him in the same way,' DS Wallace said.

'Is Phillip the type that would commit murder?' Thomas asked. 'Not every man is capable.'

'True,' DCI Kent said. 'It's early on in the investigation. We have a lot of evidence to sort through.'

'Should I find another place to stay?' Thomas asked.

'That won't be necessary,' DCI Kent said. 'I think it would be useful for you to stay here. I'll arrange it with Mrs Broadbent, if you don't mind.'

'I don't. Thank you,' Thomas said.

DCI Kent stood. DS Wallace followed. 'Thank you for the brandy, Mr Charles. I appreciate your candour.'

Thomas walked the men into the foyer.

'Oh, one more thing,' DCI Kent said. 'Your friend, Mrs Carlisle, has been asking questions around the village about David Broadbent, James' son-in-law, the illustrious Carmona's grand-father. Tell her to stop. Mr Broadbent is a leader in the community. He and his wife give tirelessly to charity. I'm assuming Mrs Carlisle has forgotten about life in a rural village. But inquiring into the character of a respected solicitor is a sure way to trouble. Pass that along for me, would you?' DCI Kent didn't wait for a response. 'Very good. Pleasure to meet you, Mr Thomas.'

Thomas watched while DS Wallace got behind the wheel and the car sped away. His thoughts were on Sir Reginald. He would be furious to know Cat had found a way to stir up trouble in the village. He chuckled. It served the old man right. He wondered why she was asking questions about David Broadbent. Something must have happened to arouse her suspicion about him. Why hadn't she confided in him? *Because she no longer trusts you.* The epiphany stung.

He took the tray with the sandwiches and brandy up to his room. He would have to talk to her, find out what she knew. He knew full well by asking the questions, he would give away his real reason for being here. Once Cat discovered Thomas had come to Rivenby for anything other than rest and research, she would be furious with him. The tenuous connection they shared would sever. He would find himself lumped into the same cate-gory as her scoundrel of a husband, and any chance of a future together would go up in a cloud of smoke.

CHAPTER 12

Cat woke up with the sun and dressed quickly. She was eager to speak to Beth, but try as she might, she had been unable to catch her at home. In the kitchen, she poured tea and gulped it down as she slipped into her walking shoes.

'Miss?'

Cat turned.

'Mrs Hargreaves wakes of an early morning to do her baking. She usually leaves her house by eight-thirty or nine to deliver the cakes and breads she has made. And some days she spends the day away.'

'Thank you, Bede,' Cat said.

'Is anything the matter, miss?'

Cat shook her head. 'No. Nothing that can't wait.'

'There's no shame in knocking on her door as early as seven o'clock. I've done it.'

'Thank you, Bede.'

'Now, if you'll forgive me for being bold, why don't you go and enjoy the sunshine while it's out? Rain's coming within the next day or two. Best enjoy the fine weather while you can.'

Cat checked her camera bag for film and lenses and headed out the door. She walked to the end of the lane, through the turnstile and took the long route across the moor to St Anne's, the church where her parents were buried. The sunshine was bright, the sky blue, a perfect day for taking pictures.

Although Cat's parents weren't terribly religious – her father was an intellectual and encouraged Cat to ask questions about God rather than blindly believe – they did attend church at Christmas and Easter. How could they not, when their local church was so hauntingly beautiful? The exterior was fashioned in sandstone of cream, yellow, and brown. Although parts of the church dated back to the ninth century, the main body of the church never failed to take Cat's breath away. Added in the nineteenth century – Cat wasn't sure what year – the mosaic floor was loved by Cat, as were the stained glass windows.

Made redundant shortly after Cat's parents passed, the door to the inner sanctum was now locked. Outside the church, grave slabs dating back hundreds of years held a place for those who came before. As a child, Cat had spent many a happy hour here, meandering along the shaded lanes, studying the graves, making up stories of those who were buried. The grounds were now overgrown with grass and weeds. Cat decided the neglected landscape would accentuate the age of the building. With clever composition, it would enhance rather than detract from her photos. She walked the familiar paths around the church taking various shots, close-ups of windows and doors, long shots with several gravestones together. Soon she arrived at her parents' graves. For the first time since returning home, a rush of childhood memories threatened to overtake her. She pushed them back, saving contemplation of her childhood for another day. After shooting three rolls of film, Cat was ready for tea at Gilly's.

She packed her camera away and continued past the church to the turnstile that led to the high street. A leisurely tea at Gilly's would be the perfect end to a productive morning. With luck, there'd be enough biscuits left over – Gilly's was known to sell

146

out – for Cat to take some home to Annie and Bede. The door to the café jangled as Cat let herself in. A quick glance around the room told her that all the tables were taken, so she stood in the short queue to purchase biscuits.

'Are you Cat Carlisle?' Cat turned to face a middle-aged woman with light brown hair and a smattering of freckles staring at her with intelligent brown eyes.

'Hello,' Cat said. 'Do I know you?'

The woman's cheeks flushed. 'You don't know me, but you were rather intimate with my husband yesterday.'

When Cat looked at her quizzically, the woman snapped, 'I'm Sybil, Cliff Swan's wife. Did you think you could go to the Duck together and no one would know?'

Cat looked around the café. A hush filled the room as all eyes focused on them.

'I wasn't intimate with your husband,' Cat whispered. 'We were just having tea.'

'Liar. You're up to trouble. I know all about you and your life in London, Mrs Carlisle. We've got enough trouble with these murders. You have no business poking your nose in where it doesn't belong.' Sybil looked Cat up and down, scrutinizing her shoes, skirt, and jumper. 'You and your fancy London ways.' She stepped closer. 'Stay. Away. From. My. Husband.'

And with that, she turned and walked away.

'Wait!' Cat chased after her, her camera case banging against her hip. Sybil Swan ignored her. Cat persisted, committed to making things right with Cliff's wife. 'You're going to hear me out,' Cat said. She grabbed Sybil's arm. Out of the corner of her eye, she saw the faces pressed up against the window in the café. Let them watch. She didn't care. 'You've no right to speak to me that way in public, or at all for that matter.'

Sybil stared at her. She looked along the street, as if checking for witnesses.

'Cliff and I were childhood friends. When I saw him yesterday,

147

you were the first thing he spoke about. He wanted me to come to dinner and meet your children.' Cat let go of Sybil's arm. 'He wanted us to be friends, so did I. But I guess that is no longer a possibility.'

'This is a small village, Mrs Carlisle. Word gets around. There's no secrecy here, no privacy. Everyone knows everyone's business.'

'Which makes me question why you felt the need to confront me in a public place,' Cat said. 'I assure you, Cliff is just a friend. And you've nothing to worry about. I've known him since childhood. He's head over heels in love with you.'

Sybil stared at Cat.

She forced a smile. 'Never mind that. Can we start over?' Cat put out her hand.

Sybil took Cat's hand, albeit reluctantly.

Cat sighed with relief. 'Thank God. Let's put this nonsense behind us, shall we? They're watching us from the café. Wave at them. Let them see we're friends.'

Sybil waved.

'Good. Now that should give them something to talk about.'

'I'm sorry,' Sybil said. 'I shouldn't have spoken to you that way. Claris Broadbent said my husband was having a tryst with a beautiful woman from London. I didn't know what to think.'

'You should trust your husband, Sybil. He is not the philandering sort.' Cat wanted to warn Sybil to stay away from Claris Broadbent, but she caught herself just time.

'I know.' Her voice was subdued. 'I'm so embarrassed.'

'Let's forget it,' Cat said. 'Call it a misunderstanding, okay?'

Sybil smiled at her. 'You're a remarkable woman, Mrs Carlisle. I wouldn't have been so understanding. You won't mention this to Cliff, will you?'

'I'll leave the explaining to you.'

'Thanks,' Sybil said.

Cat waved once again at the crowd in the café and hurried down the high street, wondering if her feeble attempt to repair the damage done by Sybil Swan had helped. Word of their altercation would spread, of that she was certain.

***

Cat took Bede's advice, and headed over to Beth's house at 6.55 the next morning. The front door stood open, the familiar smell of baking met her as she approached the house.

'Hello?' Cat called out.

'In here.'

Cat stepped into the kitchen. The work table in the centre of the room was covered with scones, biscuits, and three cake rounds. Beth added sugar and butter – real butter – to a bowl and stirred it with a spoon.

'Cat. So good to see you.' She cracked an egg and stirred it into the mixture. After a minute, she set the spatula in the sink and wiped her face with the back of her hand, smearing flour across her cheek. 'You must have heard. We were all quite shocked. I've got tea. Can I pour you a cup?'

'Thanks. Heard what?'

'About Claris Broadbent's father? We don't have details yet. Edythe tried to call Carmona, but she couldn't get through. I thought you might know something we don't. I assume he had a heart attack.' She poured tea for both of them, took four pieces of toast out of the cooker and brought the rack to the table. 'Poor Carmona. She and her grandfather were so close. The poor child doesn't get along with her mother, and I know for a fact that she used to take refuge at her grandfather's house. Where will she go now?' Beth shook her head. 'I'm sure Claris will cope. She always does. Carmona will suffer the most. Help yourself.' Beth nodded at the toast as she sat down at the table. Cat stood by, staring at Beth as though she hadn't heard a word she said. 'What's wrong?'

Cat sat down at the table, not wanting to frighten her friend.

'Cat?' Beth set her toast down and waited.

'I watched your house that first night – when it was raining so hard – and I saw someone. He came from the bushes near the lane. Crept right up to your house and peered in the window.'

Beth cupped her cup of tea with both hands. 'Was it a man? Woman? Did you get a look at his face?'

'I'm sure it was a man. He was tall, moved like a man. I'm sorry. I didn't get a very good look at him.' She reached out to Beth and put a hand on her arm. 'Listen, Beth, I have a friend who is staying here. He knows how to deal with these things. He's going to speak to the police. Meanwhile, why don't you and Edythe come and stay with me, just to be on the safe side.'

'No. I won't be driven from my home. It was probably someone associated with my cousin. He's famous for bringing unsavoury characters with him. He owes money, but he's gone now.'

Cat sipped her tea. 'What if it has to do with your aunt's murder?'

'Why would it?' Beth sighed. 'I'll talk to Edythe. Tell her what you saw.'

'Thank you. I'm sure you heard about my altercation with Sybil Swan.'

'I did. Everyone's talking about it. They didn't know what to make of the situation, actually. I heard that Sybil confronted you in Gilly's, but that you chased her outside and by the time you were finished talking to her, you were friends.'

'It's Claris Broadbent,' Cat said. 'Apparently she's been telling people that I was intimate with Cliff Swan at the pub. Did she grow into a meddlesome and odious adult?'

'Remember how you two used to argue in school? You were the only one with the guts to stand up to her. She's still strong-willed, always organizing things, running charities. Her new pet project is the evacuee situation. She really does try to help.' Beth giggled. 'But Cliff Swan?'

'Hello? Anyone home?'

Both women froze as the sound of Claris Broadbent's high heels clicked along the hallway.

Beth recovered first. She stood and pulled out a chair. 'Claris, I'm so sorry about your father.'

'Thank you. It's horrible. I've decided the best course of action is to stay busy. I've come for the clothes. I thought I could drop off Lady Swyndale's order for you.' Claris spoke in a frenetic voice. She noticed Cat.

'This is Catherine Carlisle. Used to be Catherine Paxton. She's taken St Monica's.'

The mention of St Monica's got Claris's attention. She smiled at Cat. 'Of course, I remember you. Welcome back to Rivenby!' Unsteady on her feet, Claris reached for a chair. 'I don't know what's come over me. Feel a bit light-headed.'

'Have a seat.' Beth pulled a chair out for her. 'I can make tea.'

'No, thank you. I'm a bit tired, that's all.' Claris turned her attention back to Cat. When she spoke, her voice came out shrill and high. Cat wondered if the woman had been drinking. 'I heard about your altercation with Sybil Swan. Don't pay her any mind. Everyone knows she's possessive over that husband of hers. You'd think she was married to a prince the way she carries on about him.'

'We've come to an understanding,' Cat said. 'Sybil understands that Cliff and I were friends catching up. Nothing more.'

'Claris, are you all right?' Beth asked.

Claris ignored Beth and continued hurling her questions and comments at Cat. 'How are you liking St Monica's? How are you getting settled in?'

'Getting there. Still lots to do, but—'

'I would love to discuss our evacuee situation with you. I was thinking maybe you could take on a family, or a young mother with a child?'

'Of course,' Cat said. 'I'm not prepared at this point, but if you give me a week? Why don't you call round and we can make arrangements?'

A sheen of sweat broke out on Claris's face. She seemed to swoon on her feet. For a brief moment Cat wondered again if she had been drinking.

'Are you all right?' Cat asked. She turned to Beth. 'I think she's going to faint.'

Beth hurried over to Claris. She pulled out a chair and guided her into it.

'Bend over, put your head down between your knees.'

Claris held up her hand. 'Please don't make a fuss. I just haven't been feeling very well.'

'Have you slept at all?' Beth asked.

'I haven't slept. I haven't eaten. I am utterly numb. My father – car crash –' Claris looked from Cat to Beth and back again. She took in deep noisy breaths through her nose. The cadence became quicker and quicker until Cat thought she might faint. Finally, she sucked in one final gulp of air before a sob broke through, one lone sob so deep and guttural it nearly knocked Claris off her chair. Claris hunched over and wept silent tears, while she rocked with grief.

'She needs brandy,' Cat said. She sat down in the chair next to Claris and took one of the woman's hands. It was cold. She took the brandy Beth offered. 'Drink this.' Like an obedient child, Claris took the brandy. She took a delicate sip. 'Come on, drink the whole thing.' Claris complied.

'I'm going to take you home, Claris. I'll drive your car, if you don't mind,' Beth said.

The sobbing had stopped. Claris sat in the chair, unmoving. She stared ahead with vacant eyes.

'She needs a doctor,' Cat said.

152

'I'll get her home, so her family can care for her.'

'Do you want me to come with you?' Cat asked.

'No,' Beth said. 'Can we talk later?'

'Of course,' Cat said.

***

Cat couldn't have been happier to see Thomas waiting when she got home. She had so much to tell him. Given what she had overheard at Broadbent's office, she believed Edythe's suspicions about the solicitor now had merit. Thomas would provide the fresh perspective needed to formulate a plan of action. She watched him pace across the front lawn and wondered why Bede hadn't let him in the house. Cat watched as every now and then he would stop, shake his head, and continue pacing. When she saw her, he scowled as he walked to meet her.

'What the devil do you think you're doing inquiring after David Broadbent? You'll draw attention to yourself.'

'How did you know?' Cat snapped, ready to argue, confident she could turn Thomas to her way of thinking. She froze. How did he know? 'My God, you've been lying to me.'

'I have not been lying,' Thomas said. 'DCI Kent told me what you've been up to. Surely you didn't think you could ask questions without it getting back to me?'

'Just don't. Stop. You told me you wanted Annie and me up here to get away from London, to keep us safe.' Cat's heart broke as an unmistakable look of guilt washed over Thomas's face. 'You're here on some investigation for Reginald, aren't you?'

'Cat, let me explain.'

'Don't bother denying it. I can see it in your face. You'd make a terrible poker player, Thomas.'

Tears filled Cat's eyes. She turned her back on Thomas so he wouldn't see them. Her anger boiled, taking away the hurt.

'I can just hear Reginald now. "Take her home, Tom. Use her to ingratiate yourself into society." So what are you investigating?'

A look of anguished sorrow crossed over his face. Part of Cat wanted to run to him, wrap her arms around him, and console him. The other part wanted to kick him in the shins and spit on his shoes. She did neither, just waited for an answer she knew wouldn't come.

'I can't,' Thomas said, his voice barely a whisper.

'So that's how it's to be between us, Tom? I can bear secrets, especially given your line of work. But getting me up here under false pretence, acting like you care for me, when really you wanted to use me—'

'That's not how it is, and you know it. You know my feelings. I've not bothered to hide them.'

'And to think I was about to tell you—'

'Cat, listen to me.'

'I won't listen to anything until you explain yourself to me. What are you doing here? Who are you investigating? Is it Win's murder? Mr Churchwright? You didn't kill him, did you? Did Sir Reginald send you up here—'

'Of course, he didn't. Don't be absurd.'

'Don't you dare condescend to me. I had enough placating and deceit during my marriage. I thought you were different.'

Thomas stepped close and grabbed her arm. Cat tried to wriggle out of his grasp to no avail. 'You listen to me. Two people have been murdered.'

'Two people?' Cat stumbled over her words.

'That's right. James Churchwright's brakes were interfered with, just like Win Billings'. I don't know who did it, and I don't know why. That's for the police. Yes, I'm here at Reginald's behest. That's not the issue. The issue is you acting without thinking and putting yourself in danger. I'm not in a position to protect you. So no matter what you think of me, no matter what you do, you need

154

to be careful. Do you understand me? I should have told you. I'm sorry for that, but it doesn't change things.'

Cat went still. For the briefest second it seemed nature acquiesced to her stillness. The breeze calmed, the birds stopped singing. When she spoke, her voice was ragged with anger. 'Take. Your. Hand. Off. Me.'

Thomas complied. 'Please, can we go inside and talk? Can you try to see reason?'

'How dare you insinuate that I need to be *made to see reason*.' Rage whipped inside Cat. 'As far as I'm concerned, Mr Charles, you can go straight to hell. Now get off my property.' She stepped around him, not looking back as she hurried into the house and slammed the door behind her.

Thomas followed her. She sensed him, felt his presence on the other side of the thick ancient wood as he pounded on it, calling her name. After a few minutes, utter silence filled the air. Cat tried to quiet her own breathing. She heard Thomas on the other side of the door, felt his heartbeat. How she wanted to open it and let him kiss away her tears. But that happy outcome between them was no longer viable. He had betrayed her. There was no going back. Not now. She leaned against the door and listened as Thomas's footsteps headed down the path and faded into silence.

CHAPTER 13

The night before James Churchwright's funeral, Thomas slept fitfully, tossing and turning, as thoughts of his argument with Cat ran round and round in his head. Just as sleep overtook him, Cat's angry voice and the look in her eye would jolt him awake. *I never want to see you again.*

He sat up, placed his feet on the cold floor, and forced himself out of bed. The fire from the previous night had reduced itself to ash. Knowing Beck would have his hands full today, Thomas laid some kindling, placed a log on top, and tossed a match on the lot. Flames flickered in the grate. It would take a while to dispel the morning chill.

Half an hour later, Thomas headed downstairs, wondering how the day would play out. Beck and the missus had arranged extra help for the wake due to take place after the funeral. Young women scurried about, rearranging furniture, dealing with table-cloths and glasses and linens.

'Good morning, sir. The missus has breakfast for you in the kitchen.'

Beck disappeared so fast Thomas didn't have an opportunity to respond. He headed towards the kitchen.

'It's too early for brandy.' David Broadbent's voice wafted

156

through the hustle and bustle. He spoke in the tone reserved for a petulant child.

'My father is dead, David,' Claris's voice answered. 'I am trying to cope. This is all too much. I'm tired of it. Tired of all the responsibility. These are extenuating circumstances.'

'That's what I wanted to talk to you about, darling. After we've sold this place, we'll take a holiday. I'm tired too. Maybe Carmona would come with us—'

'Sell this place? I've no intention of selling Heart's Desire. My father loved it. I couldn't bear to part with it. Carmona may want to live here one day.'

Thomas heard the sound of the decanter and imagined Claris refilling her glass.

'Carmona? Live here?'

'Really, David. I don't need you to repeat what I said.'

'She's going to London.'

'No, she's not. Carmona is not going anywhere. She is a foolish girl with foolish notions. I'll handle Carmona. As for Heart's Desire, it's my inheritance. I'll decide what to do with it.'

'Claris, listen to me. I need to talk to you.'

When Claris spoke next, her words slurred ever so slightly. At this rate, she would be passed out by eleven o'clock. 'Don't you have something you need to see to? I've had about enough of you.'

Eavesdropping wasn't a gentlemanly pastime. Thomas had no intention of getting caught with his nose in the Broadbents' business. He scurried away to the kitchen, managing to take a tray of eggs, toast and fruit, along with a large pot of tea upstairs without seeing David or Claris. He ate his breakfast wondering what kind of a man would let himself be browbeaten to that extent.

***

Liddy let Carmona sleep until the last minute before bringing her a tray of toast, jam, and a steaming cup of tea for each of them. When Carmona's tears had come the night before, she had given them free rein in the privacy of her room. The loss of her beloved grandfather would have lasting repercussions on the Broadbent family dynamic. Carmona had visions of her mother's rampant, domineering authority. With Grandfather gone, who would serve as buffer?

Her mother had proven useless these past few days, while her father ran himself ragged, tending to arrangements and details according to her grandfather's wishes. James Churchwright had wanted a party, a grand memorial send-off in his memory. His will specified a small graveside service for the family, followed by a wake at Heart's Desire. Grandfather had taken the precaution of tending to most of the arrangements himself, even going so far as arranging help for Beck and the missus and opening his extensive wine cellar for the drinks.

The night before Carmona had raided her mother's wardrobe, absconding with a black dress for her, a skirt and blouse for Liddy, along with hats and stockings for both of them.

'I'm not sure about this,' Liddy said. 'Your mother won't be happy seeing me in her clothes.'

'Mother won't notice,' Carmona said. She slipped into her mother's dress, surprised it wasn't too tight through the waist. 'You're coming to the service today as my friend, not as my mother's employee.'

Carmona stared at her haggard face in the mirror. Dark rings under her eyes spoke of her lack of sleep. She dabbed some of her mother's make-up on them, but the colour was wrong. She ended up washing it off, knowing she didn't look her best. She jumped at the knock on her door and girded herself to face one of her mother's unpredictable moods.

'Come in.' Carmona watched through the mirror as her father, dressed in his dark suit, came into the room, red-eyed and pale-faced.

'The car will be here in half an hour.' He gave her a sheepish smile as he pulled a footstool over next to her, locking eyes with her in the mirror. 'Do you mind?'

'Of course not,' she said.

'Your mother isn't coping well at all. I've never seen her like this before.' Her father looked at her with sad eyes. 'Is it true what she told me about you and Phillip Billings?'

Carmona spun around to face her father. 'It is, Daddy. And I'm sorry you had to hear it from Mother. Phillip and I should have told you ourselves. We would have, but this happened.' The tears came. She took the handkerchief her father offered and dabbed at her eyes.

'Do you love him?'

Funny, her mother had never asked her that. 'I do.'

'Why?'

'Why do I love him?' The question gave her pause. 'It's my heart, Daddy. I don't need a why. But I will tell you Phillip has treated me with respect. He's made me grow up. Mother thinks he only loves me because of the money, but he doesn't. I'm afraid the police think he may have been involved in his mother's—'

'Don't worry about that. I'll help him. We'll help him. He's family now. I'll serve as his solicitor if I need to. If he is charged, we'll find him someone good from London. I knew a few chaps. After this is over, I'll make some calls.'

Carmona's forced maturity dissipated as she turned to her father. 'Thank you. I've been so worried.'

'Don't be. I'll always help you, Carmona. You know that.' Her father stood, gave her shoulder a squeeze. 'Half an hour.'

'I'll be ready.'

After he had gone, Carmona let out a sigh of relief. She and Phillip had her father's support. Phillip would be pleased. She would tell him today. Surely he would come to her grandfather's funeral and stand by her in this time of grief. Once her mother saw Carmona and Phillip together, she would understand the love between them.

***

Despite the rain, the mourners came in droves. They braved the weather and stood near the grave, clad in black, hunched under umbrellas. Carmona listened to the sound of raindrops on the taut fabric, a macabre lullaby for her grandfather's eternal sleep. A quiet desperation too personal to share with anyone, even Phillip, had come over Carmona. Her father – in an effort to comfort her – had said the pain of loss would get worse before it got better. He had been right.

She kept turning around, stealing glimpses of the crowd when possible in hopes of seeing Phillip among the mourners. He wasn't there. Carmona hadn't spoken to him since their fight. She expected him to come to her, to rush to her side. His show of support would impress her parents, even her mother. In her fantasy Phillip would be next to her, solicitous with concern and worry, a representative of her grieving family. The rain dripped down the back of her neck as she followed her mother and tossed a clump of dirt onto the coffin that held her grandfather's body.

Something was going on between her parents. Her father, usually kind and caring towards his domineering wife, kept his distance at the funeral. Carmona expected him to be near her, to have a comforting arm around her shoulder. Instead, he acted as though she wasn't even there and put his comforting arm around Carmona's shoulder. While she was grateful for her dad, she longed for Phillip today. Carmona wanted to lean on the man she loved.

Claris had sought solace in a bottle of fine cognac. She hadn't made any effort to help with the arrangements for her father's service, instead she chose to spend her time shut up in her room.

Her husband had turned her over to the care of the doctor, an ageing man who did her mother's bidding and eschewed any new sort of treatment. Certain her mother was suffering beyond the norms of grief, Carmona had asked the old man what exactly was wrong with her mother. He had given her a pat on her shoulder and relayed his condolences for her loss. When she pushed back – like mother, like daughter – he gave her a condescending smile and told her to leave the medical issues to the experts. She had let it go, let him go. For now. If her mother continued on like this, Carmona would take her to another doctor.

The sun came out just as the service ended, as if heaven above welcomed James Churchwright into her domain. By now Claris was reduced to a state of silent torpor. She allowed herself to be ushered to the limousine, which took the Broadbents back to Heart's Desire – a stupid name for a house in Carmona's opinion – for a lavish feast prepared by the missus and served by Beck and a handful of helpers from the village. Duty bound, she girded herself to stand near her parents in a receiving line, thankful for the black veil that covered her eyes. The line seemed to go on forever. Carmona shook hands and accepted condolences from the nameless faces as they filed through the house. Phillip never came. Carmona couldn't help but feel irritation towards him. What kind of a man left his love to bear her grief alone? Her spirits sparked when she saw Edythe and her mother come through, but plummeted when she saw Beth take her place in line and Edythe move off to the food.

Carmona turned to her father. 'Excuse me, please.' He nodded, dismissing her. She followed Edythe.

'Edythe,' Carmona called. 'Wait.'

Edythe stopped walking and turned around to face Carmona. When she got close enough, Edythe put her arms around Carmona. 'I'm so sorry for your loss.'

'Were you going to come through the line?'

'Yes. I was actually going to the loo first.'

'It's that way,' Carmona said, pointing in the opposite direction Edythe had been walking.

'Oh—' Edythe blustered.

'Why haven't you returned my calls? I haven't seen you in weeks. Tell me why. Please.'

'I can't talk about it, Carm.'

'Please, Edythe. You're my best friend. Tell me.'

'I'm your best friend? You've not been confiding in me either. You've changed. You don't dress the same, you don't even act the same. Why? What's happened?'

Carmona glanced behind her, making sure they were far enough away so no one would hear. 'I've met someone. I'm in love.'

Edythe smiled in spite of herself. 'Really? I admit, you have been looking rather beautiful these past few weeks. Who's the lucky fellow?'

'I can't tell you. Not yet.'

'A secret lover?' Edythe raised an eyebrow, teasing Carmona.

'I'll tell you as soon as I can. Trust me?'

'Of course,' Edythe said.

Carmona felt a pang of guilt at not telling Edythe about Phillip. 'Your turn,' Carmona said. 'Why have you been avoiding me?'

Edythe shook her head. 'Not here. Let's go outside, okay? You're not going to like this, Carm.'

They didn't speak as they walked through the house and – grabbing coats on the way out – stepped into the back patio area. The sun was bright, but didn't quite cut through the chill. Tables and chairs had been arranged for guests, but no one had ventured out yet. Carmona and Edythe were alone. They sat down at one of the tables in a far corner.

'I don't know how to begin,' Edythe said.

'At the beginning,' Carmona said.

Edythe arranged her chair so it faced the view of the moors

and the forest beyond. 'First of all, I'm sorry I've kept this from you for so long. I think your father has been embezzling the money my dad left us.'

'My father? Embezzling?' Carmona laughed, saw the grave look on her friend's face and became silent.

'Now you understand why I didn't come to you sooner. It's horrible. I feel horrible about telling you this.' Edythe hurried on. 'My dad had money. You remember that, Carm. He worked hard and didn't spend. My parents were frugal. My mum didn't ask questions about finances. She doesn't have a head for figures, so she left all that up to my dad. But I did. He told me he had enough saved so I could go to university if I wanted or buy a house of my own. He told me – promised me – there were provisions made for Mum and me.' A stray curl fell loose over Edythe's forehead. She tucked it behind her ear. 'He wanted me to get an education. He told me – over and over again – he had money put back for my education. He wanted me to be independent.'

'Your father was a farmer. You can't know what happened. Maybe he had some setback, a bad crop or something.'

Edythe shook her head. 'I don't think so. But if he did, we should have received the accounts.'

'Didn't your mother ask for one?'

'Three times. There's been no response.'

'But now your mum's inherited from Win, you'll be all right, won't you?'

'This isn't about the money. This is about my dad, the promise he made to me. You're my best friend. I don't want to hurt you, but I need to know what happened. Something's not right. I'm not going to let this go. My dad wouldn't have lied to me.'

'If your father wasn't lying, then mine stole your family's money.' Carmona closed her eyes and took a deep breath. 'Why would he do that? He has money of his own and a good job,' Carmona said.

'Does he?' Edythe met Carmona's eyes for the first time. Carmona didn't like what she saw there. 'Your grandfather on your father's side owned a dairy farm. He lost it in a card game.'

'You've been snooping in my family's business?'

'I've been taking care of my family's business because my mother can't seem to do it,' Edythe snapped. 'Ever since my father died, we've been struggling to keep afloat. My mum is useless when it comes to business, but I'm not. I tried to get her to push your father for the accounts, but she won't do it. Every time I bring the subject up, she gets mad.' Edythe stood. 'I asked your father directly. Do you know what he told me? "Little girls should not bother with adult matters."' Edythe walked to the edge of the patio. With her back to Carmona, she faced the grassy field which abutted the deep woods behind Heart's Desire. 'I've changed my mind about going to London, about auditioning for a company. I'm sorry, Carm, but you'll have to find someone else to room with. I'm going to sign up.'

'Sign up? But what about the dancing?'

'This isn't the time for princesses in pink skirts. We are at war. I mean to make a difference. But I'm going to see this issue with my family's money sorted before I go, one way or another. I'll hire my own investigator if I have to.'

Thoughts went round and round in Carmona's head. Edythe was right, Carmona knew very little about her father's history or his financial situation. His family were all gone. Carmona never thought about money. She had always had a generous allowance from her parents. If she needed a major purchase, all she had to do was ask her grandfather. More importantly, she trusted Edythe implicitly. Edythe wouldn't make up such a painful story. Her friend had never been motivated by greed. There was no reason to think she would be so motivated now.

'I'll help you,' Carmona said.

Edythe turned to face her. 'What?'

'I said, I'll help you. We're going to find out what's happened with your family's money. You deserve an answer. You're my best friend. I'm going to help you.'

'I don't think it's a good idea to speak to your father about this. He'll be so angry.'

'That's not what I mean,' Carmona said. 'I'm going to prove to you my father isn't embezzling. He wouldn't. I hate to say this, but he doesn't have the backbone for it. I'm going to find out what happened to your father's money. Don't worry. No one will know. Except us.' Carmona stood. She was cold and ready to go back into the house. 'My father's not a thief. I'm going to prove it.'

'How?'

'I'll start with looking at his accounts records. They're in his office. Should be pretty easy to find out where your father's money went.'

'You're not mad?'

'Of course not,' Carmona said. 'Well, maybe a little. You should have come to me sooner.'

'I know.' Relief washed over Edythe. She wrapped her arms around Carmona. When she pushed away, Carmona was surprised to see tears in her friend's eyes.

'What a burden this has been for you,' Carmona said.

'And now you've taken it on,' Edythe said. 'I'm so sorry, Carm. Sorry for your grandfather and for having to tell you all this.'

'We'll get it sorted. I need to go back in. Are you coming?'

'No,' Edythe said. 'I think I'll just walk home. Tell my mum, would you?'

Carmona watched as Edythe walked down the drive to the road that led to the high street. What a mess they were in. What if her father had been stealing from the Hargreaves all these years? It would be easy for him, as he had control over the estate. Was he stealing from other clients, too? Things would have to be made right. Claris would have to be involved. The situation didn't bear thinking about. At least not today.

Longing for Phillip, Carmona moved towards the open door. She heard a champagne cork pop. Someone put a jazz record on Grandfather's turntable. The party, it seemed, was in full swing.

***

Cat had no business attending James Churchwright's funeral. But her argument with Thomas and the knowledge that he would surely attend pulled her to the graveside like an enchantment. Cloaked in a black raincoat with a capacious hood pulled over her hair, she approached the cemetery, following the throngs of mourners as they meandered through the graves to the freshly dug plot. A thick-trunked maple provided a resting spot just out of vision of the mourners. Her heart beat a little faster at the sight of Thomas, sharing his large umbrella over two village ladies, looking painfully handsome in his fine Savile Row suit.

Her temper had got the best of her. Although she had expected Thomas to come back – and beg for forgiveness – he hadn't. His presence had been missed. Now there were issues to be dealt with, like their work. Did she still have a job? This book was not off to a productive beginning. Cat knew full well if efforts weren't made to repair the damage her hateful words had caused, she could lose Thomas forever.

Cat loved Thomas Charles, but she did not want to get married. Not yet, anyway. The question remained: Could she relinquish her independence to a man with so many secrets? After her initial anger passed, Cat realized Thomas hadn't deliberately deceived her. He was following orders. She watched him, his head bent in prayer, surprised at the ache of longing she felt for him. *I've been a fool.*

The rain stopped. The sun came out just as the vicar's voice, deep and sorrowful, broke through the crowd. Cat recognized the text from Corinthians. 'We know we have a building from God, a house not made with hands, eternal in the heavens.'

Rather than walk on the road with the other mourners to Mr Churchwright's house, Cat decided to walk through the woods, taking her time. She planned to mingle among the crowd after everyone had a chance to consume the champagne and booze that in all likelihood would loosen tongues. Maybe she would discover some nugget of gossip relevant to Win Billings' and James Churchwright's death. The two were related. How could they not be?

James Churchwright's wake was in full swing by the time Cat arrived. The house was what some would call 'bachelor's quarters', smaller than most country houses, but well crafted and sheltered by a woodland garden. The green front door – which stood open now – was surrounded by embellishments Thomas would find a bit much, but which Cat liked. The entry area was packed with people, so Cat moseyed around the back, savouring the sweeping view of the woods on one side and the moors on the other. Now that the rain had stopped, young men were busy arranging tables on the stone patio.

Three large French doors opened as a handful of people stepped outside, champagne flutes in hand, lighters at the ready for cigarettes. Cat kept her back to them as she took in the view.

'Champagne, madam?' She turned to face an older man with a silver tray of champagne flutes.

'Thank you.' She took off her coat and laid it over the back of a chair before she stepped into the house. People had broken off into small clusters, talking and laughing, many of them telling stories about James Churchwright's reckless adventures and his misspent youth. Apparently, Mr Churchwright had been a wild young man, a war hero, who had made a fortune and married a woman half his age – Claris's mother – late in life. Cat paused before a portrait of the man hanging over the fireplace. She recognized the strong jaw and intense gaze that had been passed down to Claris and Carmona.

Cat moved into a room with a large desk, and two winged chairs placed before a fireplace. Claris sat in one of the chairs, another woman sat next to her. She held a glass in her hand, which tipped precariously. A crystal brandy decanter sat on the table next to her. Her eyes had a glazed unseeing look. When she saw Cat, she glared.

'What do you think you're doing here?' The words ran together in one long garbled mess.

Claris Broadbent was drunk.

Cat forced a smile. 'I've come to see how you're doing, to pay my respects.'

'Excuse me,' Claris said to the lady who was sitting next to her. She rose from her chair and wobbled on her feet. It took her a moment to collect herself before she strode towards Cat, impervious to the brandy that sloshed out of the glass and onto the floor. 'Could I have a word, please, Mrs Carlisle?'

'Of course,' Cat said.

'This way.' Cat followed Claris down a dark corridor to a small sitting room in the back corner. Light flooded into the room, catching the honey-coloured oak floor and the beams of the same colour.

'What a lovely room,' Cat said. She turned to Claris. 'How are you holding up?'

'Don't you dare act like you are a friend or that you care about how I'm holding up.' Claris stepped close enough for Cat to smell the alcohol vapours.

'I don't know what you mean,' Cat said.

'I know you've been asking questions about my husband in the village. You might be from London, but this is my village. There's such a thing as criminal slander, Catherine Carlisle.'

Cat didn't back away. She stepped so close to Claris their noses almost touched. 'You don't scare me. You didn't when we were young. You certainly don't now. You want to sue me? Fine. Your money doesn't intimidate me, Claris. You see, I now have plenty of my own.'

Claris raised an eyebrow. 'What about Cliff Swan?' Her voice taunted.

'What about him?'

'Your childhood friend. I know you were talking to him about my husband in the pub the other day. Maybe I can't ruin you – not immediately anyway – but I can certainly damage Mr Swan.'

'You do what you need to do, Claris. Rest assured, if you do decide to go after Cliff Swan, I'll use my considerable resources to help him.' Cat reached over and straightened the collar of Claris's jacket. 'You might want to freshen up a bit, darling. Your lipstick's smeared and you've missed a button.'

'Get out,' Claris hissed.

'Very well. Good day.' Cat walked out of the little room, head held high, and weaved her way through the crowd.

Once outside, she grabbed her coat and headed back the way she came. At some point Claris would seek revenge. Cat vowed to be ready. She stepped into the woods, feeling very much alone.

***

Assuming she could slip away from the festivities without being missed, Carmona weaved through the party goers towards the kitchen. It seemed that everyone was well and truly drunk. Her coat was in the pantry – strategically placed there earlier to facilitate a speedy exit. Her mother wouldn't be happy to discover that Carmona had not stayed until the bitter end. Grandfather's death was too raw for her. The happy celebration did not sit well. Liddy, looking very proper in Claris's borrowed clothes, danced with a gentleman old enough to be her father, a broad grin on her face as he swung her round. In the kitchen, Beck and the missus were at the sink, washing and drying dishes. Carmona thought of that day at Phillip's cottage when they had washed up together, after Carmona had brought him food and supplies, the day he had called her his love.

'You ready to go home, Carmona?' The missus set her towel on the countertop and came up to Carmona, her eyes full of kindness and concern. 'We didn't think this sort of celebration would suit you. Can I make you a proper cup of tea? Then Beck could take you home.'

'No tea, thanks,' Carmona said. 'I'm just going to grab my coat and slip out the back.'

'Wouldn't do that if I were you.' Beck came out of the larder, Carmona's coat over his arm. 'Your mum's out there. Imagine you'll want to avoid her.'

Carmona flashed Beck a grateful smile. 'In that case, I'll just slip out the front.'

'Sure you don't want me to drive you?'

'The walk will do me good,' Carmona said. She headed through the house towards the front door, towards freedom. Smoke filled the air. The dining table had been cleared out of the dining room. A gramophone had been placed on the side board. Swing music blared. Champagne flowed. Carmona weaved through the crowd, quickly losing her temper as she was jostled. All she wanted to do was make it to the front door. She felt trapped as she squeezed through the myriad of drunken revellers, all the while thinking of Edythe's suspicion and wondering how she could prove her friend wrong. So wrapped up was she in her own problems, that she almost missed Phillip.

He stood across the crowded room, in conversation with Carmona's father. The cuts and bruises on his face had faded a bit. Her father leaned close and said something in Phillip's ear. Phillip nodded and the two men headed towards the library, which Carmona knew had been locked for the party at Beck's direction.

170

Thank God. Carmona chided herself for not having more faith in Phillip. Of course he wouldn't abandon her in her time of grief. Weaving through the crowd to get to the office felt like swimming upstream. When Carmona saw her mother surveying the crowd with glazed eyes, she ducked down, out of sight. Keeping a low profile, she scurried her way through the crowd, down the corridor, and to the library without her mother seeing her. Mumbled words came through the closed door, but the music made it impossible for Carmona to hear what her father and Phillip were saying. She burst into the room, a smile on her face, confident that all would be well.

'Darling, I'm so glad you've come—'

Phillip turned to her, pale-faced and white-lipped. He seemed to barely see her as he headed to the door.

'Carmona …' His voice caught in the back of his throat.

'What's happened?' Carmona looked from her father to the man she loved.

'I'm leaving.'

'Why? Where are you going?' Carmona hated the desperation in her voice. She grabbed at Phillip's arm, but he pushed her away.

'I'm so sorry. Stay away from me, Carmona.' He flung open the door and hurried out.

'Wait!' Carmona hurried after him. Like a flash, her father blocked her way.

'Don't chase him, love.' He shut the door and stood before it, preventing her from running after Phillip.

'What did you say to him? Why did he run like that? I thought you supported us. You said—'

'As God is my witness, I said nothing. Actually, I gave him permission to court you properly.'

'What upset him?' Carmona persisted. 'Tell me exactly what was said.'

'I asked him about Scotland. He used to live there, as I am

sure you know. He just – it was so strange. I asked him if he planned on returning there, taking you with him, maybe. His face turned white. He simply panicked.'

'Why would he panic? What did he say?'

Her father ran his hand over his face. 'God, I'm tired. Can we discuss this later, Carmona?' Someone turned the gramophone up. Loud music filled the air. 'It's hard to think with all that racket.'

Carmona wanted to shake him, demand that he tell her exactly what had transpired between Phillip and him. She would have to wait.

'Don't worry about him, Carmona. I'm sure it's a misunderstanding. Give Phillip some room. Men like to think things through. Why don't you slip out and get Liddy to take you home? Get some rest. You can talk to Phillip tomorrow.'

Carmona didn't want Liddy to take her home. She wanted to know what was wrong with Phillip. She had no intention of standing by, waiting for Phillip to tell her what the hell had just happened. Her father, however, did not need to know of her plans.

'Thanks.' She kissed her father's cheek.

'There's a good girl.'

CHAPTER 14

Carmona didn't go home, rather she burst outside, driven by pent-up rage at her father – she was certain he had said something to put Phillip off – and fuelled by fury at Phillip for not having the backbone to come to her. They should have spoken to her father together. *What was Phillip thinking? Idiot.* Fast and furious, Carmona strode towards the high street, mumbling to herself, impervious to the strange glances she received from those who passed her.

Three women – evacuees, Carmona guessed, based on their shoes and their heavily powdered faces – stood outside Phillip's cottage. Carmona would have bumped into them, but she happened to look up, surprised at the commotion.

'What's going on?' she asked.

One constable stood outside the front door of the cottage, as though keeping watch. Two other men rifled through the shed in the corner of the property.

'Not sure,' one of the women said. 'Just out doing some shopping and came across this' – she nodded at the policemen – 'on my way back.'

The lady who stood next to her smiled at Carmona. She was a pretty blonde, despite the thick make-up. ''Bout time this here town had some action. I was just about ready to take my kiddies and go back to London.'

'Sir,' one of the constables called out. He came out of the shed carrying a saw and what looked like a wad of pound notes. 'Look here.'

One of the other constables noticed Carmona and the group of women watching. He started over to them. 'Move along, ladies.'

Carmona hurried away, unsure what to do. Phillip was in trouble. Where the devil was he?

***

While Carmona watched the police search Phillip's shed, Phillip – well hidden in the shrubs that abutted the woods – watched Carmona. For the first time he realized that toying with her may have been a mistake. While he was grateful for the money she gave him – he had paid off his gambling debts after hours in the pub, with Jem bearing witness. Never mind that Jem had been holding his hunting rifle. The men had taken the money and left without a backwards glance – he hadn't contended that the child would be so strong-willed. In the past week, Carmona Broadbent had grown up. The gullible young girl he had seduced had undergone a metamorphosis and was now an intelligent, thoughtful woman. A small part of him was sorry that he couldn't see the relationship through. Phillip usually liked his women compliant and biddable. Carmona Broadbent was neither of those things.

Now she watched the police, a look of worry on her face. Nothing to be done about that. The time had come for Phillip Billings to leave Rivenby. The copy of his mother's letter to James Churchwright rested in his pocket, tucked safely away. He could use it for monetary gain. In fact, he thought it might be easier that way. Safer. He could send a letter demanding payment to an anonymous mailbox. If he was careful, he could make his money last three months, six if he lived on the cheap. With fresh resolve, Phillip headed into the woods, unaware that he was being watched.

***

Like a cat after a mouse, Thomas had stalked Cat the minute she arrived at the funeral. She had no specific reason to attend James Churchwright's wake. He knew in his gut that she was up to something, and given her propensity to land herself in the middle of trouble, it stood to reason she was there with regard to the ridiculous promise she had made to her childhood friend. With a little luck and timing, he had managed to keep an eye on her without her knowing. After he followed her home, he returned to Heart's Desire, his trousers sodden to the knees. How could he protect her, when she was so angry at him? Once again, he'd made a mess of things.

He slipped in the back door, through the kitchen, and up the back staircase to his room. Luck was with him. He saw no one. As far as he knew, no one saw him. Once he'd changed into clean, dry clothes, he would go to Cat. The time had come for them to have it out. With fresh resolve, he took the key to his room out of his pocket, but stopped cold when he saw his bedroom door was ajar. He peered through the crack. The curtains were drawn. He liked his windows open to the sunshine and fresh air, and was certain they were in this state when he had left his room earlier.

Thomas tiptoed back down the hall, turned around and walked to the door, careful to make enough noise to alert whoever waited for him. He stepped into his room, prepared for the attack. A brute of a man grabbed Thomas from behind. Thomas let himself go limp before he leaned back into his assailant, pushing them both off balance. They crashed to the floor. Thomas popped up onto his feet. The other man – at a disadvantage as Thomas had landed on top of him – tried to stand, but Thomas knocked him over and placed a muddy foot directly on this chest.

'Can I help you?'

'Let me up. I need to talk to you.'

'Who are you?'

The man tried to grab at Thomas's leg. Thomas pressed down harder.

'I'm Elliott Markham. I'm here with a message from Sir Reginald.'

Thomas took his foot off the man's chest. He reached out his hand and helped the man up.

'So talk.'

'I've been here for a few months on a mission. We have reason to believe a group of operatives are smuggling blank passports out of the country into Scotland. Once there, they are forwarded to a deeply inculcated Nazi spy ring.'

'Scotland's a bit circuitous, isn't it?'

'Not really. The scenario is rather perfect. We believe they are getting agents in place before an invasion. This is a large operation, Mr Charles. I'm only aware of this small component. I'm sure the passports are coming through Rivenby and are being transported by someone who lives here. I've got intelligence about a drop that's going to take place this evening. I'm going to be there. This is about to spring wide open.'

'You said you had a message from Sir Reginald?'

'He wanted you to be aware of what is going on. There's a chance Phillip Billings is involved. It's possible Win Billings discovered this, confronted her son, and he killed her.'

'And James Churchwright?' Thomas asked.

'Found out about it. The rest is self-explanatory.'

Elliott Markham ran his hands through his hair and let out a heavy sigh. He was a brute of a man, tall, big feet, thick blond hair cut short, and a strong jaw that spoke of a stubborn temperament.

'Forgive me, Markham, but you don't sound convinced.'

Elliott lit a cigarette. 'I'm not. It's too easy. I show up and everything just falls into place. I've got my eyes on another party. I'm waiting for a witness to confirm a photograph. Sir Reginald just wanted you to be informed.' Elliott reached into his pocket and handed Thomas a card. 'If you need to reach me, call that number. Tell the woman who answers that you're an old friend and you wondered if we could meet for a pint. When I get the message, I'll come to you. Understand?'

'Yes,' Thomas said.

Elliott stuck his cigarette in his mouth, as he raised the window all the way and started to climb out. 'I'm sorry I broke into your room. Oh, one more thing. Sir Reginald wanted me to tell you to keep the redhead in check. He said you'd know what he meant. She caught me watching Billings' old house. Came after me. Reckless of her. She could get herself hurt – or worse – carrying on like that.'

'Leave her alone, Markham. I mean it.'

'I will.' Elliott Markham put his hands up. 'I didn't tell Reginald about it. I understand women. I understand redheads.' With that parting comment, Elliott Markham winked at Thomas, climbed out the window and shimmied down the drainpipe. Thomas leaned out and watched as he landed on the ground and scurried off into the woods, surprisingly nimble for someone his size.

CHAPTER 15

The rain started again just as the sun fell from the sky, bringing a chill wind with it. Try as she might, Cat couldn't get warm. She made herself a cup of tea and sat in the great living room, before the fire. Annie and Bede joined her. For a while, things had seemed normal as they listened to Charles De Gaulle on the wireless. Bede said that she prayed France would find her way back to a position of strength. Cat wished the same for her relationship with Thomas. Damn him. Her mind raced through all that she had discovered since she promised to help Beth. After the wireless programme ended and the dance music started to play, Bede and Annie moved to the kitchen, where they experimented with a new vegetable dish. Cat attempted to busy herself with a magazine, but she found herself staring at the same advert over and over again. She tossed it to the side, leaned back into the chair and closed her eyes.

'Miss!' Cat yelped when Annie touched her arm. She jolted, sloshing tea all over the front of Annie's dress.

'Oh, Annie.' Cat jumped up, startled. 'I'm sorry. I was so lost in thought that I didn't see you there.'

Annie ignored the tea stain and stared at Cat with a knowing expression that belied her sixteen years. She pulled a footstool next to the chair and sat down on it. 'I know you've been worried about Mr Charles. But you don't need to worry, miss. He's nothing like Mr Carlisle is – was.' Her eyes took on the familiar dreamy look when she spoke of Thomas. 'You think he's going to smother you, but he's only protecting you. And – don't get mad at me for saying this – there are times when a woman needs protecting.'

Cat felt like pulling Annie into her arms and hugging her tight. She didn't dare. The child was uncomfortable with physical affection of any kind. Instead Cat gave her a warm smile. 'Your devotion to Mr Charles is commendable, Annie.'

'I want you to be happy. I think you love him, but you won't admit it to yourself.' She stood. 'Anyway, I came to tell you dinner is in fifteen minutes. Bede says we'll eat in the kitchen if that's okay with you. Can I stay up and listen to the wireless tonight?'

As she spoke a flash of lightning illuminated the night sky, followed by a loud boom of thunder. Annie screamed. The house went dark as the electricity went out.

'It's the Germans,' she cried.

'It's not.' Cat put both hands on Annie's shoulders.

She felt Annie tremble. Cat's heart broke for the girl. 'Annie, it's just a bad storm. This old house has withstood storms like this – worse than this – for over a hundred years. I promise you, we are quite safe from the Germans. Now, let's go and find some candles and see if Bede needs help.'

They found Bede, calm as you please in the kitchen, with three oil lamps scattered about the room, and a candelabra which held six tapers on the table. The flames cast dancing shadows on the walls, filling the room with its warm glow. A shepherd's pie cooled on the rack, ready for their dinner.

'That will be the last lamb for a while. Let's make sure we enjoy it. What's wrong, Annie?'

'It's the thunder and lightning.'

'Never fear, lass,' Bede said. 'The electricity always goes out

179

during bad storms. I've worked in this house for almost thirty years, and I can tell you it has survived worse storms than this one. Once in 1919 – just after the war – a bad storm came through. Wind so strong it knocked over trees, pulled the thatch off Miss Worsted's cottage. Worst storm I've ever seen. St Monica's didn't have a bit of a damage. It would take a mighty wind to damage this old house.'

Cat caught Bede's eye and mouthed 'thank you' over Annie's head.

'I think we'll go up and change before dinner, Bede,' Cat said. 'I've spilled tea on Annie's dress.' She headed up the stairs with Annie on her heels. 'Would you like to sleep in my room tonight, dear? If the storm keeps on, I might want the company.'

Relief washed over Annie's face. 'Yes.'

'Very well. I'm famished. Will you be all right to go and change? We can get your dress sorted tomorrow.'

Annie nodded, carrying the oil lamp Bede had given her.

They ate their dinner and spent a pleasant evening playing gin rummy for raisins. Annie won, delighted with the pile in front of her.

'You're a regular card sharp, young lady,' Bede said. She stood up from the table. 'I'll be off to bed then.'

Cat and Annie followed. Annie had brought her nightgown in earlier. She changed in the bathroom and crawled under the covers on the daybed. By the time Cat had washed and changed into her nightgown, Annie was fast asleep. Cat got under the warm counterpane but sleep eluded her. Would Thomas be domineering and controlling like Benton? Frustrated, she got out of bed and lit a candle. Annie didn't stir. The bedside clock said 12.15. Cat decided hot milk with a dollop of brandy would be just the thing to make her sleep. She put on her dressing gown and had just tied the sash when someone banged on the front door.

Heart beating, Cat hurried down the stairs. Thomas. Who

180

else would come at this time of night? Something must have happened. She opened the door and found Carmona Broadbent, dripping wet, her dark hair soaked and clinging to her scalp. Carmona pushed past Cat into the house, without waiting to be invited.

Like mother, like daughter.

'Carmona? What are you doing here?' Cat stood aside.

'I'm sorry to barge in like this, Mrs Carlisle. I know I'm taking a chance – in addition to being utterly rude – dropping in on you in the middle of the night. But I need your help. There's no one else I trust to keep their mouth shut.'

'You'll catch your death. Come with me.' Cat led the way into the kitchen. She helped Carmona off with her coat. She found a large bath towel in a stack of folded laundry and handed it to the girl. 'Here, dry yourself. I'll get you some brandy.' She stopped herself for a moment, wondering if Claris would get mad at her for giving Carmona spirits, but dismissed the thought. If Claris was stupid enough to let her daughter out in the middle of the night in the pouring rain, she would hardly complain if the child was given something to warm her.

Cat took off the girl's coat, shoes, and wrapped her hair in a towel. She pulled a chair in front of the Aga and went for the brandy. When she came back, the girl was shivering uncontrollably. Cat wondered if Carmona was in shock. Should she fetch a doctor? 'Drink this. Just down it in one go.' She moved to the stove and made hot cocoa, using extra sugar. She added more brandy to it, and gave it to Carmona.

'Thank you.' The shivering stopped. Carmona wrapped her hands around the cup and sipped it.

'Does your mother know you're here?'

'She doesn't know anything. She's drunk herself into a stupor. Father's useless. Phillip – the police were searching his house today.'

'Phillip Billings?' Cat sat across from Carmona. When the girl wiped her eyes with the back of her arm, Cat realized her face was no longer damp from rain but from tears.

'We've been seeing each other. And don't look at me like that. I'm aware of the age difference. Phillip's special. He just needs someone to love him.'

'And the police?' Cat wasn't too interested in Carmona's schoolgirl crush. She was interested in the police searching Phillip Billings' house.

Cat sat down across from Carmona. Lightning flashed. A boom of thunder followed seconds afterwards. 'I'm sorry about your grandfather. What brings you out so late? You realize it's after midnight.'

'I know. I couldn't sleep.' The girl stared at her empty cup, as if collecting her thoughts. 'I need you to help me break into my father's office.'

'What?'

'I need a witness and I can't bring Edythe. Too risky. If we get caught, there will be hell to pay.'

'Carmona—'

'Edythe thinks my father has been embezzling from her family's estate. Long story, really. She's been avoiding me. I asked her why. She suspects my father has been stealing from her family. Of course, I resisted the idea at first. My father? He wouldn't do anything like that. He is an upstanding citizen, respected in the community. But Edythe put forth a rather detailed and compelling argument to support her position.' Carmona took a deep breath. Cat was struck by the girl's forthright intelligence, at her ability to tamp down her emotion and deal with Edythe's accusation directly.

Carmona finished drying her hair. She rose to hang the towel over the chair nearest the cooker.

'I'm going to break into my father's office. I'm hoping you'll come with me. We can go through the books, or search for a second set of ledgers. Isn't that how people cheat at bookkeeping?

Don't they keep two sets of records or something? In any event, we'll see what we can find. I've spent my summers doing odd jobs in my father's office. I know where the files are kept.'

'Where do I fit in?'

'You're the only responsible adult who isn't afraid of my mother. I can't very well go to Edythe and tell her I looked at my dad's books, and he's not cheating. Someone – you, hopefully – needs to back up my story, so Edythe will believe me. I just want things back to the way they were between us. I need to know if my father has been stealing. Phillip's going to need help. My family is – was – in a position to help him. My father promised to represent him and support him. But how can we help Phillip if we're in trouble too? Will you help me?'

'What if Edythe's right? What if your dad has been cheating her?'

'My mother will have to be involved, of course. Everyone will need to be paid back. Phillip will be on his own. I will have failed him.' Carmona wiped her eyes.

'You're taking on an awful lot, Carmona.' Cat ticked off all the things that could go wrong, but dismissed them just as quickly as they came into her mind. She knew that she couldn't let Carmona go to her father's office alone. The child needed help.

As if reading her thoughts, Carmona said. 'It's not like I'm breaking in like a common criminal. It's my family's building, and' – Carmona reached into her pocket and pulled out brass key – 'I've got a key.'

'When do you want to do this?'

'Tonight. Now,' Carmona said. 'When the rain stops. If you could see your way to loaning me some dry clothes?'

Cat paused for a moment, while her logic and reason did battle with the impetuous spontaneity that had caused her so much grief over the years. Carmona waited, patient as a saint, a knowing look in her intelligent eyes.

183

'Fine. Wait here. I'll get you dry clothes.' Cat took the cups and saucers and set them in the sink.

'We need torches.'

'Check the pantry,' Cat said. 'And keep quiet, please. I'd rather not wake the entire house.'

***

The stars winked above Cat and Carmona as they crept out of St Monica's. Once in the lane, they stood for a moment gazing up at a moon so bright and full, it seemed they could reach out and touch it.

'At least we won't need torches,' Cat said.

'Let's take the path through the woods. Safer that way. We don't want anyone seeing us.' Carmona set off in the dark.

Cat followed, wondering who in the world would see them at this hour. Carmona knew the footpath to town by rote. Cat stayed close, careful to step where Carmona did. As they approached a clearing, the sound of hushed voices caused Carmona to stop short and look back at Cat with wide eyes. She motioned Cat to follow her as she stepped onto a side trail and circled the clearing, coming to a halt in a bushy area near a fallen log. Cat sidled up next to her and peered into a meadow covered in grass and bathed in moonlight. Next to her Carmona stiffened, stuffing her fist in her mouth just in time to stop the cry.

Cat peered through the bushes and saw two figures having what looked to be a lovers' tryst under the moonlight. Phillip Billings sat next to Miss Hinch on the fallen log. He lit a cigarette and blew a plume of smoke into the night air.

'I need to leave.'

'No, you need to turn yourself in. You should cooperate with the police. It's the best course of action.'

'And what about you, Emmeline? Will you turn yourself in? I

have the letter. I know what's been happening. Should I give it to the police?'

Emmeline Hinch stood and wheeled around to face Phillip, her hands clenched into fists. 'I'll go to prison.'

'No, you won't. Tell the truth.'

She shook her head and collapsed back onto the log. Phillip went to put his arm around her, but she pushed him away. Her shoulders shook, as she silently sobbed.

'Oh, Emmeline.' Phillip put both of his arms around Miss Hinch, pulling her to him. This time she leaned against his chest, like Carmona had done. 'It'll be all right, love. Let's leave together. Once we're away from here, we'll figure something out.'

Carmona shuddered. 'I can't believe this.'

Cat tugged on Carmona's arm. 'Come on. Let's go. You don't need to see this.'

'Oh, yes I do.' Carmona hissed. Cat said a silent prayer she wouldn't do anything rash. She could see Carmona charging into the clearing, driven by rage, vengeful and furious. But Cat should have known better. Carmona Broadbent was too intelligent to act rashly. She would plot and plan and get her revenge in one merciless stroke, God help Phillip Billings and Miss Hinch.

'What are you going to do about Carmona? She needs to be told the truth.' Miss Hinch took Phillip's handkerchief and wiped her eyes.

'Carmona Broadbent fancies herself in love with me. It's nothing more than a schoolgirl crush.'

'That's not what her father thinks. You need to talk to her, Phillip. Tell her the truth about us. You're probably the first man who's ever shown her affection. You must consider her feelings. You're going to destroy her, you know.' Phillip rose up and tried to pull Miss Hinch into his embrace. She pushed him away. 'No. Not until you understand my position. Carmona Broadbent doesn't deserve to be lied to. We'll sort out your problems. You're to give her the money back – all of it – and tell her the truth. I'm serious, Phillip. You tell her, or I will.'

'I think we should just leave. Somebody's trying to set me up for murder. You weren't there today. You didn't see the police with the saw and the cash they found in my shed. My shed!' Phillip started pacing in the clearing, his voice rising. 'I didn't put it there.'

'I know that,' Miss Hinch said.

'The police think I murdered my mother. They'll come for me. It's just a matter of time.'

'I will not spend my life as a fugitive. We're going to sort the police out.' Miss Hinch took Phillip's hand. 'We'll face it, together.'

'Face what together?' Carmona stepped out into the clearing before Cat could do anything to stop her. 'Hello, Phillip.'

Phillip stepped away from Miss Hinch, like a guilty child caught with his hand in the biscuit tin. 'Carmona. Love. What are you doing out here?'

Carmona stepped closer. Cat marvelled at her calm. She felt guilty witnessing this intimate confrontation which should have been held privately between Carmona and Phillip.

'I could ask you the same thing,' Carmona said.

'Carmona, it's not what you think. I swear ...' Phillip shot Miss Hinch a pleading look.

'Oh, Phillip, for heaven's sake, tell her.' Miss Hinch moved next to Phillip and wove her arm through his. 'We're a couple, Carmona. We've been together for years. We just keep it a secret because we don't want the entire village knowing our business until we marry.'

Carmona wobbled on her feet. Cat moved close, ready to catch her if she fell. After a few seconds, she was steady again.

'Why do the police want you, Phillip? Did you do it?' Carmona's voice rang loud and clear in the cool night air. 'Did you kill my grandfather? Did you kill your mother?'

'Of course he didn't,' Miss Hinch said. 'And you'd better watch what you say.'

'Don't threaten me, Miss Hinch. Remember, my father is your employer. I'll see you lose your job before I take a moment of grief from you.'

'Stop acting like a child,' Phillip said. 'It's not like I asked you to marry me. We carried on a bit, flirted. But you were more of a friend, and you know it. I realize you lent me money. And I'll pay you back, I promise.'

'I despair for you, Phillip Billings. You are an utter idiot. As far as I'm concerned, you can go to hell.'

Carmona turned on her heel and walked away.

Miss Hinch chased after her. 'Carmona, wait.'

'Don't worry, Miss Hinch. I won't tell my father.'

Carmona strode away, her step strong and sure. Cat chased after her, clunking along in the Wellies that were a size too big. By the time Cat reached David Broadbent's office, her heart felt like it was about to explode in her chest. She found Carmona sitting in the doorway of the office, head in hands, rocking, while she sobbed so hard her body heaved from the effort of it. Cat sat down next to her, reached out a hand, and patted Carmona's back.

'Mum was right. I've been so stupid.' Cat reached into the pocket of her coat, found a handkerchief, and handed it to Carmona. She blew her nose. 'How could I have been such a fool?'

'You're not the first woman to fall for someone like Phillip Billings,' Cat said. 'When we've more time, I'll tell you the story of my horrible marriage.'

'Your horrible marriage? I thought women like you had their husbands swooning at their feet.'

Cat snorted. 'My husband was a bully. He did his swooning with his mistress.'

Carmona stopped crying. She stared at Cat, her head cocked to one side.

'Someone murdered him. The police thought I did it. And God knows I wanted to. I spent too many years of my life married to the wrong man. Tonight was a gift, Carmona. Phillip would have continued to use you. Best know what he's made of, so you can get on with your life.' Cat patted Carmona's knee. 'You'll get over him, dearest. That's a promise. It'll hurt for a while. These things always do. But with time, you'll recover yourself.'

'You know the worst part? I saw him and Miss Hinch – Miss Hinch, for heaven's sake – with my own eyes, yet there's a part of me that rationalizes his behaviour. If he walked up to me right now and said he didn't love her, I'd want to believe him. Ridiculous, isn't it? I'm a fool. I'm so angry at him – no, I'm angry at myself. I cannot believe I fell for him.' She dried her eyes and stood up. 'Let's get this over with. I'm exhausted all of a sudden.'

She unlocked the door to her father's office. Cat followed her into the dark office. 'It's these velvet curtains,' Carmona said. 'They block all the light. My mother's decorative touch.' She flipped on her torch. Cat did the same.

'The accounts are in here. Come on.' Carmona opened the door which led to the office on the right of the reception desk. She went to a filing cabinet and tried the top drawer. 'This is where my father keeps his ledgers. Blast. It's locked.' She turned slowly around the room. Her eyes lit on her father's desk. She hurried to it, opened the top drawer, and started pulling things out. Finally she reached in and pulled out two small keys, which she used to open the locked drawer in the filing cabinet. Soon she had four ledgers tucked under her arm. 'Here we go.' She motioned to a low table with two chairs in front of it. 'Let's set up there. We'll go through these first.' She set the ledgers down on the table.

Cat opened one on her lap. 'What exactly am I looking for?'

'Anything to do with the Hargreaves Estate, I suppose.'

Cat held a torch with one hand and the heavy ledger with the other. She read until her neck ached.

'No luck?' Carmona asked.

'Not a bit.'

Carmona shut the ledger she was holding and set it on the table. 'My father is a fastidious record keeper. If he's been skimming from his clients, he would keep a list.'

'Why? Wouldn't that incriminate him?'

'Not necessarily. He would have a back-up plan. He always does. If someone found out he was skimming, he would go to my mother for money to pay everything back. I know it sounds far-fetched to you, but you don't know my father.'

'Any idea where he would keep a document of that nature?' Cat looked around the room for a hiding place.

The office door sprung open. The overhead light went on. Two constables burst into the room, an older man with a sizable girth and handlebar moustaches, followed by a younger man with spots on his face. 'All right, gents. Don't—'

The older man stopped speaking mid-sentence, his mouth hanging open, as his eyes darted from Carmona, to Cat, and back to Carmona again. 'What the devil?'

'What do you think you're doing barging in here like this?' Carmona snapped.

The younger man, in a burst of youthful indignation, pushed past the senior constable. 'You're breaking and entering. Don't think you're going to charm your way out of this.' The young man towered over Carmona, who had remained seated on the couch.

Cat stood, appealing to the older officer. 'I think we should explain. This office belongs to this young lady's father.'

The younger officer sneered. 'You don't expect us to believe that. We're not stupid. You've broken into this office. What are you looking for?' He surveyed the ledgers on the table. 'Bank checks? Cash?'

189

'This is my father's office,' Carmona said.

'I don't believe you,' the younger man said. 'Even if it were true, what are you doing here in the middle of the night?'

'That's none of your business,' Carmona said.

'When I find ladies of questionable repute in an office in the middle of the night' – the constable's eyes swept over the open ledgers – 'looking through financial documents, I become suspicious. That's my job.'

The older constable stood in front of the door, his arms crossed over his chest, a smirk on his face.

'Her father owns this building. This is ridiculous.'

The older policeman looked at her and smirked. 'Hear that? The young lady's father owns the building.'

'What, do you think we're stupid?' The young constable said.

'Why are you letting him go on like this?' Cat asked the older man.

He shrugged. 'Just doing his job, ma'am.'

The younger constable continued to harangue Carmona, relentlessly pushing the poor girl.

'Is that how you pay for your fancy clothes? Stealing? You're coming with me, young lady. We'll lock you up overnight and see what you have to say in the morning.'

'Wait a second,' Cat said. 'You're making a big mistake.' She looked at the older constable, hoping he would see reason. 'Can't you call the constabulary and get someone who knows this woman?'

The young constable looked at Cat. 'You be quiet, ma'am.' He stepped close to Carmona. He reached out a hand and touched her cashmere jumper. 'Thieving, that's what you're up to. How else would a stupid girl be able to afford clothes as fine as this? You certainly couldn't earn your money whoring. No one would pay for the likes you.' The young man laughed.

Cat watched as Carmona's already frayed nerves unravelled and her rage boiled over, surprised that neither of the policemen

190

noticed it. The poor thing had buried her grandfather, seen the man she loved with another woman, and now she was being abused by an upstart young constable who had overstepped his position. The young man clearly didn't have the temperament for his job. His superior wasn't much better.

'Get out of here. Now.' Carmona stood nose to nose with the constable.

He didn't back down. 'You'll lose your high and mighty ways once you're locked up in jail.'

'Carmona …' Cat moved to stand between the two, hoping to dispel the tension between them. One phone call to Carmona's father would resolve the situation. *Too late.*

Carmona slapped the young man across the face so hard it knocked him to his knees.

CHAPTER 16

For the first time since he arrived in Rivenby, Thomas slept. He dreamt he was stranded on a desert island with Cat, the involuntary cohabitation forced them to spend time together, forced them to hammer out the unresolved issues that lay between them. Their conversation was spirited, fuelled by passion. In Thomas's dream, Cat realized she was loved. She came to understand everything Thomas did that made her feel smothered was motivated by a deep desire to protect her. They sat on sand as white as sugar, wrapped in each other's arms, watching the orb of sun shrink into the sea. And the phone rang.

Jolted awake, Thomas bolted upright sending his wounded shoulder into spasm. He wondered who would call at this late hour. The ringing stopped. He sighed and lay back down, knowing sleep would elude him now. The ringing started again.

Damn. He hurried into the other room and answered the phone.

'Mr Charles?' The voice didn't wait for Thomas to respond. 'Markham here. We've a bit of a problem. Seems your friend and Carmona Broadbent decided to do a little snooping tonight.'

'What are you talking about?' He looked at the clock on the desk. 'It's two o'clock in the morning. Surely you're mistaken.'

'I am not. Catherine Carlisle and Carmona Broadbent were discovered by two constables in David Broadbent's office, going through records from the looks of things.'

'But it was her own father's office. What's the problem?'

'It seems Miss Broadbent slapped one of the constables. Rather hard. He wasn't happy, so he took both Carmona and Mrs Carlisle into the police station. You'd better get down there.'

Thomas slammed the phone down. He dressed and was headed down stairs, when Beck intercepted him in the foyer. The man was still dressed in his uniform, not a hair was out of place.

'Is everything all right, sir?'

'No, Beck. It's not. I hate to bother you with this, but I'll be bringing a friend who is in trouble back here. Would you mind preparing a guest room? And tea wouldn't be amiss. I should be back within the hour.'

***

The Rivenby Constabulary – a three-storey brick building, which had once served as a textile mill – sat at the top of the high street, overlooking the village with regal nonchalance. The owner of the mill had lived to the ripe old age of 97, and had often told how he wished he could have grown up to be a policeman. He had no children and surprised the village by leaving the mill to the constabulary in his will. A harried-looking WPC waited for Thomas as he walked to the front door.

'Mr Charles?' She didn't wait for him to answer. 'They're just this way.'

'Trouble?' Thomas asked.

The woman stopped and spun around to face him. 'Your friend is busy making enemies. She should be careful, sir, if you don't mind my saying so. Constable Warwick is young, but he's mean.'

'Point taken,' Thomas said.

Thomas followed the female constable down a corridor of closed doors towards the sound of shouting. Impervious to the vigorous argument taking place in the corridor, David Broadbent and Carmona sat in a room with a window into the corridor, heads together in deep conversation.

DCI Kent, two constables, and Cat were huddled together in the corridor. DCI Kent bristled with anger. The old constable stood just out of Kent's line of fire, while the younger constable attempted to tower over Cat. He stepped so close to her, their noses almost touched. Thomas watched as a jolt of anger shot through Cat's body. With one breath, she calmed herself. Most women would have stepped away from an infuriated policeman. Not Cat. She clenched her hands into fists and leaned in closer. Something in her eyes reached the young constable for he moved away from her. Thomas resisted the urge to slam the young constable against the wall. Would he ever learn not to be so protective of Cat?

'You could have avoided this whole situation had you simply asked an intelligent question or two,' Cat said.

'Stand down, constable,' DCI Kent said.

The young man stepped away from Cat. 'I'm telling you, sir, they weren't cooperating.'

'But we weren't even doing anything wrong. Miss Broadbent had a key to her father's office. We were in there looking for something.'

'She hit me!' the young constable cried out.

'That's because you called her a whore,' Cat said.

'What?' DCI Kent said.

'Forgive me,' Cat said. 'His exact words were, "How else would a stupid girl be able to afford clothes as fine as this? You certainly couldn't earn your money whoring. No one would pay for you." Your young constable reached out and felt the fabric of Miss Broadbent's sweater. And this man' – Cat pointed to the older constable – 'didn't do a thing to stop the situation from escalating.'

'Constable Perkins, Constable Warwick, you are both suspended. Go home. I'll deal with you tomorrow.'

'Cat.' Thomas made his presence known, gratified to see she was relieved rather than angry at his presence.

DCI Kent nodded to him. 'Let's go into my office, shall we?'

Thomas placed his arm on the small of Cat's back, as they followed DCI Kent into a spacious office, the floor of which was covered with what appeared to be an Aubusson rug.

'Fancy office,' Thomas said.

'The furniture came with the mill. Long story.' DCI Kent sat at his desk. He pointed to the two chairs opposite. Thomas and Cat sat down. 'I won't keep you, Mrs Carlisle. Would you mind telling me what you and Carmona were doing in her father's office?'

Cat shook her head. 'I'm sorry. That's Carmona's story, not mine.'

DCI Kent sighed. 'It's the middle of the night and I'm not in the mood to argue.' He faced Thomas. 'I'm going to leave it with you to tell her how important it is to cooperate with the police. Someone is going to tell me what those two were up to tonight. Rest assured, if Carmona Broadbent isn't forthcoming, I'll be looking to Mrs Carlisle for elucidation. Are we clear?'

'Yes,' Thomas said.

'Very well. You can go.'

DCI Kent strode out of the room.

'Let's get out of here,' Thomas said.

'I'm still mad at you,' Cat said. 'But thanks for coming.'

'I know.'

'My car is out the back.' Cat followed him out the back of the police station. She spoke for the first time when he turned towards Heart's Desire.

'Where are you taking me?'

'Heart's Desire. I've a guest room made up for you. We have some talking to do and I don't want Bede or Annie listening to

195

it. I want you to tell me what happened tonight. I need you to trust me and confide in me, Cat. There are some serious issues at play.'

True to his word, Beck had not only arranged a room for Cat, he had lit a fire in Mr Churchwright's study, and had left a tray with tea and a plate full of sandwiches. Cat didn't speak as Thomas poured a cup for her and for himself. She moved closer to him on the sofa.

'Brandy?' he asked, nodding at the decanter.

'Please,' Cat said.

'Tell me what happened tonight, with Carmona. Start from the beginning. Don't leave anything out.' He half expected her to argue with him, respond to his request for information with questions of her own. Thomas watched her by the light of the fire. Her face was pale. Her hand shook a little as she lifted the cup of tea. She shivered.

'Carmona came knocking at midnight. She barged into my house. I should have taken her home, but she was sodden and shivering, and I felt sorry for her. Apparently, Edythe confronted her today with her suspicions about Carmona's father.' She flashed a rueful glance at Thomas. 'Edythe is convinced David Broadbent has been embezzling from her father's estate. She has expressed this concern to her mother, but Beth dismissed her. She even went so far as to ask Mr Broadbent for the accounts, but he waved her off, told her some nonsense about how young women shouldn't worry over such matters.'

'You believed her, though. Didn't you?'

'I didn't disbelieve her,' Cat said. 'She asked me to help her. She needed to know the truth. And the question remains. Why have they not received the accounts of her father's estate? My intuition is telling me something is going on.'

'You and your intuition. We need to deal in facts. You know that. You can't start asking questions based on female intuition. It just doesn't fly. Especially not in a village like this.'

'And therein lies the problem between us, Tom. You dismiss women's intuition, call it hysteria or illogical emotion. Yet you don't flinch when the intuition comes from a man. You've told me yourself when you are in the throes of an investigation you follow your well-honed instincts. Why are you so quick to dismiss mine? Or any woman's, for that matter? Women have finely tuned senses, much more so than men.'

'Cat—'

'I know my feelings on this matter seem absurd to you, and you're entitled to your opinion.' She leaned back and crossed her legs. 'You see women as weak, in need of protection. In some sense, that's true. But you use this seeming physical weakness as a reason to dismiss our intuition as emotional nonsense. I just expected more from you.'

'I'm sorry,' Thomas whispered.

'Don't be.' Cat's manner became brisk and business-like. 'You should have seen Carmona standing there in the rain, looking lost and in need of rescuing. You would have helped her too, I'm sure of it. She's been carrying on an affair of sorts with Phillip Billings.'

'I know,' Thomas said.

'How?'

'I caught Carmona snooping in my room when I first arrived. I have a dossier on Phillip. Carmona saw it. Told me she was in love with him, and that she was going to tell him about it.'

'Beth thinks Phillip killed his mother,' Cat said. 'I think David Broadbent did. And don't look at me that way. What if he's been embezzling and Win found out? What if Win told James Churchwright, so he had to go, too?'

'I just don't see him as someone who would risk losing everything. There could be more to his business relationship with Mrs Hargreaves. Maybe she received the accounts, and simply hasn't told Edythe. I don't understand what motive David Broadbent could have for committing two murders.'

197

'Love or money,' Cat said. 'In any event, Carmona is determined to prove Edythe wrong. She said she needed a witness. If she looked at the records and found nothing amiss, Edythe could have said Carmona was just making things up. I went with her.' She gave Thomas a rueful glance. 'Probably acted a little impetuously, but there you have it.'

'Did you discover any evidence against him?'

Cat had the good grace to look sheepish. 'No. But Cliff Swan heard that he mortgaged his wife's house without telling her. And he cheated Cliff out of money. Wouldn't pay him for services rendered.'

'Conjecture,' Thomas said.

'Agreed,' Cat said.

'Well, it's done,' Thomas said. 'I'm not going to reprimand you about your actions, Cat. The only thing I can do is implore you to be careful. I'm not close enough to the investigation to protect you. Let's say hypothetically David Broadbent murdered Win Billings and James Churchwright. Once Carmona tells him why she was in his office, he will know that you are suspicious of him. What if he comes after you?'

'Point taken,' Cat said. 'I suppose it's time I turn my focus to other matters, like our book.'

Relieved at Cat's sensible response, Thomas stared at the woman he had fallen in love with. She was like quicksilver, moving and flowing in her own way, just out of reach of his protection. He got up and poured two brandies, setting one of the glasses down in front of Cat.

'Reginald sent me here to keep watch on the investigation into Win Billings' murder. She worked for him as a cryptographer in the last war. Apparently, she was rather brilliant, using her good looks to manipulate her way into the upper-echelons of the German Army. She stole battle plans, code books, and did countless heroic acts. I'm only here to make sure her death was not caused by a past grievance, for lack of a better word.'

'I understand,' Cat said.

Cat met his eyes. He saw a glimmer of emotion there, a flash of the feeling that existed between them before the kiss.

'We should talk, Cat, about what happened—'

'No.' She shook her head. 'I'm not ready yet. Please. Give me a bit more time.' Cat sipped at her brandy, her green eyes meeting his over the rim of the crystal snifter. Thomas was pleased to see the rosiness come to her cheeks.

'I'll tell Reginald that I'm finished, once and for all, Cat. Say the word. I'd do that for you.'

'You know I'd never do that. You'd resent me. Sounds to me like you have some questions about your life, about what you want to do with it. You need to find your own way here, Tom.' She reached up and touched his cheek. He resisted the urge to take her hand and kiss it. 'Would you mind taking me home? I just want to crawl into my own bed.'

He drove Cat home, enjoying the comfortable silence between them. When he pulled to a stop in front of St Monica's, she leaned over and gave him a peck on the cheek. 'Good night, Tom.'

He watched while she walked up to the dark house and waited while she used a key to let herself in. He resisted the urge to follow and make sure she had locked the door behind her. As he drove, he replayed their conversation. Was he dismissive of women's intuition? Did he have a double standard? Her accusation made him defensive, but at least they were talking. She had assured him that she would step back, focus on their book. His cheek tingled where her hand had touched it. That simple touch would have to do for the time being.

CHAPTER 17

Carmona sat in the back seat while her father slid into the driver's seat, perplexed at the change in her parents' relationship. She had expected her mother to make mincemeat of the young constable who had pushed Carmona to the breaking point. Instead, her mother had waited in the car while her father had used his logic and reason – along with his connections to the village – to see that Carmona was released into his custody.

Her mother – who usually did the driving – sat in the front seat, docile as a lamb. She didn't chastise Carmona for her reckless behaviour. In fact, she didn't look at Carmona at all. Carmona couldn't help but wonder what had brought about this change. What had thrown her mother so off centre that she had willingly ceded her power, her utter sense of self, to her husband?

Worries of family slipped away as the memory of Phillip's arms around Miss Hinch played in Carmona's mind, like a horrible film she couldn't stop. The scene ran in slow motion, each second a painful reminder not only of Phillip's utter betrayal, but of Carmona's stupidity. What a gullible idiot she had been, basking in the security of a love that didn't exist.

'I think I'm going to be sick. Can you pull over?'

'We're almost home. Can you hang on?'

She wanted to scream, to weep, to throw a tantrum. At least the old Carmona did, the childish Carmona who fell prey to handsome men with sweet words and false promises. Her grandfather's death, Phillip's betrayal, and the nagging worry her father had a secret galvanized her desire to get away from Rivenby, go to medical school, and avoid marriage and family altogether. She did not want to follow in her mother's footsteps, of that she was certain. Carmona knew she was strong. She made no apologies for it. But there were different sorts of strength. Look at Mrs Carlisle. She was strong, yet she managed to be kind and feminine. And then there was the strength of her mother, who over the years had grown more and more domineering and pushy. Now look at her. Carmona would never be like her mother, nor would she give her heart away so recklessly again. She hunkered deeper into the backseat, resolved to spending the rest of her life alone and grateful to do so.

Her father pulled up in front of the house. Carmona waited while he held the door for her mother. He spoke to her in the same tone he used on Carmona when she was a child. 'Claris, go to bed. I'll bring you something to make you sleep in a minute.'

'I really think—'

Carmona watched as her father led her mother into the foyer, amazed that she shuffled off to her room without a word.

'She's nearly catatonic. I think we need to get her a doctor. Aren't you worried?'

'You're not a doctor, Carmona. Stop with the diagnosis, please. Your mother's suffering from grief.'

'And you're being cruel. What's happened between the two of you?'

'Your mother is the least of my problems,' her father said. 'Come with me. We're going to have a little discussion about why you felt the need to snoop through my office.'

Carmona longed to tell her father about Phillip and Miss Hinch, longed for the days when he would kiss her forehead and say just the right thing to make her feel better. They went into the study. Her father poured himself a brandy.

'Can I have one?' God knew she could use it after what she had been through tonight. Finding out the truth about Phillip was enough to make her want to drink until she passed out.

'Don't try my patience, Carmona. Please, sit.' Her father pointed to one of the chairs before his desk. Carmona did as he bade, while he remained standing. 'What were you and that Carlisle woman doing in my office? Clearly, she made you take her there. What did she say? What was she after?'

'It wasn't her—'

'Don't lie to me, Carmona. I know she's been asking questions about me in the village. She thinks I've done something. I'd like to know what. My reputation – the reputation of this family – is at stake. You realize that, don't you? The newspapers will be here before too long. They'll be hounding us, looking for a story.' He rubbed his face with his free hand. Carmona saw the stress in the deep lines etched around her father's eyes.

'You're mistaken about Cat Carlisle.' Carmona closed her eyes and tipped her head back. God, she was exhausted. 'Edythe thinks her father had money when he died. She wants the accounts.'

'Not this again,' her father said.

'If you hadn't dismissed her, if you'd given her the accounts when she asked for it, this wouldn't be a problem. Now she's convinced you've been embezzling money from her. She's like a dog with a bone, Dad. She won't let it go.'

'So you decided to see if she was right?' He refilled his brandy before he sat in the chair next to Carmona.

'I decided to prove she was wrong. I know you didn't embezzle from her. But she needed proof. And I couldn't very well say, "I verified my father wasn't stealing from you. Problem solved.

Thank you, very much." So I brought Cat Carlisle with me as a witness. She's a respectable adult and I trust her not to say anything.'

'Why didn't you just come to me?'

'Because you would have dismissed me like you dismissed Edythe. She needs proof. Surely you can see that.'

'I suppose you're right.' He refilled his brandy before he sat on the footstool near Carmona's chair. 'I'll make arrangements to see that Edythe's concerns are addressed. I'm not used to you modern young women.'

'Thank you.' The last of Carmona's resolves slipped away. She dabbed at her eyes with the back of her sleeve. 'It seems my world is falling apart.'

'Phillip?'

'I saw him with Hinch, Daddy. Hinch.' She shook her head. 'It's over. It wasn't anything, really. I made too much of the relationship.'

'Sorry about that, love. Probably for the best.'

Carmona stood. 'I'm sorry to drag you and Mother out of bed in the middle of the night.'

'All is forgiven.' Her father stood too. He opened his desk drawer and took out a chemist packet. 'Take this. It'll make you sleep. Have a lie-in tomorrow. We'll discuss Edythe's accounts and get things squared away. All right?'

'What about Mum?'

'I'll ring the doctor in the morning. I was inclined to just let her do what she needs to do to grieve, but maybe you're right. She needs help now.'

'Good night.'

'Good night, Carmona.'

***

203

Phillip was hiding in the back shed at the Dirty Duck when the police found him. Too exhausted to run, he didn't give the constables any trouble, following them like an obedient puppy. Ten minutes later, Phillip was sitting in a windowless room so small it had to have been a closet at one point. A small table and two chairs were the only furniture. The room was painted a hideous shade of green that made Phillip want to vomit. He started to shake. The tears came soon thereafter. Utterly diminished, Phillip Billings wept like a baby.

After what seemed like hours, DCI Kent came into the room and sat down in the chair opposite Phillip. DS Wallace remained standing, blocking the door. He found Phillip hunched over his chair, a desperate look in his eyes.

'I've got something to say, but I'll not say it to you.'

'You'll talk, laddy,' DCI Kent said.

'Not to you I won't. I know who killed my mum and James Churchwright. And I've got proof. Get that bloke that's staying at James Churchwright's house. I'll talk to him.' Phillip sat back in his chair, arms crossed over his chest.

DCI Kent nodded at DS Wallace, who left the room. When they were alone, DCI Kent walked over to Phillip and leaned down so close that Phillip could feel his hot breath. Phillip whimpered.

'Mention my sister's name again, and I'll wring your neck.' DCI Kent straightened, fussed with his jacket, and sauntered out of the room.

***

Carmona fell into the deep sleep that accompanies emotional exhaustion, helped by the sleeping powder her father gave her. The morning dawned grey and misty, and still Carmona slept. By the time Liddy came in with the tea tray, it was noon. She opened one eye and watched as Liddy went through the usual routine, setting the tray on the table, pouring out for both of them. They would talk while Liddy tidied Carmona's room, with Carmona helping so Liddy could finish early and get back to her family. Today there was only one teacup on the tray. Liddy's hand shook while she poured. When she was finished, she leaned against the table for a moment, sighed, and wiped her eyes with the back of her hands.

'What's wrong?' Carmona sat up and reached for her dressing gown. 'Why are you crying?'

Liddy turned to face Carmona. 'He's given me the sack. Today's my last day. Actually, I'm leaving now. I just wanted to bring you this and say goodbye.'

Carmona grabbed her clothes and headed into the bathroom. 'Wait. I'll take care of this.'

'You can't fix it this time, Carmona. There's nothing to be done. Your mother sat right there while he gave me my notice and didn't say a word. She looks like she's still wearing the same clothes from yesterday and she's drinking brandy.' Liddy cocked her head and stared at Carmona. 'What's happened? You could cut the tension in this house with a knife.'

Carmona thought back to her conversation with her father last night. Was he more upset than he let on, or had something happened during the night?

'I've never seen him like this. And your mum – it's like she's not even aware of her surroundings.' Liddy shivered. 'They're waiting for you in the dining room. You'd better hurry.'

'What will you do?' Carmona asked.

'I'll manage. I've saved some money. I'll look for another post. Maybe join the land girls. Your dad said he'd give me a glowing reference.' She gave Carmona a weak smile. 'Please don't worry about me.'

'Of course I'll worry about you, Liddy. You're a dear friend. I'm so sorry about all this.'

'Don't be,' Liddy said. 'Things change, Carmona.'

'For both of us,' Carmona said.

Her parents were indeed waiting for her in the dining room. Her father ate heartily from a plate piled high with eggs, kippers, and toast, while her mother sat sullen, a very full glass of brandy in front of her.

'Brandy, Mother? In the morning?'

Liddy was right. Her mother looked as though she hadn't slept. She still wore the black crepe skirt and the blouse – made of a fine dove-grey silk – she had on yesterday, but she had missed a button. A stain spattered the front of it. Her hair had come loose from its pins, the wildness of it accentuating the jutting cheek-bones and the dark half-moons under her mother's eyes.

'Dad, she's worse,' Carmona said.

Her father ignored her. 'Grab a plate and sit down. There are things we need to discuss.'

Carmona sat down. She waited while her dad used a piece of toast to soak up an egg yolk. A small dribble of it, yellow and gelatinous, stuck to his chin. The sight of it brought on waves of nausea. She poured herself tea and took a small sip.

'You fired Liddy? Why? You didn't even ask me.'

'Ask you?' Her father met her eyes. Carmona recoiled, taken aback by the look she saw there. The kind-hearted man of last night had now been replaced by someone hard and strong.

'What's happened?' Carmona asked.

'Phillip Billings has been arrested with the saw that was used to hack through the brakes of his mother's car. It won't take long for the police to charge him with your grandfather's murder.' He tossed his napkin down on top of his plate before he pushed it aside.

'He's not—'

'Do not speak.'

'But I'm not going to—'

He slammed his fist down on the table so hard the cups rattled

206

in their saucers. Claris looked up.

'Mum.' Carmona started to get up and go to her mother, who looked as though she were about to faint.

'Do not move. Your mother's fine. Aren't you, dear?'

Claris nodded. Carmona had never, not once in her entire life, seen her mother acquiesce to her father. The walls closed in around her. A heavy weight sat on her chest, encircling her heart.

'You have brought disgrace to this family, Carmona. Everyone in the village knows you've been carrying on with Phillip Billings. I don't know how we are going to face our friends and neighbours. I do know you have had way too much freedom. As of now, that is going to change. Your mother has agreed to give me control of your inheritance from your grandfather.'

'I made a mistake,' Carmona cried out.

'Your privileges are revoked. Your car is to be sold. This afternoon we will go to your bank, and you will close your account and turn those funds over to me. This is for your own protection. Your mother told me you've given Phillip money. Is that true?' He didn't wait for Carmona to answer. 'Never mind. You clearly aren't capable of making good decisions. You are restricted from doing anything or seeing anyone without my approval. Do you understand?'

'No. You think treating me like a child will save your precious reputation? I haven't done anything wrong. You know it. Yes, I fell for a man. As I told you last night, I made a stupid mistake. Believe me, I'm not seeing him anymore. It's over between us.'

'It's over between you? You think the fact that you are no longer sneaking around in the middle of the night with him matters in the grand scheme of things? Did you think you could carry on with Phillip Billings, go to his house – to his house, Carmona, without a chaperone – and not be seen? The village is abuzz with it. Our family is going to be dragged through the mud.'

'Fine. I'll leave. That should make things easier on you. If I'm out of the picture, you can just blame me for everything. I don't care. But you won't sell my car. Grandfather gave it to me. It's in my name. And I'll not give you my bank account. I don't have much, but at least I can get away from here. From you.' Carmona's eyes blazed with anger, at the injustice of it all, at Phillip's betrayal. 'Mum, do you have anything to say about this?'

Claris's eyes locked onto her husband's for the briefest second.

'Mum, say something.'

Claris rose from her place at the table, the crystal glass that had held her family's brandy for generations in her hand. In one fluid motion, she hurled it against the fireplace, where it shattered into pieces. Then she turned and walked out of the room. Carmona waited while her father followed. In the distance, a door slammed, her father's voice – aggressive and insistent – echoed through the hall.

Carmona bolted to her room, locking the door behind her. Without thinking, she grabbed her two best suitcases, started throwing clothes in them, and stopped. Now was not the time for impetuous behaviour. Careful thought was in order. Once Carmona left home, there would be no coming back. In the end, only the best pieces of clothing, those that were well made and would withstand the test of time, made their way into her cases.

As she packed, she planned. First, the car would be sold to the first dealer who offered a fair price. She recalled one man in particular who was a friend of her grandfather's. He would treat her fairly, of that she was certain. When she got to London, she would sell her fur, find a job, and a flat. After she packed as much as she could into the two cases, she grabbed a small valise from under her bed. This she filled with items that she would need for the next day or two.

Twenty minutes later, she tossed her suitcases out the window, loaded everything into her car and drove to Edythe's. She half expected her father to try to stop her, but she did not see him as she drove away. Avoiding the high street, she turned onto the lane which led through the woods and pulled onto the back of Edythe's property. *Please, Edythe, be home.* She parked the car in an overgrown layby, well hidden from the road. Secure in the knowledge her dad couldn't find her here, she left the car and crept up to the Hargreaves' house.

She didn't knock on the front door and let herself in as she usually did. Instead she crept around the side of the house – careful to duck as she passed windows – and found Edythe sitting on her bed, reading her dog-eared copy of *Lady Chatterley's Lover*. Carmona watched her friend for a moment, so beautiful, so peaceful, so at ease in her austere surroundings. How did Edythe manage to make the few things in her room appear so warm and inviting? She rapped on the window. Edythe looked up and smiled. She lifted the sash and leaned out.

'What are you doing here?'

'I'm actually running away from home. I'd be happy to tell you the sordid details, if you'd invite me in.'

'Sure. Come around to the front door.'

'I'd rather not have anyone know I'm here.'

Edythe stepped back. 'Can you climb in here?'

Carmona hoisted herself in through Edythe's window, coming to rest in a heap on the floor and tearing her skirt in the process.

'What's happened?' Edythe held out her hand. Carmona took it, allowing herself to be pulled to her feet.

Edythe sat down on the bed, pointing to the chair that sat next to it. 'Have a seat.'

Carmona sat. 'I need to tell you something. I've been a fool, and I've kept things from you. You're not going to like it. I told my mum and dad I wanted to go to medical school.'

Edythe sat up a little straighter. 'What? Oh, Carmona. I'm so sorry. How did they take it?'

'My mother was dead against it. We got into a horrible argument. I climbed out my window and went walking.' Edythe knew Carmona often took night walks when she couldn't sleep. 'On this particular walk, I encountered a man. He led me to believe he had loved me. For the first time in my life, I had someone who cared about me, who was willing to share my dreams and help me achieve something on my own.'

'Who was this man?' Edythe asked.

'Phillip.' She watched the emotion – shock, surprise, and realization – play across the familiar planes of Edythe's face. 'I'm a fool. I made more of the relationship than it really was. How desperate is that? He used me. Asked me for money, which I gave him. And then I saw him in the woods with bloody Miss Hinch. Miss Hinch. Can you even believe it?'

'Phillip? My cousin?' Edythe said. She stood and started pacing across her bedroom, her lovely hands clenched into fists. 'I'm so mad at him. I swear, I could kill him. You know he's been arrested?'

'My dad told me. There's more, Edythe.'

Edythe stopped pacing and stared at Carmona. 'More?'

'Last night I took Mrs Carlisle to my dad's office, to act as witness while I went through the accounts. The police came.' Carmona rubbed her face with her hand. She had never lost control like she did last night. She couldn't stop herself from hitting that smart-mouthed young man. He deserved it. And dear God, it felt good. When it was over, Carmona realized the gravity of what she had done. Her utter lack of control scared her to death.

'I hit one of them.'

Edythe gasped.

'I couldn't stop myself.' Carmona spoke quickly, as if to rush past her humiliation. 'Mrs Carlisle and I were taken to the constabulary. My father is furious. He revoked my privileges. He wants to take control of my money and sell my car. He's forbidden me

210

to see anyone he doesn't approve of. I'm leaving. I packed my suitcases – they are in the car, parked on the layby behind your house. I'm going to sell the car and put the money someplace where my father can't get to it. I'm finished with Rivenby, finished with my parents for the time being. I'm going to move to London as soon as I can.'

'You can stay here,' Edythe said.

Carmona shook her head. 'This is the first place my parents will look for me. Never mind that now.'

'Oh, Carmona.' Edythe sat down on the bed. She put her arm around Carmona. 'You've had a horrible time, haven't you?'

'It's been hell. You should see my mother. She's changed into a docile, compliant wife.' Carmona shuddered. 'Everything's falling apart. I'm on my own now, Edythe. It's all on me.'

'What are you going to do once you get to London?'

'Find a flat. Get a job.' Saying her plans out loud to Edythe gave Carmona strength.

'Did you find anything? You and Mrs Carlisle?'

Carmona shook her head. 'We went through records for about an hour. Not a mention of your family. You know how fastidious my dad is. There's got to be something. If he's been stealing, he'll have a record of it. I just wish I knew what I was looking for—'

'What about the safe?'

Carmona stared at Edythe. *How can I be so utterly without a brain? Of course, the safe.*

'You didn't look there, did you?'

'No,' Carmona whispered. 'But I'm going to. Tonight.'

'I'll go with you,' Edythe said.

'I don't know if you should. My dad is pretty angry at me. You might want to stay out of it.'

'Nonsense. I'll come with you and keep watch.'

'I'll need to stay out of my father's way. I'll search the safe and then leave for London tomorrow. Do you think I could stay here without your mum knowing?'

'Of course,' Edythe said. 'She never comes in here. If you keep quiet, she won't know the difference.'

'I don't think Phillip killed his mother,' Carmona said.

'Nothing about Phillip would surprise me,' Edythe said. 'He is so greedy, I can't even begin to explain. He never has enough money.'

'No,' Carmona interrupted her. 'He's too weak. Think about it. While I agree he is greedy, and I believe he would lie, cheat, and steal for money, he doesn't have the guts to kill someone. He'd run away first.'

'Are you saying you want to prove his innocence?' Edythe asked, her voice laced with a fair measure of incredulity and sarcasm.

'No. He can rot as far as I'm concerned.' Carmona walked to the window. She stared out at the Hargreaves' sloping lawn, and the hedgerow that blocked the house from the lane.

'I'll help you,' Edythe said.

Carmona turned to face her.

'We'll help each other,' Carmona said.

'And then we'll leave,' Edythe said.

'And then we'll leave. I'm not telling my parents I am here. As far as they are concerned, I'm gone.'

'Okay,' Edythe said. 'You can hide in my room until you sell your car. I'll even go with you. We can ride the train back, have a final dinner with my mum – she won't be happy, but she'll understand – and leave the next day. I'll sign up for the service in London.'

Carmona nodded. Edythe talked about the plan as if they had conjured a sure-fire way to resolve everything and leave Rivenby for good. Carmona wished she could be so certain things would work out. Her outlook on life, however, had been forever tainted thanks to Phillip's betrayal.

Edythe came to the window. She wove her arm through Carmona's. The two young women stood shoulder to shoulder.

Carmona – historically the stronger of the two – leaned on her friend.

'We're growing up, Carm,' Edythe said.

'I know,' Carmona whispered.

CHAPTER 18

For the first time since James Churchwright's death, Heart's Desire was quiet. Beck and the missus were in residence, but they stayed out of Thomas's way. He and Cat had spent a productive morning together, sketching out the idea of the chapter outline that would, eventually, become a book, discussing Cat's photo ideas, and mapping out the day trips they would take for research. Neither of them had mentioned David Broadbent or Phillip Billings. It seemed – thank the Gods – that Cat was doing her level best to stay out of trouble. Dusk fell as he capped his pen and set it on top of the sheaf of papers. He stood and stretched, massaging at the kink in his neck, ignoring the car that pulled into the driveway. The missus wasn't back from her daily shopping, but she had left Thomas a sandwich covered in a linen cloth on the kitchen worktop. He had just sat down to eat when Beck appeared.

'Gentleman to see you, sir. DS Wallace.'

'Sorry to bother you, sir, but you're needed down at the constabulary.' DS Wallace eyed the sandwich.

Dread washed over Thomas. He put the sandwich down and pushed the plate away, his appetite replaced by a knot in his stomach. Heart thumping, he said, 'What's happened? What's she done? Is she injured?'

'What are you talking about?' DS Wallace asked.

'Mrs Carlisle. I thought she—'

'This isn't to do with Mrs Carlisle. It's Phillip Billings. He's been arrested. We found a saw similar to the one used to tamper with the brakes in his mum's and Mr Churchwright's car. We also found cash and a packet of blank passports. Mr Billings says he's got proof that he didn't kill anyone, but he will only talk to you.'

'Very well,' Thomas said. 'I need to call Elliott Markham. He'll be interested in the passports.'

'He's already on his way,' DS Wallace said.

'How did the police come to search Billings' property?'

'Anonymous tip,' DS Wallace said.

'Isn't that convenient?' Thomas said. 'Bit too easy. The police received an anonymous tip to search the shed. Lo and behold, they discover the saw and the passports, not very well hidden.'

'I agree, sir,' DS Wallace said.

Cat's words floated into Thomas's mind. *You dismiss women's intuition. Call it illogical, female emotion.* Here he was, trusting in his own intuition, yet he was so quick to dismiss Cat's.

They found Elliott Markham and DCI Kent tucked away in Kent's office. Elliott Markham looked like he had been living rough. Dark stubble graced his chin and jaw. His eyes were bloodshot. Lines of exhaustion were etched around his mouth.

'Thomas,' he said.

DCI Kent nodded at Thomas and pointed to the empty chair next to DS Markham. 'Would you mind repeating your story, Mr Markham. Slower this time, please.'

Thomas didn't envy Elliott Markham's position. He listened as Elliott laid out the logic of his deductions, and the evidence to support his theory – albeit anecdotal at this point – and was impressed by his attention to detail and the articulate way in which he made his case. By the time Elliott had finished speaking, DCI Kent was on board with David Broadbent as the most likely suspect.

Elliott took a deep breath. He took a cigarette from his pocket and put it in his mouth. When DCI Kent offered him a light, Elliott shook his head.

'Thomas is aware of the passport scheme.' Elliott sat back and crossed his legs. 'I've now confirmed who the involved parties are. David Broadbent was seen a month ago, delivering blank passports to a man in Edinburgh a week later. In exchange he received a considerable sum of money.'

'Are you sure it's Broadbent?' Thomas asked.

'An operative took pictures. It's Broadbent all right.'

'If you're wrong about this, Markham, heads will roll. The Broadbents are not without influence.'

'If I'm wrong – and I am certain I'm not – I'll see that none of the blame falls to you or your men. Mr Broadbent is a small piece in this Fifth Column syndicate. We want the men at the top.'

'Why would he do this?' DS Wallace asked.

'Money,' Elliott Markham said. 'I've confirmed that Mr Broadbent mortgaged his wife's house without her knowing.'

'How could he do that without her signature?'

'By forging her name,' Elliott Markham said. 'He took a woman with him who claimed to be her. She signed for Mrs Broadbent. He's up to something.'

'I have something to add,' Thomas said. 'Cat Carlisle believes that David Broadbent has been embezzling from his clients. That's why she and Carmona were in her father's office. Apparently, Edythe Hargreaves was suspicious and confronted Carmona. Carmona was trying to get to the truth. She brought Cat – Mrs Carlisle – along as a witness.'

'Why are we just hearing about this now?' Elliott Markham didn't bother to hide his irritation.

'Because it's conjecture. She found no proof,' Thomas snapped.

'And the Broadbents are certainly not short of cash,' DS Wallace said.

'Well, wait a second,' Elliott Markham said. He stood and started to pace. 'We know that Mrs Broadbent has money, but what if her funds didn't flow to her husband? I wouldn't be surprised to find that James Churchwright kept his daughter's money protected from her husband.'

'Gentlemen ...' DCI Kent held up his hand. 'Let's stay focused and take our obstacles one at a time. Phillip Billings has insisted that he speak to Mr Charles. Let's see what he has to say. Agreed?'

***

In the end, Thomas spoke to Phillip alone. Phillip showed Thomas the letter that his mother wrote to James Churchwright. Win Billings – as was her custom – left no stone unturned when she investigated David Broadbent. She, too, had broken into his office, but she had got into the safe and discovered the second set of false ledgers, which depicted an accurate accounting of the money he had stolen. Two dozen blank passports were also in the safe, and at that time, she had reached out to Sir Reginald Wright, certain that David was going to sell them – probably to an inculcated group of German agents – for profit. Reginald had sent Elliott to Rivenby to investigate, without bothering to tell Thomas.

'I didn't murder anyone. I don't know anything about those passports.'

'Why didn't you come to the police immediately?' Thomas asked.

'DCI Kent wouldn't have believed me.'

'So you weren't planning on blackmailing David Broadbent?'

Phillip gave Thomas a pleading look. 'I just needed a little cash so I could get away and start over.'

'I think we need to bring Mr and Mrs Broadbent in.' Elliott Markham spoke to Thomas and DCI Kent. They had left DS Wallace in the room with Phillip. 'I don't mean arrest them, I mean bring them in under the guise of clearing up a few things. They know Phillip's been arrested. Everyone in the village knows that by now. David Broadbent should not know we suspect him of any wrongdoing. But let's bring them in and separate them. After they are here, I plan on tricking Mr Broadbent into a confession.'

'Trick David Broadbent into a confession?' DCI Kent didn't bother to hide the sarcasm in his voice. 'You realize David Broadbent is an intelligent, educated man? No disrespect, Markham, but I wouldn't bank on tricking him.'

'I'll get him to confess. We'll have your men search his safe for the second set of ledgers. If things go wrong, I'll take the blame.'

DCI Kent opened the door to his office. 'Constable, fetch DS Marshall. Stay with Mr Billings.'

DS Marshall came into the room. He nodded at Thomas and Elliott.

DCI Kent shut the door. 'I want you to pick up Mr and Mrs Broadbent and bring them in. Tell them Mr Billings has been arrested and we need their assistance to clear up a few questions. When they get here, separate them.'

'What? Sir—'

'I'll explain everything after you've got them.' DCI Kent handed the DS a set of keys. 'Use my car. Take Gibbons with you. Go now.'

'Yes, sir.'

After DS Marshall left, DCI Kent sat down at his desk. He picked up the telephone. 'They'll have my guts for garters if you're wrong.'

'I'm not wrong,' Elliott said.

CHAPTER 19

St Monica's attic took up the entire third floor. Furniture, rugs, broken china, and dubious pieces of art had accumulated over the centuries, along with an accompanying layer of dust and grime. Cat spent the better part of the afternoon going through it, organizing and cleaning as she went. Bede and Annie had offered to help, but Cat needed to be busy. It took all of her discipline not to go into the village in search of gossip about Phillip Billings' arrest. She thought about sending Bede on a reconnaissance mission, but her better judgement prevailed.

An old trunk lay in the corner. Inside she found a cache of toys and books including a beautiful doll, along with a complete wardrobe of clothes. The doll's hair was matted, her face grimy. The clothes smelled of mildew. Cat thought of the children coming from London, often with nothing more than a suitcase. Surely some child would appreciate this find.

'Mrs Carlisle?' Bede called out.

'I'm up here,' Cat said. She heard Bede's footsteps on the stairs. Soon she poked her head into the room. 'You need more light. You realize what time it is? You've been up here for hours.' Bede came all the way into the room. She eyed the neat rows of boxes and trunks, now dust free. 'And you've made good use of your time, I see.'

'I found these toys and books,' Cat said. 'I thought we could clean them up a bit and share them with the evacuee children.'

Bede opened the trunk. She fingered the dresses. 'They may as well be put to use. I'll take them downstairs and let them soak in sudsy water. Meanwhile, Emmeline Hinch is here to see you.'

'Tell her I'll be right down. I need to change my clothes. Can you give her tea or something?'

'Something's more like it,' Bede said. 'She's right upset. Looks like she's seen a ghost. I've got a fire going in the drawing room. I'll just put her there, if that suits.'

'Perfect. I'll be right down.' Cat changed her clothes, splashed water on her face, and re-pinned her hair. She found Emmeline Hinch in the drawing room, clutching a cup and staring at the fire.

'Miss Hinch?'

She jumped at Cat's voice.

'I didn't mean to startle you. Don't get up. Would you like a brandy?'

Miss Hinch nodded. Cat poured a generous dollop of brandy into her cocoa before she settled into a chair.

'What can I do for you?'

'You said it would all come crashing down. You said I could come to you. Here I am.' She spoke in a whisper. Her hand shook as she lifted the cup to her lips. 'We're in trouble, Phillip and I. He's been arrested for murder.'

'I heard.'

'He didn't kill anyone.' Miss Hinch downed her cocoa. She set the cup on the table and leaned back in the chair. Cat watched as the woman regained her composure. 'I am going to tell you a story, Mrs Carlisle. When I'm finished, I'm hoping you'll help us. I don't have anyone else to turn to.

'After I tell you the truth, you may not want to get involved.

220

I won't blame you for that. I've decided to tell the police every-thing I know. I've enough saved to get Phillip a lawyer, and me if I need one. I'm tired. Tired of the lies and the subterfuge.

'When David – David Broadbent, my employer – and Claris first started dating, James Churchwright took David aside. He told David he didn't think he was good enough for his daughter. But he told him if he and Claris married, and if David could keep Claris happy and content until their eldest child came of age, he would receive a legacy, a monetary gesture of goodwill. If Claris wasn't happy at the time the child came of age, David agreed he would give her a divorce, leave Rivenby, and never darken the Churchwright door again.

'Of course, David agreed. How could he not? He and Claris were in love, and David was tempted by the Churchwright money and influence.' Miss Hinch fussed with her skirt. 'Never under-estimate the corruptive power of money, Mrs Carlisle.

'I've worked for David since the beginning. He's a hard worker, but he never had quite enough money. Claris was used to having her way. The amount of money that woman spends would surprise you. She didn't bother to ask her husband what their financial situation was. She assumed he would support her in the manner to which she had become accustomed. Women can be so stupid. Ten years ago, I discovered David had been embezzling from clients. He convinced me that I was complicit too, since I managed the accounts. He offered me money to keep silent. A lot of money. I took it and bought my cottage. Now I'm guilty, too, you see?' She sat silent for a moment, her head bowed. Her shame emanated around her in waves. 'In any event, David intended to pay everyone back with the legacy from Mr Churchwright.

'When Carmona came of age, David approached his father-in-law about the money. Mr Churchwright laughed at him. Told him it was just a jape. He was just trying to motivate David to do well. That was in February. There were no funds to repay the clients. Creditors were growing impatient. David became desperate.'

'Why didn't he just go to Claris?' Cat asked. 'Surely she's got sufficient funds to help him?'

'He wouldn't dare. Claris would run to her father. He controls her money, you see.' Miss Hinch shook her head. 'No. That wouldn't have done. You didn't know James Churchwright. Win Billings found out what David was up to. She is so smart – was so smart. Three months ago, she approached me, told me she knew that David had been embezzling. I confessed my role – I had no choice. Win convinced me to cooperate with the police. I agreed.

'I'm sure David killed her. He knows about cars. I know Win Billings and James Churchwright were very good friends. It stands to reason she told him what she knew. In all likelihood, James Churchwright threatened to go to the police, or confronted him in some fashion. I'm sure David killed them both. I should have gone to the police. But I'm as guilty as David. I kept quiet for money.' She pinched the bridge of her nose, as she took a deep breath. 'I can't bear this anymore. I'm going to confess to my part. The police need to know they've got the wrong person. Phillip didn't do anything.'

'Is there any proof of David's embezzling scheme? He seems like a fastidious man. Surely he kept records.'

'He's kept track of everything. There's a second set of ledgers in the safe, along with one sheet of paper with a running balance of how much he owes each client.' Miss Hinch sniffed. 'We could go and get it, if you think it would help.'

'I think that's a good idea,' Cat said. 'Would you like me to go to the police with you?'

'Would you?'

'Of course. And I can certainly help you find a good solicitor, should you need it. Help yourself to more brandy. I'm going to grab my handbag.' Cat excused herself. She went into the kitchen and used the telephone to ring Thomas. She needed his help now.

No answer. She grabbed her handbag, anxious to get to Broadbent's office before Miss Hinch changed her mind.

CHAPTER 20

Carmona spent a quiet day pent up in Edythe's room, pacing the
floor and wondering about her future, while Edythe carried on
about her business. She half expected her mother to come
storming up to the front door and demand she return home
immediately, until she remembered her mother's actions earlier
and realized in all likelihood her mother wouldn't even miss her.
How could her mother have changed so quickly? Carmona understood the physical pangs of grief, especially in light of her
grandfather's murder. The ensuing anger and need for justice for
whoever murdered him gnawed at her relentlessly. Despite this,
Carmona still had the same virtues, the same flaws. Her mother's
metamorphosis boggled the mind.

Mrs Hargreaves hummed in the kitchen. The smell of warm
sweet biscuits and scones permeated the house. Carmona
imprinted these sensations, along with the way the light came in
the windows and the chip in the floor where she had dropped a
pail of seashells years ago into her memory. This house was
imprinted in Carmona's heart. She would miss Mrs Hargreaves
and her gentle ways.

The girls set out on foot just as the sun went down. The old
solidarity between them – missing since Carmona had fallen for

Phillip – had returned. They moved in quiet communication, both of them expectant, nervous, and more than a little afraid. She expected to feel the tug of nostalgia as she walked past the stationer's, the dressmaker's, the land agent. These buildings – and the people that inhabited them – had formed the backbone of Carmona's life. These were the people who knew her history, knew her as a child. *They won't know me in my shame.* Phillip's betrayal still stung, even though she no longer had feelings for him. Her father had said everyone in the village knew of their midnight trysts. How could they not? This was Rivenby. Everybody knew everything about everybody. How naive Carmona had been to think she was exempt from this credo. Thank God she would never have to show her face here again.

'Are you all right?' Edythe asked. 'You've been so quiet.'

'I'm fine. Ready to be finished with this.'

'Are you going to leave tomorrow morning?'

'Maybe. It depends on what we find. If you're right, I need to see things get sorted with the police. I'm also afraid to leave my mum.' They approached her father's office, ducked into the doorway which hid them from prying eyes. Carmona took the key out of her pocket. 'I'd like to get the car sold tomorrow. Then I can find a place to live.'

'You could take your mum with you,' Edythe suggested. 'Just a thought. Maybe it would do her good to get her away.'

Carmona felt the weight of the world pressing on her shoulders. Could she get her mother to come with her? So much hinged on what they discovered at her father's office. If he embezzled from his clients … Carmona pushed that thought away.

'It'll be all right, Carm. Why don't you just stay with us for a few days? Just wait a bit and see what happens. That way you don't have to spend your money on a place to live.'

'I'll think about it.'

'I don't blame you for what your father may have done. I want you to know that.'

'I know. And if it turns out you are right, I just want you to know I am so dreadfully sorry.' She opened the door. The girls stepped into the outer office. 'Let's leave the lights off in here, just so we don't attract any attention. Do you mind tucking yourself into the corner alcove out there? You can see out the window. If someone comes into the office, they won't see you. If my father comes, move close to the door. If you need to, get the police.'

'I wish I'd never started this,' Edythe said.

'Too late.'

'How will you get out? If he comes in this door, you'll be trapped.'

'Let's hope I'm not in danger from my own dad. Don't worry. I'll climb out the window if I have to.' She saw the fear reflected in her friend's eyes. 'Are you sure you want to do this? I'll be okay on my own.'

By way of an answer, Edythe tucked herself into the corner alcove, out of sight.

Carmona moved into her father's office, flicking on the banker's light on his desk. She stood for a moment, reliving a childhood filled with summers spent working here, filing, banging away on the typewriting machine with two fingers, anything to be near to her father. She had entertained the notion of becoming a solicitor, but her mother had put the kibosh on that idea the minute Carmona put it into words. She had grown up loving her father, a soft gentle buffer against her mother's hard edges.

This is not the time for sentiment. She girded herself to the possibility her father – a paragon of virtue in Carmona's mind – could very well be up to criminal activity. Squatting down before the safe, she twirled the dial left, twice right, and left again, hoping her father hadn't changed the combination. He hadn't. With a click the door sprung open.

Her father used the safe to keep confidential client documents, her mother's good jewels, deeds, money for emergencies, along with an old service revolver her father had brought home with him in 1919 when he returned from the war. The gun was gone – thank goodness. Carmona hated guns. A box lay on top of the pile. Carmona took it out, set it on the floor, and started to rummage through the loose papers. She picked up a musty ledger book and fanned its pages. An unsealed envelope fell to the floor.

She fumbled with the flap as she removed a folded sheet of paper, worn at the creases. Her father's tight perfect penmanship covered the page. Carmona read the names of village residents, Swyndale, Banders, Maxwell, Hargreaves. Each name had a date, the words *amount due*, and a figure written next to it. The names were written in pen, but the dates and the amounts due were written in pencil. Some of the figures had been crossed out with a new figure – always higher – written next to it.

Edythe was right. Her father had been stealing from his clients. Carmona ran her eyes down the figures, coming up with a sizable amount of money he had stolen over the years. This would ruin her family. Her mother would have to get involved, as her money would be needed to settle the accounts with these people. Would her father go to prison? The magnitude of what he had done washed over Carmona, an unexpected tsunami that would destroy her family's standing in the village. She was leaving. For good. Her mum, so beleaguered and embattled with grief, wouldn't be able to cope. How could she leave her to face this alone? She couldn't. Her mum would have to come with her; otherwise, there would be no move to London. There would be no medical school.

She folded the sheet of paper into the envelope and tucked it into the pocket of her skirt. She picked up the box and set it on her father's desk. Inside were stacks of passports. She reached a hand out and opened one. It was blank, pristine. Carmona knew the significance of this find. She scoured the newspapers and had read about the Nazi sympathizers who were laying the ground work for the invasion – if it came. What a perfect scheme to get German agents into the country, undetected. She recoiled. 'Oh, my God.'

She felt her father's presence before she heard his words. 'That's our ticket out of this mess, Carm.'

She wheeled around. He stood in the doorway, dressed in the grubby clothes he wore when he worked in the garden. He carried a can of petrol in one hand and his gun in the other. The gun – thank God – was pointed at the ground. At least the man looked like Carmona's father, same height, build, but the soul behind the eyes belonged to a stranger.

'What mess, Dad?' Her voice came out in a whisper. She thought she heard Edythe's footsteps outside the door.

'I'll explain everything later,' he said. 'You've found the pass-ports, I see.'

'You've been swindling from your clients. Taking money from our friends and neighbours. How will Mum hold her head up? You'll go to prison.' Carmona didn't recognize her own voice. God help her, she sounded like her mother.

'This isn't my fault.'

'Not your fault? Is that the best argument you've got? You've committed treason. You've been stealing—'

'I needed the money. I borrowed from clients. Borrowed. Nothing more. All would have been fine, if your grandfather had honoured his word. He didn't. I had to find a way to pay people back.'

Carmona stood still, as though her feet were riveted to the ground. She watched, unable to move, as her father went to the window. He pushed the curtains aside and opened it wide. Her father took the can of the petrol and started pouring it over the drapes. He moved towards Carmona, drizzling petrol on the floor as he did so.

'You killed them. You killed Grandfather and Win.' Carmona

felt her eyes well with tears. She sensed movement outside the office, heard the door shut as Edythe let herself out. If her father was aware of Edythe in the foyer, he didn't let on.

'I had to. Win discovered what I was up to – meddling old bitch. It was easy enough to tamper with her brakes.'

'And Grandfather?'

Her father continued, as if he hadn't heard her. 'I wasn't sure she told anyone, but I should have known better. She and your grandfather were in cahoots. She told him, gave him copies of the evidence she had against me. He threatened me. Told me he was going to the police. But first he had to see that you and your mother were away from the village. He couldn't bear the idea of the two of you facing the scandal.' He shook his head. 'God, I hated him.'

'So you tampered with his brakes too?'

He laughed. 'And put the saw and a few of those passports in Phillip Billings' shed.' His face became tender. 'I had to avenge you, Carm. Phillip Billings made a fool out of you. I couldn't have that. Once I deliver those' – he nodded at the box of pass-ports – 'I'll have the means to settle everything. We'll leave, go somewhere where no one knows us, America maybe.'

'Who are you selling them to?'

'It doesn't matter, Carmona. All that matters is the money.' Her father gazed off into the distance, his eyes glazed, his pupils a pinprick. Carmona wondered if he was on drugs. 'He promised me a legacy after twenty years of marriage, if I could keep your mother happy.' He laughed, a dry croak which held no mirth. 'Keep your mother happy. God, that's absurd. Your mother was never happy. Nothing was ever enough. I wasn't enough. She reminded me of my shortcomings every day. I would have left her, if you hadn't come along. Do you know how much money your mother spends on clothes, food, linens, flowers, nonsense? She had to keep up appearances, you see.'

'Dad, we'll get through this. Mum won't want a scandal. We'll make her see reason.' She edged towards the door. She had the proof she needed. She had always been a fast runner.

He set the petrol can down and walked over to her.

'The police know I'm here. You need to tell them what you've done. Mum will help you. It will be fine.' He was getting closer to her now. She moved around to the front of the desk. He parried and blocked her way. She should have been frightened. She should have recoiled or ran. Instead – in typical Carmona fashion – she got angry. White hot fury started at her feet and vibrated up her body until her scalp tingled from it. Her hands clenched into fists. She launched herself at him.

She pounded and pummelled, sobbing while she beat him. He recoiled, blocking his face while she gave into her all-consuming primordial anger. He never hit her back. The gun stayed pointed to the ground. Later she would wonder why he didn't shoot her. When her rage was spent, Carmona stood facing her father, heaving like a beast of burden, tears streaming down her cheeks.

He looked at her with those blank, soulless eyes. 'You were always a little headstrong, Carmona. I've changed my mind. I'll not be bringing you with me. I'm sorry I can't let you see this through to the end.'

He's going to kill me.

He smiled a little as he stepped close and backhanded her across the face so hard she fell to the ground, hitting her head on the floor. Everything went black.

CHAPTER 21

By the time Cat and Miss Hinch reached David Broadbent's office, Miss Hinch had filled in all the details of David Broadbent's embezzlement scheme, driven by Claris Churchwright Broadbent's insatiable craving for social position and power in the village.

'I'm going to help you, Miss Hinch,' Cat said.

Miss Hinch walked beside Cat, rigid with determination. 'I don't deserve help. I committed a crime. I need to pay for what I've done.'

'We'll see about—'

Miss Hinch had just taken a ring of keys out of her handbag when Edythe burst out of David Broadbent's office.

'Edythe?' Cat said.

'He's in there – he's got Carmona. Petrol. Gun.' Edythe gasped. She was shivering.

'Stop,' Cat said. She put her hands on the girl's shoulders. Edythe wrested away.

'I'm going for the police.' Edythe bolted.

'Maybe we should wait for the police. If he's got a gun ...' Cat said. But Miss Hinch was already in the office.

Cat followed her, catching the end of Carmona's rage as she

231

pummelled her father. David Broadbent didn't notice Cat and Miss Hinch as they stood by, helpless to do anything until Carmona's tirade ended. When he knocked Carmona to the ground, Cat and Miss Hinch gasped in unison. David Broadbent turned to face them.

'What are you doing here, Miss Hinch?'

'I've come to get evidence of your malfeasance.'

Cat hurried over to Carmona. She made a feeble attempt to check her pulse. Carmona moaned.

'You're okay,' Cat whispered to her. 'Stay still. The police are on the way.'

'What are you going to do? Take it to the police? You're as guilty as I am, Emmeline. You benefited from this crime, too.'

'I am well aware of that, David. You've reminded me daily over the past ten years.'

'You'll go to prison.' David Broadbent emptied the petrol can, pouring it around his desk, splashing it on the books and client files in the bookcase. He tossed the empty can aside and went to the desk.

'I'm prepared to pay for what I've done.'

He put the top on the box that held the passports, scooped it up and tucked it under his arm. He trained the gun on Emmeline. 'Go over there.' He waved the gun at Carmona and Cat.

'No,' Miss Hinch said. 'I'm tired of you telling me what to do. Go ahead and shoot me, David. I couldn't care less.'

He pointed the gun to the ceiling and fired.

In a surprising show of strength, Miss Hinch remained calm as she walked over to Cat and Carmona.

Carmona moaned. Cat helped her sit up.

'I'm going to mourn the daughter who betrayed my family. Claris will be shaken when she discovers Carmona and you were embezzling from my firm. I'll take her away from here. Maybe we'll sell everything and go to America. Such a shame you three had to perish while trying to destroy the evidence.' He walked

232

over to the office door, took a key out of his pocket, and locked them all inside.

With the turn of the key, Cat realized that he intended to burn them alive. They would perish in the fire and Thomas would never know she loved him. Why wasn't Miss Hinch concerned? She prattled on, impervious to their fate.

Miss Hinch snorted. 'No one will ever believe that, and you know it.'

'Doesn't matter, Miss Hinch,' David Broadbent said. 'By the time the police sift through the ashes, I'll be long gone.'

A sheen of sweat broke out over Cat's back and shoulder blades. What did one do in the event of fire? *Aside from scream and cry.*

'Wait,' Cat cried. Laying Carmona's head back on the floor, she stood and approached David Broadbent, stepping between him and Miss Hinch. 'Are you sure you want to do this? You'll hang.'

'Don't be an idiot, Mrs Carlisle. No one will catch me.'

'Thomas Charles will.' As Cat said the words, she took comfort in them. Forcing herself to speak with a confidence that she did not feel, she continued. *Keep him talking.* 'He's ruthless, Mr Broadbent. He'll hunt you down and see you hang for your crimes. Murdering your own daughter. You should be ashamed of yourself.'

'Ashamed of myself?' His face paled with rage. He stepped towards Cat, but caught himself and gave her a sly smile. He pointed at her. 'I know what you're doing, Mrs Carlisle. Shame on you. Trying to keep me talking?'

'Something like that,' Cat said. 'The police will be here before long.'

'Now we both know that's not true, don't we?'

'You're an idiot, Mr Broadbent. Edythe Hargreaves was outside the whole time. She was going for the police when we got here—'

'Mrs Carlisle—' Hinch interrupted.

'And even if you burn us alive, Edythe knows everything. What

233

are you going to do, kill her too? I assure you, you won't get away with this.'

David Broadbent tossed the box containing the passports out the window. Emmeline Hinch grabbed his leg, trying to pull him back in.

'Let go of me, you cow,' he said. With a strong kick he sent her flying backwards, where she landed with a thump. Straddling the windowsill, he pulled a gold lighter out of his pocket. The click of the ignition seemed to happen in slow motion. In one fell swoop he tossed the lighter in the direction of the curtains. With a *whoosh* they went up in flames. Cat swore she heard him say, 'Goodbye, ladies,' before he climbed out the window.

The fire ignited and spread like a chain of dominoes. It followed the trail of petrol that David Broadbent had traced around his desk, over the chairs, and onto the bookcases that held the client files, deeds, and the account books. By some stroke of luck, he had forgotten to pour the petrol by the locked door. Noxious smoke stung Cat's nostrils. She gagged as she jumped over the licking flames, trying to get to Carmona. Hinch tried to speak, but the sound of the flames sucked the words out of the room and consumed them.

'Stay down,' Hinch screamed over the roar of the fire as she dropped to the ground. 'I've got keys. We need to crawl to the door. Stay down to avoid the smoke.' A flame licked at the hem of her skirt.

'Hinch.' Cat pointed. Hinch pounded the flame out with her hand.

'Carmona, you must crawl,' Cat said. 'Go first. I'll be right behind you.'

She crouched down, the grit of the rug digging into her knees. Carmona tried to hoist herself onto all fours, but toppled over. By some unspoken agreement, Cat and Hinch each took one of Carmona's arms and dragged her to the door.

'When I open this door, the fire is going to travel towards the oxygen. You have to get her out fast, so I can shut the door. We won't have much time. Do you understand?'

Cat nodded.

Hinch held her breath and stood into the cloud of smoke, her upper body encased in the black of it. When she opened the door, the fire raged closer to them. Cat bent down and grabbed Carmona under her armpits. The bookcase was an inferno, the fire a pulsating source of roaring energy. The can that held the petrol exploded, along with the glass lamps that sat on the credenza. Holding her breath, she dragged Carmona out into the foyer. Hinch followed, shutting the thick oak door behind them. The latch engaged. Thick smoke furled out of the office, hanging thickly in the air once the door was shut.

'Let's get out of here,' Hinch said. 'Carmona, you need to stand up and try to walk.' With a strength driven by the will to survive, Cat and Hinch managed to pull Carmona to her feet. She put an arm around each of their shoulders, and the three women hobbled out of the office.

When they burst onto the walkway and into the clean night air, the sound of popping glass filled the night.

Anxious to get away from the burning building, Cat practically carried Carmona over to the green.

She heard someone say, 'Look, there!' before she lost consciousness.

CHAPTER 22

DS Wallace knocked on DCI Kent's office. 'Mrs Broadbent's here, sir. She wasn't happy at being forced to come in.'

'And Mr Broadbent?' Elliott Markham asked.

'Not at home. She doesn't know where he is.'

'Very well,' DCI Kent said. 'Markham, it's your funeral. You do the talking.'

Claris Broadbent sat at the table, an unlit cigarette hanging from her mouth. Her clothes were clean, and her hair was washed, but she smelled of drink, expensive cognac in particular. She looked at Thomas with bloodshot eyes. He recalled the hale and hearty woman who ushered him to her father's home when he first arrived in Rivenby. Now Claris's face had a gaunt look, a physical manifestation of grief, exhaustion, and lack of food.

'What's the meaning of this? You've no right to bring me here without my husband. He's a solicitor, you know.'

'Look, lady,' Elliott Markham said.

Thomas shook his head. He sat down near Claris Broadbent. She gave him a startled look, as if realizing he was there for the first time. 'And what are you doing here? Are you some sort of policeman? I insist on seeing your credentials. I knew you would bring trouble. I've lost my father. My daughter is trying to get away from me. My husband ...' Her eyes filled with tears. She stared at her lap, unable to finish the sentence.

Careful to keep his voice calm, Thomas said, 'Mrs Broadbent, where is your husband? We really need to speak to him. Once we talk to him, we should be able to clear things up and you can go home.'

She gave Thomas a befuddled look. When she spoke, her voice was tremulous. 'I don't know where he is.'

'Mrs Broadbent,' Thomas spoke in a gentle voice, 'you know Phillip Billings has been arrested. We just want to ask you a couple of questions, just so we can clarify a few points. It won't take long. When we're finished, we'll drive you home. I know things have been difficult for you. I'll try to get this taken care of as quickly as possible.'

Claris nodded. She wouldn't meet Thomas's eyes. 'Thank you.'

He handed her a handkerchief. She dabbed at her eyes.

'Would you like tea? Maybe something to eat? DS Marshall could find something.'

'No.' Claris responded to his gentle voice. 'I'm sorry. Things have just been ...'

Thomas wondered for a moment what she was going to say about how things had been. Careful to keep his voice quiet, he spoke. 'Tell me about your daughter's relationship with Phillip Billings. Do you know what their plans were?'

'Relationship? My daughter has been given to fanciful imaginings, Mr Charles. I assure you, there was no relationship.'

'I understand. He's not exactly worthy of Carmona.'

'Of course he's not.'

'When did you last see your husband?'

'I don't know. He was gone when I woke up. I've taken to napping lately—' Claris looked up, startled by the question. 'What is all this? I get the feeling you're not being honest with me, Mr Charles. What can I possibly tell you about Phillip Billings?' Her voice rose in anger. 'I demand to know why I am here. Why do you want my husband?'

Thomas ignored her questions. 'Where's Carmona?'

'Gone. She and my husband had a horrible row. She packed as much as she could carry and drove away in her car. She probably went to Edythe's. Those two were always thick as thieves.'

'Aren't you worried about her?'

'Honestly, no. Carmona is very resilient. And smart. She can take care of herself.'

Thomas rose. 'I think we're close to being finished, Mrs Broadbent. I'll see about getting someone to take you home. Would you mind waiting here? I'm sure DS Marshall can get you some tea.'

'I'll wait. I don't want anything.'

'DS Wallace is going to stay here with you, Mrs Broadbent,' DCI Kent said. 'Thank you for coming down. I'll send you home in a few minutes, all right?'

'Of course. Thank you.' Claris Broadbent's hand shook as she took the cigarette out of her mouth.

Elliott Markham and Thomas stood in the corridor.

'That was a waste of time.'

'She doesn't know anything,' Thomas said. 'She doesn't even know where he is. I think finding Broadbent should be a priority.'

'Agreed,' DCI Kent said. 'I'll get my men on that. Give me a minute, and we'll meet in my office to decide what to do next. I don't like that David Broadbent is missing—'

They were interrupted by the hysterical sound of a young girl's shrill voice at the front desk.

'It's David Broadbent. He's got Carmona. Miss Hinch and Mrs Carlisle are there, too.'

DCI Kent, Elliott, and Thomas broke into a run at the same time. They skidded to a stop – nearly knocking each other over – just as Edythe said, 'And he's got a gun.'

238

Edythe looked at them with wild eyes. Her breath came in short gasps. 'Hurry!'

Thomas ran out the door at a sprint, ignoring the slicing pain in his shoulder, thanking heaven above David Broadbent's office was within running distance. He sensed rather than saw Elliott Markham on his heels for a moment, but Markham ducked down a side street and disappeared. A crowd had gathered outside David Broadbent's office. A constable was trying to keep them away from the building. 'Move back. Make room for the fire brigade.' Thomas heard the sirens in the distance. Fear pushed him as he sprinted towards the building, towards Cat.

He skidded to a stop at the door just as Cat, Carmona, and another woman whom Thomas didn't recognize burst onto the walkway. The crowd gave a collective gasp. Thomas felt his heart stop for a moment and then leap into his stomach. Carmona Broadbent had an arm draped across Cat's shoulders. Cat all but carried her over to the green away from the fire. After Cat eased Carmona to the ground, her knees gave way, and she collapsed onto the grass next to Carmona. Thomas ran to her, reaching her side just as the windows started to pop, shattering from the heat, releasing acrid plumes of smoke into the night air.

'Cat,' Thomas cried out. He grabbed her with his good arm. She smelled of smoke and fear. Crouching down next to her, he cradled her head in his lap.

'I love you, Thomas. I thought I was going to die without you knowing.' Her eyelids fluttered shut. 'We need a medic,' Thomas shouted. A man hurried over, medical bag in hand.

'Move over, man, so I can tend to her.' Reluctantly Thomas scooted away.

A black saloon skidded to a stop. DS Marshall, DCI Kent, Edythe and a befuddled looking Claris Churchwright got out of the car. Edythe and Claris ran over to Carmona. Claris fell to the ground and took her daughter into her arms.

'Carmona, talk to me,' Claris said, her voice frantic.

Edythe gazed at Cat. She was awake now, sitting up, while the doctor checked her over.

'She'll be all right,' the man said.

The doctor moved over to Carmona, who had pushed herself into a sitting position. She rubbed her head where it hit the floor. 'I may be a bit concussed.'

'What happened to Carmona?' Thomas asked.

'He hit her. Knocked her to the ground. She hit her head when she fell.'

Elliott Markham came around the far side of the building, dragging David Broadbent – whose arms and legs flailed as he tried to escape – by the collar of his coat.

'I haven't done anything,' David said. 'My daughter and my secretary have been stealing. Let me go.'

Claris Broadbent disentangled herself from Carmona and stood. She walked towards her husband. A hush fell over the crowd.

When Claris spoke, her voice rang clear and true. 'My God, David, what have you done?'

David Broadbent looked at Claris with a hatred so pure, even Thomas – who had fought in the trenches and lived to tell about it – was taken aback. David Broadbent stopped struggling and fell limp in Elliott Markham's grasp, diminished and defeated. Elliott made the mistake of releasing his grasp.

Cat cried out, 'Don't let him go!'

Too late. David Broadbent wriggled out of Elliott's grasp and ran back to the burning building, charging into the flames.

Claris covered her mouth with her hand, her eyes riveted on the horror as it played out before her.

Carmona stood. On wobbly feet she chased after her father, but fell to her knees after a few steps. When the roof caved in, sending flames shooting into the sky, her scream rent the night.

CHAPTER 23

The next morning, Thomas drove to St Monica's to escort Miss Hinch to the police station. Despite DCI Kent's protestations, Miss Hinch had been left in Cat's care, after securing a promise she would arrive promptly at 9 a.m. to give a detailed statement of the events leading up to last night's fiasco. Cat explained how Miss Hinch had saved their lives. The smell of smoke still lingered over the whole village. Thomas avoided the high street. He could only imagine what the gossip mavens were up to.

True to her word, Cat and Miss Hinch were ready when he pulled up. They came out of the house and got into the car without a word. Miss Hinch held her handbag rigidly on her lap and stared straight ahead. When Thomas pulled his car to the constabulary, DS Marshall met the car. He nodded at Thomas as he opened the door.

'Miss Hinch can come with me now.' He offered an arm to her.

'I'm coming too,' Cat spoke from the backseat.

'I'm sorry, ma'am. No one will be allowed into the room except DCI Kent and Elliott Markham.'

'Nonsense,' Cat said. 'She is not going—'

'Thank you, Mrs Carlisle. It's all right. I just want to get this over with.' Miss Hinch got out of the car and followed DS Marshall into the building.

'Ring my house when you're finished with her,' Cat said to DS Marshall. 'If I don't hear from you in two hours, I'm getting her a solicitor.'

Cat and Thomas sat in the car for a few minutes, neither of them speaking, each of them reflecting on the events of the past twenty-four hours.

'Do you think they will be fair with her?' Cat asked.

'I do. It's obvious Broadbent forced her to work with him. Her story is too far-fetched to be made up. Carmona's list supports her position.'

'Do you think they will charge her with a crime?'

'We'll have to wait and see.' Thomas put the car in gear.

They passed the morning pretending to read the newspaper. Neither one of them could focus. Cat kept watching the clock, ready to start calling solicitors if they didn't hear from DS Marshall. Fifty minutes had passed when they received the phone call saying Emmeline Hinch was free to go and Phillip would be set free later that afternoon.

Miss Hinch didn't speak until she was safely tucked into Thomas's car and on her way back to St Monica's, where Bede had lunch waiting for them.

'They are not going to charge me with a crime. I'm going to sell my cottage and give the money back. That's the fair thing to do. I know you must think I'm silly, letting myself love Phillip. He's a scoundrel, I know that. But I love him. He needs to be taken in hand. With love and looking after, his good will shine through.' She looked from Thomas to Cat, as though seeking approval. 'You see, we're to be married. As soon as possible. We'll live in Phillip's cottage. I think I'm going to start a secretarial school. I've always had good business sense. Why not pass that along?'

'What a splendid idea,' Cat said.

After lunch, Thomas made his excuses and left the women to their plans for Miss Hinch's future. Cat, of course, offered financial help in exchange for a stake in the business. He had his own future to worry about. Sir Reginald would require a detailed explanation of the events of the past few days. Thomas decided to submit his report in writing. The sooner it was in the post, the better. Sir Reginald would not be happy with the chain of events nor with Cat's involvement. Thomas didn't care.

CHAPTER 24

The morning after the fire, Carmona woke up with a banging headache. The hideous image of her father running into the flames played over and over in her mind's eye. Did she drive her father to his death? Would her mother ever forgive her? How in the world would she pick up the pieces of this shattered life?

Her mother rapped once on the door and came into the room carrying a tea tray and two cups.

'Mum?' Carmona couldn't keep the surprise from her voice.

'Don't get up.' She watched as her mother set the tray on the desk and poured steaming cups for both of them. She sat down next to Carmona on the bed, an intimate gesture that took Carmona back. 'We need to talk about our future, how we want to go forward.'

One lone tear spilled onto Claris's cheek. 'Your father never loved me. He wanted my family's money and influence. Everyone could probably see that but me. I've been such a fool.'

Carmona set her teacup down. She took her mother's hand.

'I've wasted my life, Carmona. I don't want you to waste yours. If you want to go to medical school in January, you can, with my blessing. I'll buy you a house in London and do everything I can to help you.'

A lump formed in Carmona's throat.

'I've been so horrible to you all these years. I've bullied you, tried to make you into something you're not.' Claris's teacup rattled in its saucer. She set it on Carmona's nightstand. 'Can you ever forgive me?'

Carmona knew that she and her mother were at a crossroads, and how she responded at this moment would affect her for the rest of her life. Her father was gone from them. Her mother was the only family she had left. Her mature self knew that her mother deserved a second chance – everyone did.

'I already have.'

Claris opened her arms. Carmona leaned in, and for the second time in Carmona's life, her mother held her.

Later that afternoon, Carmona was sitting at her father's desk, a stack of paperwork in front of her, when Phillip came in carrying a bouquet of flowers.

'Hello?'

'What are you doing here?'

'I've come to apologize to you.'

Carmona set her pen down and stared at him. *Is he serious?* Gone was the cocksure arrogance. Gone was the devil may care attitude. Now Phillip was just an average looking middle-aged man. Before long, his lean athletic body would thicken and the blond hair – already thinning on the top – would recede. *Whatever did I see in him?*

'Come in,' Carmona said.

'I knew you had feelings for me, Carmona. I took advantage of you. I'll pay you back the money you gave me, I promise.' He held out the flowers. 'These are a peace offering.'

'Thank you.' Carmona took the flowers and set them on the desk.

'I don't expect you to forgive me right away. I treated you terribly.'

'What will you do, Phillip?'

'I'm going to marry Emmeline Hinch and work at that school of hers. Mrs Carlisle is putting up the money to get it started. There will be scholarships for people who can't afford tuition. Emmeline's beside herself. She's busy planning and organizing. I've never seen her so happy.' Phillip smiled sheepishly. 'I might surprise everyone and turn out to be a businessman after all. We're getting married.'

'Do you love her?' Carmona asked.

'We've been friends for a long time. Emmeline seems to see the good in me,' Phillip said. 'Goodbye, Carmona. I hope you go to medical school. You'll make a good doctor.' She let him kiss her cheek and watched as he walked out of the house and out of her life.

CHAPTER 25

Summer officially arrived in Rivenby, bringing with it sunshine and clear skies. The morning air still held its chill, but by noon the sky was bright and the air was warm. Families picnicked on the village green, while children played outside.

Cat didn't know why Thomas had summoned her so urgently to Heart's Desire, but something in his tone caused her to take extra care with her appearance. He had rung the previous night, with the cryptic message that he had something to do and he wanted her to bear witness. She put on her best suit, a new hat and matching gloves, and set out on the bike she had salvaged from the old barn.

The late morning sun warmed her back. The day would be fine, bright with sunshine but tempered by the brisk northern air. The high street was the quickest route. As she rode along, people waved and smiled at her. It seemed as though the people of Rivenby had accepted her back into the fold. She got off the bike at the gate, surprised to see a taxi parked in front. Cat tucked her bike around the side of the house and approached the front door. She had just raised her hand to knock, when Beck answered.

'They are just in the drawing room. If you'll follow me.'

'Thank you,' Cat said.

Beck held the drawing-room door open for her. Thomas grinned when he saw her.

'Here she is.' He stood and walked up to her. His guest sat hidden in the winged chair, which faced the fireplace. Thomas beckoned her to sit next to him. She sat down, surprised to see Sir Reginald, surveying her with his usual smirk. Once upon a time they had been very good friends. But Reginald had used her. Now she didn't trust him.

'Hello, Catherine,' Sir Reginald said.

'Hello.' Cat looked at Thomas, and back at Sir Reginald. Why was she here?

'Thank you for coming,' Thomas said.

'Now you can explain why you've dragged me to this godforsaken place. You know the rules, Thomas. I don't travel. You come to me. I am interested in the details of how you botched this investigation. There's a building burned down, a man's dead—'

'No,' Thomas said. 'I'm doing the talking. You're going to listen. Cat's here because I want her to hear me say this to you. I'm finished. Finished with you, finished with your orders and your unreasonable demands. I'm tired, Reginald. The game doesn't suit me anymore.'

Sir Reginald looked at Cat, not bothering to hide his feelings for her. 'I suppose this is your doing. You've bewitched him, haven't you? Have you kissed him? Told him you love him?'

'Say one more word about her and I'll give you a beating, old man,' Thomas said. 'This has nothing to do with her. This is all me.'

'I don't accept your resignation, Thomas.' Sir Reginald stood. He took his time tending to his hat and his ridiculous driving gloves. He took his cane and sauntered out of the room. When he reached the door, he turned to Thomas. 'If I need you, I'll call.'

When the sound of the taxi's engine faded into silence, Cat spoke. 'I hope you didn't do that for me.' She walked over to the window. Thomas followed, coming to rest next to her. She stepped close to him, so their arms were touching. 'Don't you think you'll be bored? I know you like writing, but is it enough?'

'Turns out there's a shortage of policemen due to the war. DCI Kent has offered me a job. Claris has offered to rent me Heart's Desire for a reasonable price, so I'll have a place to live—'

'You're going to be a policeman?'

'No,' Thomas said. 'I'm going to do investigations for him, help out when I can. We've come to a rather nice arrangement, actually. I'll still be able to write books, be involved in investigations, and I won't have to deal with Sir Reginald.'

Cat smiled up at him. 'What a perfect solution.'

Their eyes locked. Thomas reached up and touched Cat's cheek. She felt her body respond as she turned to face him.

'I love you, Cat. You know that, don't you? I'm sorry to have pressurized you about us. You can set the pace. We can take it slowly—'

'Thomas ...' she rose up onto her tiptoes and wrapped her arms around his neck.

'Yes,' he said.

'Stop talking.'

She kissed him.

Acknowledgements

Many hands helped this book morph from an idea into the second instalment of the Cat Carlisle series. Heartfelt thanks to the following people, who have supported me on my writing journey: Angela Baxter, Kim Laird, Gloria Rowland, Ann Croucher, and Janet Robinson read through first drafts of the book, making sure I kept Cat Carlisle on her interesting – albeit troublesome – path. In addition to beta reading, Janet Robinson, a professional tour guide, is a never-ending font of knowledge regarding historical and modern-day London. Saul Baxter deserves a special thanks for his mechanical knowledge, especially tampering with the brakes of an old car. Kathleen Featherstone – a retired police officer – helped me out with info about the status of roads in the 1940s. Annie Whitehead, historical novelist and doyenne of all things Anglo-Saxon has a fabulous blog, which I turn to regularly to add depth to my research. (You can visit Annie's blog here: https://anniewhitehead2.blogspot.com/) Charles Yarbrough, Starkville Fire Chief, gets a special thanks for helping me learn about fire and the way it chases oxygen. Special thanks to Nia Beynon, editor extraordinaire, who pushed me to grow as a writer in ways I've never dreamed. Thanks to my husband, Doug, for his never-ending inspiration, encouragement, and support. I would never have been able to fulfil this dream without him. Most importantly, thanks to all the readers who have read my books and taken the time to review them. When I start a new project and sit down to an empty screen, I set to work with you in mind.

#ReaderLove

Dear Reader,

Thank you so much for taking the time to read this book – we hope you enjoyed it! If you did, we'd be so appreciative if you left a review.

Here at HQ Digital we are dedicated to publishing fiction that will keep you turning the pages into the early hours. We publish a variety of genres, from heartwarming romance, to thrilling crime and sweeping historical fiction.

To find out more about our books, enter competitions and discover exclusive content, please join our community of readers by following us at:

🐦 *@HQDigitalUK*

f *facebook.com/HQDigitalUK*

Are you a budding writer? We're also looking for authors to join the HQ Digital family! Please submit your manuscript to:

HQDigital@harpercollins.co.uk.

Hope to hear from you soon!

Turn the page for a thrilling extract from
The Silent Woman…

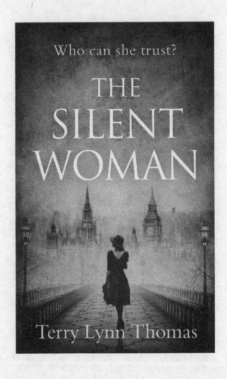

Turn the page for a thrilling extract from
The Silent Woman...

PROLOGUE

Berlin, May 1936

It rained the day the Gestapo came.

Dieter Reinsinger didn't mind the rain. He liked the sound of the drops on the tight fabric of his umbrella as he walked from his office on Wilhelmstrasse to the flat he shared with his sister Leni and her husband Michael on Nollendorfstrasse. The trip took him the good part of an hour, but he walked to and from work every day, come rain or shine. He passed the familiar apartments and plazas, nodding at the familiar faces with a smile.

Dieter liked his routine. He passed Mrs Kleiman's bakery, and longed for the *pfannkuchen* that used to tempt passers-by from the display window. He remembered Mrs Kleiman's kind ways, as she would beckon him into the shop, where she would sit with him and share a plate of the jelly doughnuts and the strong coffee that she brewed especially to his liking. She was a kind woman, who had lost her husband and only son in the war.

In January the Reich took over the bakery, replacing gentle Mrs Kleiman with a ham-fisted Fräulein with a surly attitude and no skill in the kitchen whatsoever. *No use complaining over things that cannot be fixed,* Dieter chided himself. He found he no longer had a taste for *pfannkuchen.*

By the time he turned onto his block, his sodden trouser legs clung to his calves. He didn't care. He thought of the hot coffee he would have when he got home, followed by the vegetable soup that Leni had started that morning. Dieter ignored the changes taking place around him. If he just kept to himself, he could rationalize the gangs of soldiers that patrolled the streets, taking pleasure in the fear they induced. He could ignore the lack of fresh butter, soap, sugar, and coffee. He could ignore the clenching in his belly every time he saw the pictures of Adolf Hitler, which hung in every shop, home, café, and business in Berlin. If he could carry on as usual, Dieter could convince himself that things were just as they used to be.

He turned onto his block and stopped short when he saw the black Mercedes parked at the kerb in front of his apartment. The lobby door was open. The pavement around the apartment deserted. He knew this day would come – how could it not? He just didn't know it would come so soon. The Mercedes was running, the windscreen wipers swooshing back and forth. Without thinking, Dieter shut his umbrella and tucked himself into the sheltered doorway of the apartment building across the street. He peered through the pale rain and bided his time. Soon he would be rid of Michael Blackwell. Soon he and Leni could get back to living their quiet life. Leni would thank him in the end. How could she not?

Dieter was a loyal German. He had enlisted in the *Deutsches Heer* – the Germany army – as an 18-year-old boy. He had fought in the trenches and had lived to tell about it. He came home a hardened man – grateful to still have his arms and legs attached – ready to settle down to a simple life. Dieter didn't want a wife. He didn't like women much. He didn't care much for sex, and he had Leni to care for the house. All Dieter needed was a comfortable chair at the end of the day and food for his belly. He wanted nothing else.

Leni was five years younger than Dieter. She'd celebrated her 40th birthday in March, but to Dieter she would always be a child. While Dieter was steadfast and hardworking, Leni was wild and flighty. When she was younger she had thought she would try to be a dancer, but quickly found that she lacked the required discipline. After dancing, she turned to painting and poured her passion into her work for a year. The walls of the flat were covered with canvases filled with splatters of vivid paint. She used her considerable charm to connive a showing at a small gallery, but her work wasn't well received.

Leni claimed that no one understood her. She tossed her paintbrushes and supplies in the rubbish bin and moved on to writing. Writing was a good preoccupation for Leni. Now she called herself a writer, but rarely sat down to work. She had a desk tucked into one of the corners of the apartment, complete with a sterling fountain pen and inkwell, a gift from Dieter, who held a secret hope that his restless sister had found her calling.

Now Michael Blackwell commandeered the writing desk, the silver pen, and the damned inkwell. Just like he commandeered everything else.

For a long time, Leni kept her relationship with Michael Blackwell a secret. Dieter noticed small changes: the inkwell in a different spot on Leni's writing desk and the bottle of ink actually being used. The stack of linen writing paper depleted. Had Leni started writing in earnest? Something had infused her spirit with a new effervescence. Her cheeks had a new glow to them. Leni floated around the apartment. She hummed as she cooked. Dieter assumed that his sister – like him – had discovered passion in a vocation. She bought new dresses and took special care with her appearance. When Dieter asked how she had paid for them, she told him she had been economical with the housekeeping money.

For the first time ever, the household ran smoothly. Meals were produced on time, laundry was folded and put away, and the house sparkled. Dieter should have been suspicious. He wasn't.

He discovered them in bed together on a beautiful September day when a client had cancelled an appointment and Dieter had decided to go home early. He looked forward to sitting in his chair in front of the window, while Leni brought him lunch and a stein filled with thick dark beer on a tray. These thoughts of home and hearth were in his mind when he let himself into the flat and heard the moan – soft as a heartbeat – coming from Leni's room. Thinking that she had fallen and hurt herself, Dieter burst into the bedroom, only to discover his sister naked in the bed, her limbs entwined with the long muscular legs of Michael Blackwell.

'Good God,' Michael said as he rolled off Leni and covered them both under the eiderdown. Dieter hated Michael Blackwell then, hated the way he shielded his sister, as if Leni needed protection from her own brother. Dieter bit back the scream that threatened and with great effort forced himself to unfurl his hands, which he was surprised to discover had clenched into tight fists. He swallowed the anger, taking it back into his gut where it could fester.

Leni sat up, the golden sun from the window forming a halo around her body as she held the blanket over her breasts. 'Dieter, darling,' she giggled. 'I'd like you to meet my husband.' Dieter took the giggle as a taunting insult. It sent his mind spinning. For the first time in his life, he wanted to throttle his sister.

At least Michael Blackwell had the sense to look sheepish. 'I'd shake your hand, but I'm afraid …'

'We'll explain everything,' Leni said. 'Let us get dressed. Michael said he'd treat us to a special dinner. We must celebrate!'

Dieter had turned on his heel and left the flat. He didn't return until late that evening, expecting Leni to be alone, hurt, or even angry with him. He expected her to come running to the door when he let himself in and beg his forgiveness. But Leni wasn't

260

alone. She and Michael were waiting for Dieter, sitting on the couch. Leni pouted. Michael insisted the three of them talk it out and come to an understanding. 'Your sister loves you, Dieter. Don't make her choose between us.'

Michael took charge – as he was wont to do. Leni explained that she loved Michael, and that they had been seeing each other for months, right under Dieter's nose. Dieter imagined the two of them, naked, loving each other, while he slaved at the office to put food on the table.

'You could have told me, Leni,' he said to his sister. 'I've never kept anything from you.'

'You would have forbidden me to see him,' Leni said. She had taken Michael's hand. 'And I would have defied you.'

She was right. He would have forbidden the relationship. As for Leni's defiance, Dieter could forgive his foolish sister that trespass. Michael Blackwell would pay the penance for Leni's sins. After all, he was to blame for them.

Leni left them to discuss the situation man to man. Dieter found himself telling Michael about their parents' deaths and the life he and Leni shared. Michael told Dieter that he was a journalist in England and was in Germany to research a book. *So that's where the ink and paper have been going,* Dieter thought. When he realized that for the past few months Michael and Leni had been spending their days here, in the flat that he paid for, Dieter hated Michael Blackwell even more. But he didn't show it.

Michael brought out a fine bottle of brandy. The two men stayed up all night, talking about their lives, plans for the future, and the ever-looming war. When the sun crept up in the morning sky, they stood and shook hands. Dieter decided he could pretend to like this man. He'd do it for Leni's sake.

'I love your sister, Dieter. I hope to be friends with you,' Michael said.

Dieter wanted to slap him. Instead he forced a smile. 'I'm happy for you.'

261

'Do you mind if we stay here until we find a flat of our own?'

'Of course. Why move? I'd be happy if you both would live here in the house. I'll give you my bedroom. It's bigger and has a better view. I'm never home anyway.'

Michael nodded. 'I'd pay our share, of course. I'll discuss it with Leni.'

Leni agreed to stay in the flat, happy that her new husband and her brother had become friends.

Months went by. The three of them fell into a routine. Each morning, Leni would make both men breakfast. They would sit together and share a meal, after which Dieter would leave for the office. Dieter had no idea what Michael Blackwell got up to during the day. Michael didn't discuss his personal activities with Dieter. Dieter didn't ask about them.

He spent more and more time in his room after dinner, leaving Leni and Michael in the living room of the flat. He told himself he didn't care, until he noticed subtle changes taking place. They would talk in whispers, but when Dieter entered the room, they stopped speaking and stared at him with blank smiles on their faces.

It was about this time when Dieter noticed a change in his neighbours. They used to look at him and smile. Now they wouldn't look him in the eye, and some had taken to crossing the street when he came near. They no longer stopped to ask after his health or discuss the utter lack of decent coffee or meat. His neighbours were afraid of him. Leni and Michael were up to something, or Michael was up to something and Leni was blindly following along.

During this time, Dieter noticed a man milling outside the flat when he left for his walk to the office. He recognized him, as he had been there the day before, standing in the doorway in the apartment building across the street. Fear clenched Dieter's gut, cramping his bowels. He forced himself to breathe, to keep his eyes focused straight ahead and continue on as though nothing were amiss. He knew a Gestapo agent when he saw one. He heard the rumours of Hitler's secret police. Dieter was a good German. He kept his eyes on the ground and his mouth shut.

Once he arrived at his office, he hurried up to his desk and peered out the window onto the street below. Nothing. So they weren't following him. Of course they weren't following him. Why would they? It didn't take Dieter long to figure out that Michael Blackwell had aroused the Gestapo's interest. He had to protect Leni. He vowed to find out what Michael was up to.

His opportunity came on a Saturday in April, when Leni and Michael had plans to be out for the day. They claimed they were going on a picnic, but Dieter was certain they were lying when he discovered the picnic hamper on the shelf in the kitchen. He wasn't surprised. His sister was a liar now. It wasn't her fault. He blamed Michael Blackwell. He had smiled and wished them a pleasant day. After that, he moved to the window and waited until they exited the apartment, arm in arm, and headed away on their outing. When they were safely out of sight, Dieter bolted the door and conducted a thorough, methodical search.

He went through all of the books in the flat, thumbing through them before putting them back exactly as he found them. Nothing. He rifled drawers, looked under mattresses, went through pockets. Still nothing. Desperate now, he removed everything from the wardrobe where Michael and Leni hung their clothes. Only after everything was removed did Dieter see the wooden crate on the floor, tucked into the back behind Michael's tennis racket. He took it out and lifted the lid, to reveal neat stacks of brochures, the front of which depicted a castle and a charming German village. The cover read, *Lernen Unser Schones Deutschland*: Our Beautiful Germany. Puzzled, Dieter took one of the brochures, opened it, read the first sentence, and cried out.

Inside the brochure was a detailed narrative of the conditions under Hitler's regime. The writer didn't hold back. The brochure told of an alleged terror campaign of murder, mass arrests, execution, and an utter suspension of civil rights. There was a map of all the camps, which – at least according to this brochure – held over one hundred thousand or more Communists, Social Democrats, and trade unionists. The last page was a plea for help, a battle cry calling for Hitler and his entire regime to be overthrown.

Dieter's hand shook. Fear made his mouth go dry. They would all be taken to the basement at Prinz Albrecht Strasse for interrogation and torture. If they survived, they would be sent to one of the camps. A bullet to the back of the head would be a mercy. Sweat broke out on Dieter's face; drops of it formed between his shoulder blades. He swallowed the lump that formed in the back of his throat, as the fear morphed into blind, infuriating anger and exploded in a black cloud of rage directed at Michael Blackwell.

How dare he expose Leni to this type of danger? Dieter needed to protect his sister. He stuffed the brochures back in the crate, put the lid on it, and pushed the box back into the recesses of the wardrobe. There was only one thing for Dieter to do.

CHAPTER ONE

Marry in haste, repent at leisure, says the bird in the gilded cage.
The words – an apt autobiography, to be sure – ran round and
round in Cat Carlisle's head. She pressed her forehead against
the cold windowpane and scanned the street in front of her house.
Her eyes roamed the square, with its newly painted benches and
gnarled old trees leafed out in verdant June splendour. A gang
of school-aged boys kicked a ball on the grass, going out of their
way to push and shove as they scurried along. They laughed with
glee when the tallest of the group fell on his bum, turned a
somersault, popped back up, and bowed deeply to his friends.
She smiled and pushed away the longing that threatened whenever a child was near.

She thought of the time when she and her husband had loved
each other, confided in each other. How long had it been since
they'd had a civil conversation? Five years? Ten? How long had
it been since she discovered that Benton Carlisle and Trudy
Ashworth – of the Ashworth textile fortune – were involved in a
long-term love affair? Ten years, two months and four days. For
the record book, that's how long it took for Benton's love to
morph into indifference and for the indifference to fester into
acrimony. Now Cat and her husband rarely spoke. On the rare

occasions when they did speak, the words between them were sharp and laced with animosity.

Cat turned and surveyed the room that she had claimed for her own, a small sanctuary in the Carlisles' Kensington house. When she and Benton discovered she was with child the first time, they pulled down the gloomy wallpaper and washed the walls a charming shade of buttercup yellow, perfect for a child of any sex. But Cat had lost the child before the furniture had been ordered. In an abundance of caution, they hadn't ordered furniture when Cat became pregnant for a second and third time. Those babies had not survived in her womb either. Now she had claimed the nursery as her own.

It was the sunniest room in the house. When Benton started to stay at his club – at least that's what he told Cat; she knew he really stayed at Trudy's flat in Belgravia – Cat moved in and decorated it to suit her own taste. She found she rather liked this small space. A tiny bed, an armoire to hold her clothes, and a writing table – with space between the pieces – were the only furnishings in the room. She had removed the dark Persian rug and left the oak floors bare, liking the way the honey-toned wood warmed the room. She had washed away the buttercup yellow and painted the walls stark white.

'Miss?' The maid stood in the open doorway of Cat's bedroom. She was too young to be working, 13 if she was a day, skinny and pale with a mousy brown bun peeking out from the white cap and sharp cheekbones that spoke of meals missed.

'Who're you?' Cat asked. She forced a smile so as not to scare the poor thing.

'Annie, ma'am.' Annie took a tentative step into Cat's room. In one hand she carried a wooden box full of feather dusters, rags, and other cleaning supplies. In the other she carried a broom and dustpan. 'I'm to give you the message that Alicia Montrose is here. She is eager to see you.' She looked around the room. 'And then I am to turn your room.'

'I'll just finish up and be down shortly,' Cat said.

The girl hesitated in the doorway.

'You can come in and get started,' Cat said.

'Thank you, miss.' The girl moved into the room and started to work away, focusing on the tasks at hand. 'Do you mind if I open the window? I like to air the bed linens.'

'Of course not,' Cat said.

She reached for the box that held her hairpins and attempted to wrangle her curls into submission. Behind her, the child opened the window and pulled back the sheets on Cat's bed. While the bed linens aired, Annie busied herself with the dusting and polishing.

Cat turned back to the mirror and wondered how she could avoid seeing Alicia Montrose. She couldn't face her, not yet. The wounds, though old, were still raw.

The Montrose family had always been gracious and kind to her, especially in the beginning of her relationship with Benton when she felt like a fish out of water, among the well-heeled, tightly knit group who had known each other since childhood, and whose parents and grandparents before them had been close friends.

Many in Benton's circle hadn't been so quick to welcome Cat into their fold. Not the Montroses. They extended every courtesy towards Cat. Alicia took Cat under her wing and saw that she was included in the events the wives scheduled when the husbands went on their hunting and fishing trips. Alicia also sought Cat out for days of shopping and attending the museum. And when the Bradbury-Scots invited Cat and Benton for dinner, Alicia swept in and tactfully explained the myriad of customs involved.

'They'll be watching you, Cat. If you hold your teacup incorrectly, they'll never let you live it down. And Lady Bradbury-Scott will load the table with an excess of forks and knives just to trip you up.' Alicia had taken Cat to her home every day for a week, where they dined on course after course of delicious food prepared by the Montroses' cook. While they ate, Alicia explained every nuance to Cat – *speak to the guest on the right during the first course. Only when that is finished can you turn to the left.* The rules were legion.

Cat credited Alicia's tutelage for her success at the dinner. She had triumphed. The Bradbury-Scotts accepted her, so did Benton's friends, all thanks to Alicia Montrose. One of these days Cat would need to make peace with Alicia, and talk to her about why she had resisted Alicia's overtures. Cat didn't expect Alicia to forgive her. How could she? But at least Alicia could be made to understand what motivated Cat to behave so shabbily. But not today.

She plunked her new green velvet hat on her head and pinned it fast without checking herself in the mirror. As she tiptoed downstairs, she wondered if she could sneak out the kitchen door and avoid the women altogether. With any luck, she could slip out unnoticed and avoid the litany of questions and criticisms that had become Isobel's standard fare over the years.

'I think the chairs should be in a half circle around this half of the room.' Alicia's voice floated up the stairs. 'A half circle is so much more welcoming, don't you agree?'

'Oh, I agree.' Isobel Carlisle, Cat's domineering sister-in-law, a shrewish woman who made a career of haranguing Cat, spoke in the unctuous tone reserved for Alicia alone. 'Move them back, Marie.'

Poor Marie. Isobel's secretary bore the brunt of Isobel's self-importance. Cat didn't know how she stood it, but Marie Quimby had been Isobel's loyal servant for years. Cat slunk down the stairs like a thief in her own home.

'But we just had them in the half circle, and neither of you liked that arrangement,' Marie said. She sounded beleaguered and it was only nine in the morning.

'There you are, Catherine. Bit late this morning.' Isobel stepped into the hallway.

'Catherine,' Alicia said. She smiled as she air-kissed Cat's cheek, while Isobel looked down her nose in disapproval. 'How've you been, Cat? You're looking well. We were worried about you. Good to see you've got the roses back in your cheeks.' Alicia was resplendent in a navy dress and a perfect hat.

'It was just a bout of influenza. I am fully recovered,' Cat said. 'And thank you for the lovely flowers and the card.'

'Won't you consider helping us? We could certainly use you. No one has a knack for getting people to part with their money like you do.'

Cat smiled, ignoring Isobel's dagger-like glare. 'Maybe next time. How're the boys?'

'Growing like mad. Hungry all the time. They're excited about our trip to Scotland. The invitation's open, if you'd like to join?' Alicia let the question hang in the air between them.

'I'll think about it.' Cat backed out of the room, eager to be outside. 'It's good to see you, Alicia.'

'Come to the house for the weekend, Cat. If the boys are too much, I'll send them to their gran's house. We've some catching up to do.'

'I'd like that,' Cat said. 'Must run.'

'Perhaps we should get back to work?' Isobel said.

A flash of sadness washed over Alicia's face. 'Please ring me, Catherine. At least we can have lunch.'

'I will. Promise,' Cat said.

'Isobel, I'll leave you to deal with the chairs. I'm going to use your telephone and call the florist.'

'Of course,' Isobel said.

Once Alicia stepped away, Isobel stepped close to Cat and spoke in a low voice. 'I do not appreciate you being so forward. You practically threw yourself at Alicia. Don't you realize what my association on this project could do for me, for our family, socially? This is very important, Catherine. Don't force me to speak to Benton about your behaviour. I will if I have to.'

Cat ignored her sister-in-law, as she had done a million times before. She walked past the drawing room, where Marie was busy arranging the chairs – heavy wooden things with curvy legs and high backs. Marie looked up at Cat and gave her a wan smile.

Isobel, stout and strong with a mass of iron-grey waves, was the exact opposite of Marie, who was thin as a cadaver and obedient as a well-trained hound. Marie's wispy grey hair stood in a frizzy puff on her head, like a mangled halo. Cat didn't understand the relationship between the women. Isobel claimed that her volunteer work kept her so busy that she needed an assistant to make her appointments and type her letters. Cat didn't believe that for one minute. Cat knew the true reason for Marie's employment. Isobel needed someone to boss around.

Her sister-in-law surveyed Cat's ensemble from head to toe, looking for fault. Cat dismissed her scrutiny. After fifteen years of living in the Carlisle house, she had become a master at disregarding Isobel.

'What is it, Isobel? I really must go,' Cat said.

'Before you go, I'd like you to touch up the silver. And maybe you could give Marie a hand in the kitchen? I know it's a bit of an imposition, but the agency didn't have a cook available today. I'm expecting ten committee members for our meeting this afternoon. I wouldn't want to run out of food. I need these committee members well fed. We've much work to do.'

'I can manage, Izzy,' Marie said.

'I've asked Catherine,' Isobel said. 'And those chairs won't move themselves.'

'I'm going out.' Cat paused before the mirror. She fixed her hat and fussed with her hair, taking her time as she drew the delicate veil over her eyes.

'You should be grateful, Catherine. Benton has given you a home and a position in society. You've made it clear you're not happy here, but a little gratitude wouldn't go amiss. You and Benton may be at odds, but that doesn't change things. You'd be on the street if it weren't for us. You've no training. It's not like you are capable of earning your living.'

'I hardly think any gratitude I feel towards my husband should be used to benefit you. I'm not your servant, Isobel. I'm Benton's wife. You seem to have forgotten that.'

Isobel stepped so close to Cat that their noses almost touched. When she spoke, spittle flew, but Cat didn't flinch. She didn't back away when Isobel said, 'I suggest you take care in your dealings with me, Catherine. I could ruin you.'

Cat met Isobel's gaze and didn't look away. 'Do your best. I am not afraid of you.' She stepped away and forced a smile. 'Silly old cow,' Cat whispered.

'What did you call me?'

'You heard me.' Cat picked up her handbag. 'I don't know when I'll be back. Have a pleasant day.' She turned her back on Isobel and stepped out into the summer morning.

She headed out into the street and took one last glance at the gleaming white house, one of many in a row. Benton's cousin, Michael Blackwell, Blackie for short, stood in the window of Benton's study, bleary-eyed from a night of solitary drinking in his room. Blackie spent a lot of time in Benton's study, especially when Benton wasn't home. She knew why – that's where the good brandy was kept.

Blackie had escaped Germany with his life, the clothes on his back, and nothing else. A long-lost cousin of Benton and Isobel, Blackie turned up on their doorstep, damaged from the narrow escape and desperate for a place to live. Of course, they had taken him in. The Carlisles were big on family loyalty. Now Blackie worked at a camera shop during the day and spent his nights sequestered in his room with a bottle of brandy and his memories of Hitler.

Cat often wondered what happened in Germany to frighten Blackie so, but she didn't have the heart to make him relive his suffering just to satisfy her curiosity. He saw Cat, smiled at her, and held up a snifter of Benton's brandy, never mind that it was only half past nine in the morning. Everyone knew Blackie drank to excess. They didn't care. He was family. Cat waved at him, anxious to get as far away from the Carlisle house as fast as she could.

The next book from Terry Lynn Thomas is coming in
April 2019

If you enjoyed *The Family Secret*, then why not try another heart racing read from HQ Digital?

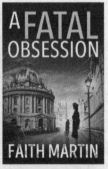